EXCAVATIONS

KATE MYERS

Excavations

a novel

HARPERVIA

An Imprint of HarperCollins*Publishers*

Excerpt on page vii from "The Sanctuary" by Elif Batuman. Published in the December 19 & 26, 2011, issues of *The New Yorker*. Used by permission.

HarperCollins books may be purchased for educational, business, or sales promotional use. For information, please email the Special Markets Department at SPsales@harpercollins.com.

FIRST EDITION

Designed by Janet Evans-Scanlon

Art on pages 3, 143, and 215: © *alvaroc/stock.adobe.com*

Library of Congress Cataloging-in-Publication Data has been applied for.

ISBN 978-0-06-330451-2
ISBN 978-0-06-333905-7 (Int'l)

23 24 25 26 27 LBC 5 4 3 2 1

For Anna

She was leaving a cell-phone store, accompanied by a teen-age boy wearing a T-shirt that said "RELAX, MAN," over a picture of an ice-cream cone playing an electric guitar. You wouldn't think an ice-cream cone *could* play an electric guitar, or would want to. I was reminded of Schmidt's hypothesis that hybrid creatures and monsters, unknown to Neolithic man, are particular to highly developed cultures—cultures which have achieved distance from and fear of nature. If archeologists of the future found this T-shirt, they would know ours had been a civilization of great refinement.

—ELIF BATUMAN, "The Sanctuary"

It's never just a foot. It's not that easy.

First, you get the lasers. You survey the whole thing, blast a billion pin pricks into the ground, then look at the screen to see if it's even worth packing shovels in the van. Then you mark it out with yellow tape and delineate a rectangle of HERE and NOT HERE. Then get rid of the crust on top: the stuff that's been trampled over, rained on, and scorched to death. That first six inches is easy. It's wet. It's farther down that's hard, past the one-foot mark; any gravedigger will tell you that. And it's not straight down like a rabbit hole. It's wide and down: a human hole.

The only good thing about the first few feet is the Nazis. There's no one down there but them. The top—that grassy, dog-peed-on part I was talking about—that's today, or like 2002. But one, two feet in is about the time the Germans were here trying to tell us they descended from Greek gods. You don't give a shit about that nonsense, which means you can hack at it, put the word *shove* in shovel. Go for it. Doesn't matter if you hurt anything—the cigarette packets or Deutsche coins or newspapers—and you always do. Forget it; they were nothing if not determined to spread their stuff absolutely everywhere, and you see they succeeded.

Another foot down, it's the Brits. The cartoony, pith-hatted colonialists who really screwed this thing up. They came in here and dug around for the big stuff. They wanted more Elgins for all the marbles and had the balls not only to break stuff that got in their way en route, but to try and get to it like scooping your way around the vanilla ice cream for the cookie dough chunks. They were rummaging around layers of the historical record to maximally jumble things up into no particular order, so that dumber versions of you and me might think: *Man, it's wild how much Latin these Greeks spoke.* It's a mess. Thank God, at least they didn't clean it up; digging disturbs history, but cleaning up your digging reimagines it. Don't do that.

Then you're past all that, finally, and you switch to trowels for precision digging. Even though this world has enough Roman ruins, apparently it's still *frowned upon* to so much as fart on a rock engraved with Latin. The Romans are here now, and you can tell because it's stupidly overbuilt. You run into sturdy walls and real roofs and just tons of stuff that no one asked for, and everything is signed. Like, *Yes, we get it. Take your dicks out of the inkwells. No need for an autograph on every single boring-ass clay pot.*

And that's when you get slower. By now you've almost definitely encountered an earthquake or two, you're crouching about four or five feet underground, and the layers on the dirt walls surrounding you might be slanted. At first you think that's weird, but then whoever is standing six feet above you *on* earth reminds you that Greece has more fault lines than California does, which isn't comforting when you're down there. But it's the truth, and that's just the business you're in, so you switch to your toothbrush. With the bristles you can be ridiculously careful. It's excruciatingly slow, but that's the point.

Now you're in it, the part that counts. There's small stuff here because the Greeks lived here for a really long time. Thousands of years. Remember how long this just took us, how many tools we had to use, and poor excuses we had to come up with just to get down here four thousand years? It took us five feet, and you got to use a shovel for half of it. Now you're holding a toothbrush in your hand, and I need you to do another thousand, down past the white togas and way down past the white wine and philosophizing and into the naked, savage, human-sacrifice layer of this hillside.

What I'm trying to tell you: there's never some dude's foot just sticking up out of the ground. Something happened, you moron. Get up here.

Part
One

Part
One

Chapter

1

We were here.

"Oh, we were there all right, and then *bampfh!*" She honked.

"One minute, we're here, sure. The next, gone-zo. Done-zo."

"And let me tell you the pièce de résistance—the coup de grâce," she said. (She mixed those two up, so she always said them back-to-back to give herself a fifty-fifty shot.) Over the past hour she'd called a half dozen friends to recount her latest indignity, ensuring a trainful of passengers knew every conceivable detail of her most recent separation.

It was critical, in Z's experience, to tell these stories as she processed the feelings—better yet as she *felt* the feelings—so she could shape them. This way she massaged her feelings with the very words she used: pummeled them into submission, molded them into benign bon mots. The tears she had no control over. She closed her eyes, having exhausted the slew of friends who'd pick up a midday call, and shook with loud sobs at her window seat. Surrounding her was a jagged moat pixelated with empty blue cushions, beyond which sat her unwitting audience. More than one pointed cough had been shot her way as she blubbered into her phone. *These commuting squares were probably all blissfully married to their high school sweethearts*, she thought, *and unless they had an ounce of morbid curiosity left to hear how her story evolved on the sixth retelling, they'd better rip off the corners of those* Wall Street Journals *to stuff in their ears.*

She was going for it, as she felt she deserved to. Through so many similar *betweens*—between jobs, between partners—she had kept

remarkably cool, breezily propelled by the power of polished anec-
dotes. It was all explainable—fun to explain, even—and she bounced
from one doomed entanglement to another, each of which she wrapped
up in a self-deprecating yarn. But she was sick of it. Now in an idiot's
ouroboros, her own compulsive storytelling was depressing her more
than the stories themselves. She pulled a can from her tote bag and
popped open the next beer. The crack pulled gazes her way from
around the train car, eyebrows rising above their coffee cups.

Earlier that very morning she'd been feeling downright grandiose,
struck with the brilliant idea to carve this eternal, romantic sentiment
into a tree while on a walk with her beau (*boyfriend*, if he was feeling
linguistically magnanimous): WE WERE HERE. She drew neither a heart,
nor initials, nor indicated a time frame such as "forever" since they had
yet to define their relationship. Indeed, those three words would prove
painfully accurate. They were there, it was a Saturday morning, and
they were walking along one of the city's waterfront parks. They were
nowhere near forever.

She'd met this latest young man four months ago at an ice cream
truck outside the Met, where the two instantly mistook one another's
passions: his for museum work, hers for candied nuts. It wasn't the first
time that she'd clocked a foundational misunderstanding like this and
proceeded anyway. In her lifelong, misguided optimism, she viewed
these dalliances as opportunities for her to learn to care about things
like art, real estate, optometry, etc. They all seemed like things she
should care about, at some point, probably. But she never quite got
there, exactly. Her pairings were never quite right, neither comfortable
nor exciting enough to inspire her to dig in; she viewed them just as
merciful breaks from the relentless current, like a fish latching its suck-
ers onto a whale for the ocean ride. When coupled, she could at least
tell her friends and family that she was, as they all suggested, trying to

settle down. They didn't need to know exactly what this looked like: dragging a pocketknife across a tree trunk in a public park, listening to this man explain the difference between art and vandalism, and wondering aloud why hot dog carts do not announce themselves with bells so they can be easily located—for example, during long walks along waterfront parks.

A more accurate carving for the ages: A DING-DONG WAS HERE.

They walked by a series of baseball diamonds, and her eyes ran the bases longingly. She'd been a mediocre player in high school and absolutely loved it. Being an overenthusiastic, near-violent member of various corporate softball teams gave her the greatest sense of belonging she'd felt in years. But no matter how nicely she asked him to go have a few throws with her, he insisted they keep walking. All along, of course, he had an endpoint in mind.

A few blocks later she saw her opportunity for breakfast: a glimmering, silver-wheeled mirage on the near horizon heralding feasts of two-dollar franks. Her beau was motioning toward a bench nearby and trying to tell her something as her thoughts drifted into a serious consideration of condiments. Then, all of a sudden, she heard something that sounded a lot like—

"I don't know if you're *the one* for me.

"I can't really see us getting *serious*."

It might not have been in that exact order. By now, her memory had been blown out into two rolls of Amtrak toilet paper tissues. She let out a long moan, then inhaled through the gauze of snot across her nose and mouth, making alarming gargling, gasping sounds.

An uninitiated passenger rolled a suitcase toward her empty row and paused. She looked up, and a familiar splash of self-destruction gushed within her veins—*Hark, a male! What a way to meet. What a great story this would make!*—before a glob of drool plopped onto her chest, propelling her would-be soulmate into the rows ahead. "I'm fine!" she shouted to him, to no one, to everyone on the train who'd begun to conspire nonverbally about when they should band together to pick her up, jam open a door, and hurl her onto the tracks.

She was en route to her parents' place, where she'd crash-landed half a dozen times in as many years during these *between* periods, such as the one she was undergoing now.

It wasn't that she was so heartbroken over this particular man, but rather that he was the latest in a long, undistinguished line. Turning these quagmires into quips wasn't cutting it anymore; if anything, it was hastening them. Her heart hadn't broken today—not exactly—but it was breaking down, choice after choice, crack by crack.

She dreaded her arrival home, where her parents would invariably reiterate their advice to *settle down*. They would accept any form of it— romantic, professional, social—and dangled every fun phrase in the book to get her to heed their counsel: *biological clock, saving for retirement, more like your brother*. They couched this encouragement as a kindness toward her: *certainly she would be happier with a bit more structure*?

"Pfft!" She honked aloud again just thinking about it.

The Northeast Corridor rattled by, graffitied obscenities shouting to her one vacant factory at a time. She scrolled through her feed, not really able to read any of it, her finger flicking like the tail of a snake whose head's just been chopped off.

Then something stopped her.

Gary!

Gary, of all people, was blasting out an email for summer staff in Greece again. A ping from the past, her feral college years brought forth to this wretched sliver of present as if to say *My, how the tables have hardly turned*. Isn't he how this whole unfortunate pattern began? Wasn't this all Gary's fault, really? He'd been the inaugural boyfriend in the withered lineage. *Yes, it was all his fault*, she thought, *in the same way that a house burning to the ground was the chimney's fault for getting struck by lightning.*

She held her breath as she read his note. Mountain village, baklava, some light exhumation.

She'd had one great job in her life, the same job she was skimming a description of at this very moment: junior excavator on an archaeological dig. It was one of those glorious, canonical summers she thought back to often, usually on the wrong side of a desk from HR. So much of her life felt fleeting, by her own sloppy hand—the blurry parties, the never-quite-right dudes, and the shifting allegiances among friends and colleagues thanks to partings of every kind. But that job, that work in the dirt, had made her truly feel—yes—*I was here*. It anchored her to the earth. She'd studied archaeology in college, morbidly fascinated by all the skeletons and their personal effects, but working on a dig was a different sensation entirely. *Ever palmed a skull, exit interview Suze?* Once Z had worked at the Mega excavation, she'd gotten a taste of the forever—had felt what it was like to be tethered to the earth-time continuum. No wonder she'd squirmed her way out of each and every cubicle since.

She was still in touch with Elise, a lifelong British digger in her forties whom Z had glommed onto that summer. For years now they'd traded emails, and Z felt closer to Elise than she did to most of her friends here. She was spellbound by Elise's descriptions: of scrambling over a mountainside to stake out new trenches after a bone discovery; of unearthing a complete, delicate glass lamp, four thousand years old; or even the tantalizing minutiae of applying sunscreen each and every day to her neck, chest, and shoulders. Z's responses back about meetings, restaurants, and roommates felt lifeless by comparison.

Not to mention how Z had felt about Gary that summer: too-tall, wild-haired, crinkle-eyed, open-mouth-smiling Gary. They hadn't been in touch for six years, but her memory of him was preserved in the most golden amber. She pictured him forever standing on the side of that emerald Greek mountain, squinting into the sun with one foot up on some rock, his binoculars chiming in the wind against the metal ruler that hung from his belt loop. This gorgeous dork rose larger than life in her memory, affixed upon her timeline to this formative place.

They'd sneaked around the dig at night, smuggled beers in their backpacks, stargazed in the grass, and wondered aloud about *them*— the bodies lying parallel beneath their own, all the tree-carving yahoos who came before. It was like being together with someone when you experienced a death; it bonded you. And there they'd been among the ruins, surrounded by the dead, corpse-drunk and infatuated.

Gary was the resident laser guy, a budding lidar expert who straddled the two impossibly colliding worlds of 3D mapping technology and ancient pottery. He blasted pinpricks of light to render the big picture: the perimeter of the city, grade of the road, or number of buildings. He was a creator of worlds, while the rest of them scrounged around in glorified garbage piles. By the standards of the archaeology department, he was a tech god. He spent countless hours in the offices of senior professors, whom he loved like grandparents and for whom he had bottomless patience.

He'd been a football player in high school, or so he claimed; though he certainly had the size for it, Z simply could not fathom him exerting an ounce of aggression. The man got jazzed about *birds*. He'd crouch on a steep slope of grass next to his closest associate (a gray, beam-blasting box with three sturdy yellow legs), adjust his glasses, and jot down notes, only to interrupt his own focus with an abrupt—

"Quail!"

She preferred to remember him precisely like this, instead of at the moment she'd broken up with him, crying and crushed on the edge of a tangled bed in Pylos. She'd bolted, predictably, after he told her he hoped they'd be together forever. That sounded too much like *settling down*. The fact that he was still in Greece, still finishing up his dissertation, and still mapping the excavation was what bounced her from him in the first place. How could she have stayed in place at twenty-two? She blew her nose, this time on a napkin and not her sweatshirt sleeve—a testament to just how far she'd come.

In this moment, a weak one by any measure and certainly if you measured it by the number of passengers pointing the conductor in her direction, an escape plan to Greece was irresistible. She was used to taking whatever horrible feelings she most recently experienced and hauling them over into the next quagmire, like a human mancala game. This day would be no exception.

Her heart lifted its head off the floor.

Here was the eject button for her life. It always appeared, and she always pressed it, but usually not so soon. She pressed it now.

DAYS LATER, SHE SAT CROSS-LEGGED IN THE PASSENGER SEAT OF A BLUE sprinter van speeding between switchbacks up the side of a mountain. It was a profound discombobulation. Her head still spun from making this rather abrupt (even for her) change of plans to return to the excavation—though it could hardly be described as a "change" when she hadn't had a plan in the first place. It was a return to a kind of starting line for herself, back in time in every way, an opportunity to reset and even go so far as to perhaps make some non-terrible life choices going forward. Anything could happen.

Kara, a half-Korean, all-Connecticutan peer from Z's last time at the excavation, picked her up at the chaotic Athens airport. Z had barely paid attention to Kara that summer because of the woman's interest in "actually learning something" beyond finding the best make-out spots and hiding beers in the bone bags. She was gorgeous, far more so than Z remembered, with acres of gleaming black hair and skin that announced, *Yes, I take expensive care of myself.* She wore a linen top with pleated shorts and fiddled anxiously with the enormous round sunglasses dangling from one of her buttonholes. Kara now had some important letters behind her name, and had risen through the ranks at the excavation. Presently, she was trumpeting to everyone in the van forced to listen that she was in charge of the lab now. Good for her.

Up, up, up Kara drove toward the relentless sun, testing the bounds of the van's gasping air conditioning. Z was savoring it, knowing it would be the last for a while. Hours ago they'd left the city limits, then the trickle of small towns, and beyond those, miles of low green hills dotted with short trees. Now they were aimed straight up the mountain, toward the Peloponnesian peak they'd call home, slowing on the ascent past orchards full of walnut and fig trees. Z saw the occasional cluster of white Corinthian columns visible on the nearest slope, too. Some were stumps; some had fallen sideways; some were still towering stone—cracked, chipped, all alone up here, and so quintessentially ancient-looking that Z imagined she could pick one up to find it was a hollow plastic prop. But she knew from experience they were as real as it got. They passed a cluster of white, hand-painted signs for a few cities and one sea, all dozens of miles away. The olive-green mountain grass sizzled in the heat, and the last sign of civilization before they made the final climb to their summer village was a lone old woman in a navy-blue headscarf, sitting behind a tiny table selling paper plates of gooey baklava for a euro each. At the sight of their van, the woman stood and proffered one in each hand.

"Pull over. I need that," Z said. In the intervening years she'd thoroughly romanticized her Greek food experience. Now she pined for a version of it she'd never eaten at the dig: flaky phyllo, salty feta, tangy olives, syrupy sweet squares like the old woman's. In the days leading up to her departure, she'd regularly assuaged her doubts about whether or not she was making a terrible mistake by telling herself that no matter what—at the very least—she'd eat a lot of baklava.

"I think not." Kara rolled her eyes, under the impression that street treats were some kind of joke. She did not slow down. Z twisted her body backwards, near-tearfully watching the glistening snack table grow smaller and smaller in the distance.

As irritating as she was, Kara could be stomached for a summer. A "Kara" was a known quantity. The city contained hundreds of thousands of Karas, and Z had off and on been one herself, whenever she was working at a new job, trying hard for a while and attempting to date someone boring. Kara was on the intense end of the spectrum all right, and richer than the rest of them combined (from what Z remembered), but they shared a set of traditions, rituals, regimens, and probably even friends if Z had any desire to play the wretched name game that plagued her demographic.

Their proximity was unfortunate insofar as it took a brutal measuring stick to the top of Z's head—they'd both started out here as junior excavators. Now Kara was the one with "goals" and a "working" "credit card." She'd taken the interesting approach of not bailing: checked the grad school box, didn't piss off her boss, wore sunscreen, didn't throw up in the van. *We get it, you're perfect.*

And, of course, these two shared a bond from years ago, when the intellectual heavyweights on the dig couldn't stretch their minds to differentiate Kara from Zara. She'd become "Z" and stayed that way.

In the six years since college, Z had had as many jobs, each of which directly *pertained* to fun but was not, itself, fun. She'd worked entry-level roles at the corporate behemoths atop theme parks, cruise lines, and movie theaters, and her performances at each could've been best described as *phoned in*—had she at any point been willing to pick up a phone. The constant discussion and analysis of fun had been an unforeseen downer, a depressing day in, day out reminder that she was not, in fact, having any. She was fired from each of these places and felt relieved every time, hungry for the in-between stints where she could physically participate in the activities she'd been relegated to half-heartedly spreadsheeting about.

It became obvious to Z how ill-suited she was to a life behind a desk, and she regularly admitted to herself that she'd be much happier working outside. Maybe she'd thrive as a camp counselor, tour guide, or some kind of resort employee—anything where she could move around a lot, talk to new people every day, and anchor her achievements to the lowest possible stakes. Some days her body felt downright claustrophobic inside these interchangeable, stifling buildings; she was desperate for fresh air. But she felt hemmed in by her social circle—by the Karas of the world and her other lifelong, exorbitantly educated peers—and at the same time she was unable to admit that a white-collar path had defeated her. Her parents were overly supportive, if anything, of her exploratory phase, so long as she stayed within the bounds of being A Corporate Professional. Frankly, she'd thought often about returning to the excavation for its academic, *professional* version of outdoor labor. The problem was that this gig only lasted a summer. Nonetheless, she'd see where things shook out on the other side of August.

Requiring zero encouragement, Kara continued her unsolicited filling in of what Z had missed over the past half decade. She was speaking as warmly as if they were old friends, rather than one-off colleagues. Listening gave Z the feeling that, somehow, she loomed much larger in this woman's life than vice versa. When Z thought about the dig, she certainly did not think about Kara. This dynamic, combined with a stick shift and the airport beer she'd chugged upon arrival, produced quite the feeling of whiplash.

"Well, you probably read about this, but obviously the most exciting thing we found since you left was Victor." Kara drummed her perfectly rounded nails along the steering wheel and nodded as if in conversation with herself. "The biggest find of a full athletic statue in a century—I'm serious! He was about a foot tall, and his arms were raised up in the air like a winner, hence the name of course. I mean, it was nothing short of extraordinary. A century! Here! I'm sure you saw."

Z's friend Elise had mentioned this briefly in one of her emails, along with some choice words about Kara's contribution to the event. Elise despised her.

"Elise was the one who found him and removed him from the trench and . . . well, I don't know if I should say anything." Kara put a hand to her chest and appeared to be choking up. She stared straight ahead at the road for a moment, pursing her lips as they passed by a series of gray stone houses crawling with green vines. At the edge of the tiny neighborhood was a small, gold-domed church with windows rimmed in blue.

Z straightened up in her seat. "Out with it, woman."

Kara checked the rearview mirror. She confirmed that the back of the van contained four conscripted undergraduates. Each of them was strapped into headphones and completely zonked out, having blissfully missed this interminable status update on a place whose entire purpose was never changing.

"Well, it's just that. Elise was the one who found him in the dirt, and then I, of course, did the preservation part. Cleaned him properly, removed the detritus, and checked carefully for inscriptions so that he'd be ready for display. You know."

"Sure."

"And, gosh, I can't even say it without getting emotional . . . We lost him." This bitch actually produced a tear over a hunk of naked plaster; she sounded like a surgeon who'd lost one of her patients. Z would give her left nip to care about something this much. "He shattered, in this earthquake that hit near the storage facility."

"Yikes," Z offered. "But what can you do? I mean, shifts happen."

"No," Kara said sternly and turned sideways to look over at Z. "No, it was Elise's fault. I'm sorry, but it's just the truth. When she took him out of the ground, she wiggled him. Like, he wasn't coming out easily enough and she . . . wiggled. The biggest find in our field in any of our lifetimes, and she wiggles!"

Kara closed her eyes and shook her head, not the kind of emotional moment you want to witness your driver having.

"Wiggled," Z said. She tried to remember what Elise had told her about this. Something about how Kara was the one who'd damaged the thing? Now Z wasn't so sure.

"I know! No doubt about it: that is what damaged him. She cracked him. Charles and I talked about it at length." Dr. Charles Barton was the head honcho at the dig, a thousand-year-old professor of archaeology who made the royal family seem incredibly laidback. From what Z remembered of him, the man was incapable of speaking in anything but length and had always been quick to call "trowel play" when his workers inevitably fell short of his exacting standards for dirt handling.

"I mean, I'll just tell you exactly what he told me. Charles said, and I quote, 'This is squarely on Elise.' If she hadn't been so forceful, so willful, the piece never would've succumbed to that kind of damage when she removed it. It is one hundred percent her fault. She basically lost us a slice of time itself!" Kara lifted both palms from the wheel and shook them in front of her.

This was a moment made for sunglasses, and Z rolled her eyes accordingly.

"He'd still be here with us! Oh, Z, you should've seen him. He was perfect. It was just . . . Anyway, so, it's been totally impossible for me to trust her ever since. Sometimes I can barely look at her because I just, well, I can't believe Charles even let her come back here."

Kara closed her eyes again, attempting to kill them all, and took a deep breath.

"I know you and Elise are still in touch, but I just wanted to warn you before we got there. Be careful with her. And between you and me, we're missing two discuses at the moment. God knows where they are, and I would not be surprised in the slightest if she had something to do with it."

"Damn," Z said. Her old friend Elise was a stone-cold lunatic, for sure, but Z couldn't imagine her being cavalier with any finds like that. Elise's lunacy was based, in fact, on how seriously she took this stuff. Z couldn't wait to see her again.

Z steered them back to more neutral territory.

"So, you seeing anyone?"

"Well," Kara singsonged. "Guess who's marrying Gary?"

She pumped her left hand into the air, and a godforsaken diamond caught the light, lasering white-hot misery all over Z's face.

If she stumbled upon those two missing discs, now Z knew to take one in each of her hands and clap her head between them.

Chapter

2

One of the problems was that they didn't even have a pool here. Patty wouldn't be able to repurpose the oversized penis pool float. So that went in the pass pile. The penis straws were useful, certainly, but there weren't enough to go around. Pass. The penis whistles could be used in case of emergency. Keep. Penis cake mold? She'd ask the cook about that one—keep for now. Patty was only halfway done digging through this person's depraved suitcase, and there were still a dozen more plastic bags inside filled with items she blushed to even imagine.

How had this happened to her?

See, it had been Patty's first time on a plane, ever. The rest of the kids here had left the country plenty of times. Some of them flew back and forth from home to school and didn't even consider it a big deal to get on a plane. To them, the plane was the boring part. Some of them had even been to Greece before. She'd never even been to an airport, let alone used one to leave the country. When she listened to the girls in her dorm talk about various impediments to travel, a dazzling array of problems sprung up, like scheduling conflicts with weddings and lavish birthday parties, golf and tennis commitments, or even internships that sounded more glamorous than the vacations themselves. Somehow money was never, ever the impediment. Patty gulped just to imagine her parents' response if she'd asked them for additional funds to *travel*. Her mother might've easily slapped her. They were resistant enough as it was to pay her meager portion of the heavily subsidized tuition checks so far, and Patty wasn't about to jeopardize that lifting of a finger by embarrassing them and suggesting she might need even *more* money for something even *more* frivolous.

But during one such night of travel talk at school, Patty learned there were ways that these unimpeded jet-setters greased their wheels even further: summer research work funded by the university. She'd been dreading returning to her job at her uncle's nursery (*plants, not children*, she was quick to clarify), and she was blown away by the variety and exoticism that awaited her for free in places like Megalopolis, Guam, and Manitoba, should she show any aptitude or willingness for physical labor on behalf of the archaeology, ecology, or geology departments. Could she ever! The word *stipend* glimmered on the page.

She had figured it out this far, and yet she had no idea what the accepted customs and established wisdoms of traveling were—didn't even know if she was being rude when she declined the little bag of pretzels. How could she? No one ever bothered to give her any advice on stuff like this. From her family it was all, *trust your gut, follow your heart, be yourself*—as if her gut, heart, or self knew anything.

She was simply a dummy, long-suspected and at last confirmed, and now they were going to fire her. As they should, she guessed. Her parents would say so, quick to cut bait on anyone who lacked what they considered common sense. She'd be flying again much sooner than she'd hoped. At least now she'd know what to do about the pretzels: Take two. Save one in front pocket for later.

It all started because Patty had been the last to leave campus for the excavation. She had to work at her job at the front desk of the Student Health Office, where eye contact went to die, until the final day possible. She'd needed every last paid hour she could get. Thus, she was the last undergrad to fly over, right before the boss, Dr. Charles Barton. This meant she was helping him, packing and planning, until the final moments. He'd asked her to bring an extra suitcase for him filled with shovels, yellow tape, a series of knives, reams of duct tape, and special kinds of humongous plastic bags. If she hadn't been packing these items while kneeling in the hallway of the archaeology department, she would've called a homicide detective.

Dr. Charles also asked Patty to pack in this suitcase two metal discs: more than a foot wide each, thick, heavy, and recently painted, it seemed. She had no idea what those were but didn't, for that matter, know what half of this stuff was for. It didn't matter; he could've asked her to travel in the suitcase herself, and she would've said yes. She was pretty flexible.

Then the day came, the day that she was leaving the United States. She'd even penned Xs on her dorm room cat calendar leading up to the trip, something she'd only seen people do in movies. But this time she'd really had something worth counting down to.

"Have a nice trip!" The fruit-print-scarfed woman at check-in waved to the person behind Patty to step up in line. That was it. For some reason she'd pictured getting a flower lei around her neck. Something to mark the occasion.

There the luggage went, down the conveyor belt, into the abyss. How the heck was Patty supposed to know that every single piece of luggage basically looked exactly the same?

It had floored her when Professor Barton responded to one of her copy-and-pasted emails about summer internships. She saw on the department website that he was the head of the school's archaeology museum and only taught graduate students. The blurb about him read like a description of Indiana Jones meets Steve Prefontaine. Even though in her excitement she only skimmed it before getting back to his email, blurb words jumped out at her like "BBC Contributor," "Olympics," "endowed," and "foremost." He was a world-renowned expert on ancient sports history, a subject she hadn't even known had renown anywhere, let alone all over the whole world. The fact that this man had typed her name seemed like a huge mistake.

In his office she could barely look right at him, something her work experience as an STD greeter had prepared her for. He was like an oil painting diluted to life. She'd seen these dignified old people walking around campus and assumed she'd go her entire college career without ever being acknowledged by one, let alone having one half of a two-way conversation with one. She badly wished for him to have to do something important for a moment, so she could get in a good stare at her surroundings.

Stalagmites of books and binders rose from the floor. Many looked to be stacks of the professor's own book, *Running Naked* by Dr. Charles Barton, PhD. Many who heard the title were a bit disappointed—even admittedly repelled—to meet the bony, elderly man behind it, but as Charles was quick to mention, he was a much, much younger man at the time of publication. The book was the culmination of his life's work on the exploration of masculinity in the competition rituals at ancient athletic sites in pre-Olympia Greece. In other words, it was necessary to drop toga and jangle your olive-oiled manhood around the track at top speed to display or determine who was really in charge. The book had been a bestseller thanks to its glamorization of Charles's vine-swinging decades digging around in the dirt, and their connection to his brief stint as a decorated college marathoner. *Running Naked* lionized Real Men in sport throughout the centuries, and canonized them as the only true, natural participants in exercise itself, with an unimpeachable origin story that culminated seamlessly with the Super Bowl. Charles's staunch commitment to the history of testosterone had made him bulletproof to modernization, insofar as he deemed it pointless and rather corrosive to his patently successful theories. He hadn't written anything since.

The two bookshelves in his office, facing each other from either side of the room, had been emptied of reading material and replaced with dozens of silver-framed photos: Dr. Charles shaking hands with a vice president, a news anchor, two professional tennis players, and even a country singer Patty's mom called a hunk. She'd have to mention that to her. The rest pictured men in suits who she didn't recognize, which made her understand they must be all the more important. It reminded her of the Fayetteville Café, with its photos of state senators and big hunting guides—all signed and made out to Chef Tim referencing how violently hot the barbecue sauce was—hung all over the wall by the cash register. It was pretty impressive that all those guys had eaten there, and Patty was now equally impressed by Dr. Charles's display of the kind of elbows he rubbed without even having to cook them a great meal.

The professor sat behind the desk now, looking much older than he did in his website picture—at least sixty, maybe seventy even, though Patty was terrible with ages (she once asked her great aunt for a tampon). Charles was so thin that his clothes seemed to be hanging on for dear life; if one thread were tugged on that many-pocketed vest, the whole outfit would slide right off him with only slippery bones for purchase. His hair was the most vibrant thing in the dusty room, a blinding block of white. It was "styled," though that was probably the wrong word, with whatever pasty product old men use to make their hair look clipped on like a single Lego unit. When he reached to put on the tortoiseshell glasses that hung around his neck, his sleeve slid to reveal a surprisingly feminine silver bracelet inlaid with turquoise beads, like something the hostess at Chi-Chi's wore. Patty squinted at it.

"I see you used to work at a nursery," he said, peering at the bottom of her paper resume, which he must have printed out. The idea that he'd pressed multiple buttons on her behalf flattered her to no end.

Patty leaned forward, certain she'd misheard him. That was not the first bullet point she was expecting he'd pick out, and was in fact one she was hoping he missed entirely. She had been torn about including her high school summer job in the plant department at the hardware store, but unfortunately it was all the work experience she had.

"I did," she said slowly, so that if in between syllables she sensed she was giving the wrong answer she could change course. "But that was just my summer job, and I worked there on holidays. On weekends I volunteered at our historical museum." The way she said it sounded like a question, so she reached over the desk and pointed to the line on her resume that indicated the local museum's name.

"Right there. Yeah, I gave tours to a lot of . . . clients." She had never spoken that word before in her entire life. Paying the three-dollar-and-fifty-cent entry fee with a coupon from the PennySaver didn't give someone a title lawyers used. Why did she say that?

"My wife, Terry, would spend every minute in that beautiful garden of hers if she had her druthers." Charles tilted his head toward her as if trying to squash any doubt she had about how beautiful it could be.

Patty had no doubt. Her lips automatically flattened sideways into what she considered her professional smile.

"How's your landscaping experience then?"

"I've never owned a plant myself," she admitted. "But I would give the customers some good tips, you know, ideas—on how to keep things alive, for the most part. Not that they followed my advice. A lot of people end up coming back for the same plant, if you can believe it. I pretty much just mulched what we had, added those little blue fertilizer pods, sprayed them with the hose, and moved a lot of the inventory around to make sure the good stuff was out in front. Plus the outdoor register. Oh, and for Christmas: I got the sled onto the roof, sawed the stumps off of the trees, and wrapped them up in that orange mesh, you know."

With every word she was more certain that this man was making fun of her; he'd done so in such a clever way that he'd actually made her make fun of herself. It was stupid to think anyone like this would need a minute of her help. She didn't speak a word of Greek, and her whole academic "expertise" so far was in less than two semesters of novels, half of which she was still desperate to understand. How had Christmas trees come up? Mentioning her nursery work was just his way of reminding her where she'd find herself again this summer, where she belonged.

"Mmm. And you don't, uh, know anyone else? In the department here?" He said, twitching his head to the right and indicating the hallway she'd just walked down.

She blinked and shook her head slowly. "This is my first time, appearing, in this building," she explained, as if her appearance were typically required elsewhere.

"Good. And you don't know any of the other Ugs—I mean, students—who are coming along this summer?"

"No," she sighed, "I don't know them either." This had to be the nail in the coffin, she was certain.

"All right," he removed his glasses. "Now, Peggy, I require two things in this role. Physical toughness, which it appears to me you have in spades. Pun intended! And secondly, discretion. The right person in this role, if this role is performed correctly, stands to benefit immensely if they are loyal to me and can keep a secret, if need be. After all, archaeology is, at its core, all about secrets."

Color Patty dazzled. She sat perfectly still and moved her eyes sideways to glimpse, once again, at the wall of photos. There was even a picture of him with what had to be an esteemed dog.

"Does this sound like something you'd be interested in?"

"Yes," she said breathlessly. "Really?"

"Excellent!" The professor slapped the desk, stood up abruptly, and smiled. "And don't tell me you're a sports fan. Are you?"

Her eyes widened into silver dollars. Basketball was the only reason she was even here: she'd been a short but dogged high school

player, and her coach was the first and only person in her life to suggest college. She'd chosen this university because their basketball
team was nationally ranked. While she had no delusions of ever playing for the team, she'd begged her way into a second job as an assistant to an assistant coach during the season, washing towels and
collating Gatorade flavors. Merely being in proximity to these extraordinary athletes she idolized (growing up, she'd had university roster
posters in her room) was the highlight of her entire life. Sports were
the cornerstone of her upbringing; her whole family was bananas
about football, baseball, and basketball. It was the only thing Patty
felt truly comfortable talking about with anyone, anytime. A thousand
times it had been the life raft to save her from the uncertain seas of
small talk.

"Huge," she whispered. That was the only answer she had, right or
wrong.

Charles extended his hand for a shake. She took it, stunned, as she
fumbled up and out of her chair.

"Bravo. We'll have much to discuss then. I'll be in touch, Peggy. I'll
have you pack up some things for me to carry over with you. I think it's
a very strong fit, for both of us."

"Patty, but don't worry about it, it's—"

"Oh!" He palmed his forehead, again revealing the bracelet as he
held up her resume. "I'm looking right at it. I am so sorry, I apologize."

She mumbled an apology back to him for some reason and slid out
the door, before he realized it really was a Peggy he'd been looking for
all along.

UPON ARRIVAL AT THEIR GREEK VILLAGE, SHE'D DROPPED OFF CHARLES'S
suitcase by the stone steps and proceeded to her room to get settled.
They were all living in a tiny bundle of buildings that jutted out from

the top of a rock-riddled mountainside. It was a remote four-hour drive from Athens to the base of the mountain, then a vertical hour ride up from the valley to their houses, and another twenty-minute van ride higher still to get to the excavation site. The village was organized around the spine of a wide stone staircase, attached to which were several charmingly decrepit homes; unfinished patios bubbled up with the roots of intruding trees, which jabbed their branches into open windows. The houses were all made of sun-bleached stone with an appealing foundational precariousness, cracked and tilting jauntily. The constant wind rustled the towering laurels and white-flowered sage brush, giving the area an herbal scent that reminded Patty of a recently cleaned kitchen—not unpleasant at all.

Down at the stairs' base was a gravel parking area, which led to a white stone building with an enormous patio wrapped the entire way around it. This was the lab, Charles had explained, implying experiments of some kind. It was made of the same bleached stones, and the patio was half-walled in places, making nice spots to sit and look out. Dozens of plastic buckets were turned upside down all over the place, butts baking in the sun alongside drying towels and brushes she assumed were tools beyond her capabilities. Beneath the patio's outer edge was a steep drop dotted with walnut trees, the tops of which stretched their wares to jangle against the walls. The diagonal orchard stretched for miles down the mountain, interrupted only by the faded black crisscross of the switchbacks they'd taken to get here.

At the very top of the stairway sat the cafeteria, a squat, Greek-blue box with splintering pink wooden shutters open to the outside, revealing a dozen long tables within. To the cafeteria's left was the largest patio. It had plenty of plastic seating and was beset against a smooth stone wall that bore a fading Mythos mural of a laurel-wreath-crowned cat enjoying a beer. Among the houses, various sights along the climb up the stairs included a swing set that was precariously planted at best, a shed spilling rusted tools that spoke to the quality of the local construction, and ornery shrubbery.

To Patty, the place looked like a postcard of half-ancient Greece—like it had tried to hang on to the past, but a few updates had been made. She delighted in being completely clueless about what any of the Greek-lettered signs on each building meant and found it funny that a visitor would need any directions, since one could see the entire village from any point within it. The refusal of the trees and plants to remain outdoors gave the place an endearing feel of timelessness, of existing long before and after any of them were here. The wind spun each leaf and flower on its axis enough to keep the quarters livably cool and give the impression that the village itself was vibrating ever so slightly. *Picturesque* is the word Patty would use to describe it to people who wouldn't be able to see it.

The girls' house was one single large room that was magically dark and brisk despite the blistering sun outside, with a smattering of cots set up across the floor and a confusing, relatively ancient chandelier hanging above. From the outside this appeared to be a two-story house, white with blue shutters, but the interior layout didn't seem to include stairs. The inside walls were yellow stucco and rough to the touch, bare save for a single poster of the Greek alphabet and its corresponding animals, should anyone need to know during their stay that dolphin began with delta. At the back wall were two bathrooms side by side, each containing a European-style shower-and-sink combo, and an open doorway closed off as much as possible by a dense set of hanging glitter beads. As Patty unpacked beside her cot, a spherical, gray-haired woman wearing an "I ♥ Meatballs" apron swung through the opening and stopped before her.

"Don't look so nervous," the woman instructed, revealing an Australian accent Patty found exciting. A balding man, rail-thin in a pair of cargo shorts and nothing more, came up behind her, raised both palms,

and wiggled his fingers by way of hello. They were Ursula and her husband, Ian, the cook and handyman who kept this entire operation
afloat along the critical thoroughfare from pizza to plumbing.

Ian locked eyes with Patty, then pulled a tiny wrench from his
pocket and pointed it at the window. "Remember in '92? The shutters
had all fallen off," he said without further introduction. "Earthquake
most likely, or simple disrepair. Before my time, but that's how they
were when I found them. These things need tightening, which is why
I've got this. You'll see, all right. No shutters attached at all; they were
all sideways on the ground. So this year I'm going to set it all back
again, to the way it was," he assured her.

Patty stared at him and nodded, which seemed like the right thing
to do.

"Yes dear, now come on," Ursula laid a hand between Ian's bare
shoulder blades. As she very slowly made her way out the door, holding up the sides of her house dress so as not to trip, she turned her
head back to Patty to add, "If an ice pop might steel your nerves, you
come and get one. We've got some for you anytime, love. Just grape
though."

Patty smiled. She loved grape!

And then Charles's voice boomed from down the stairs, "Patty!"

A moment later the two of them stood shoulder to shoulder on the
brutally hot patio, looking down inside an open suitcase containing a
treasure trove of perverted plastic.

"Whose suitcase is this?" Dr. Charles demanded.

For the second of two times standing before this man, Patty was
certain of her absolute identity as a bozo. She'd finally risen to a place
in life where such a man felt ambivalence toward her—maybe even tilting toward warmth—and now she'd tripped herself back down.

". . . Yours?" she tried.

"This?!" He bent over and plucked forth a satin sash purporting to

"Chardon-YAY." "This is mine, you're suggesting?!" His eyeballs threatened to pop out and pelt her in the face.

"No?" Patty backtracked. "I don't know. Yes? You helped me pack?" She frantically looked around the patio, but the entire group of students had retreated into the building to feast on her demise from behind the windows.

"Did you just grab the first brown suitcase you saw? Hmm? And wheel it merrily along? Not perhaps thinking to confirm that it was, in fact, my suitcase? My essential, critical, vital suitcase?!"

That is exactly what she'd done—she would've sworn it was his!—and she was now mortified at how merry her wheeling was. "I'm so sorry," she said. "Really sorry. I'll go back to the airport! I can drive."

He palmed his forehead. "At this very moment, Patty," he snarled. Every time he uttered her name, her plans to return home grew more concrete. "Some woman, or some young man for that matter, is unzipping their luggage to commence a godforsaken bachelorette party, only to find—" he made circular motions with his open palm, inviting her to guess.

"Weird knives?"

"Yes! Among other various personal items that I require," he said. Then he lowered his voice into a terrifying whisper-growl and leaned in until his face was an inch from hers, "Like those discs."

Patty gasped. She held her breath and sincerely hoped she'd pass out and collapse, ideally hitting her head on the way down.

"Heard you got everything on your Christmas list, Chaz," a British-accented woman said as she clomped past them on the patio in ankle-high work boots. She wore one of those tank tops with a built-in bra, which was jarringly sensual when paired with her baggy, knee-length Bermuda cargo shorts. Her forearms and calves were liberally tattooed and otherwise wholly bronzed from what looked like years of working in the sun, giving her faint eye lines that extended out far beyond the bounds of her wraparound sunglasses. The ensemble was vaguely militaristic. It was a relief to Patty to see anyone else at all.

"This is just unacceptable," Charles spat. "I would not have entrusted you with these supplies had I known that this was your plan."

"Her *plan*?" The woman scoffed. "Why the hell are you making this girl haul a bunch of your crap halfway around the world? Why don't you just ship it, cheapskate?"

"Elise," Charles turned to her. "Enough. Thank you. This is between myself and this young lady."

Elise snorted in Patty's general direction and walked off toward the building, leaving her alone with him again. For a fleeting second Patty's eyes followed after her, drinking in the sweat slick on the inch of skin exposed between Elise's tight top and roomy shorts. *Jesus, Mary, and Joseph—focus, Patty.*

Charles continued. "Those supplies are critical to the specific kind of stratigraphic exploration we do here because, as you know, the earth has a tendency to move—"

She burst into tears at this news. She was so exhausted and upset that by now it felt like her face was at its melting point under the extreme heat. All along it was true: she was not supposed to be here.

"Whoa, whoa, whoa!" One of the older grad students jogged out of the lab, very cavalierly carrying two pairs of scissors. Elise walked behind him, arms crossed. He wore a faded bucket hat with the school's logo on it and a T-shirt featuring pictures of ancient pottery and the words "Pot Head." He smiled, which Patty couldn't fathom a reason on earth for.

"Elise said we lost the knives and—oh, wow." He froze in front of the suitcase. Patty had never been more grateful for the use of the word *we*.

This floppy-brimmed hero pushed his glasses up the bridge of his nose (they'd slid off during his little run) then looked directly at Patty and extended his hand. "Gary, laser guy. We'll figure this out, no sweat."

He, Elise, and Charles commenced strategizing about various tool substitutions. Patty absorbed their exchange like plastic absorbs a spill. She stared vacantly into the testicular abyss. Losing this job was not an option; she'd already given up her spot at the hardware store for the summer and used half her savings to get a daylong layover in Portugal so she could say she'd been to two countries. Her initial goal had been to use the months among these people to lift herself high enough to never have to return to the nursery again; now her only motivation was to stay, any way she could.

"I suppose we'll see you at dinner," Charles said to her, grinding out the words from between his teeth.

AT DINNER SHE SAT ALONE, AT THE SAME LONG TABLE AS OTHER students but separate, distinctly a toxic entity that warranted a buffer. While everyone else went immediately to bed afterward—jet-lagged, the most glamorous tiredness she could imagine—she instead went to see Dr. Charles in his private room. She had to. She'd traveled so impossibly far to be here, and there was no way she was going to let herself remain on the wrong foot.

Her mother had sneaked a plastic storage tub of peanut brittle into her luggage, the discovery of which nearly made Patty cry again. She took out half and wrapped it up with a ream of toilet paper to save for herself and any possible future friends. Then she carried the remaining half to give to her boss as a peace offering.

Charles's room was perched atop a narrow set of stairs that shot off diagonally from the cafeteria. Ensconced in the canopy of trees, the room's two small windows glowed like yellow eyes in the dark, looking out on everything beneath him.

She paused on the landing to collect herself and decide what exactly it was she intended to say. The view from up here was tremendous once she was above the thick tree line; the diamond lights of the city far below were so small, a cluster of tiny jewels spilled in the bottom of a bag. The breeze gently brushed the air with dill and rosemary from the little herb garden below.

Quietly, she lifted the lip of the plastic tub and slid out a nutty golden piece to fortify herself.

"Of course not, Terry!" Dr. Charles bellowed from inside.

Patty froze mid-bite.

He continued in a loud whisper, "—how much pressure I am under. I can assure you, as I am spending good money on this very phone conversation to do, that I am considering all the avenues. There is quite literally not one stone left unturned, as you well know. What I need from you, in fact, is a pronounced increase in trust, please. We cannot have any kind of hysteria at a delicate moment like this, and thus it is your job to inoculate us against talk with your confidence in my methods and abilities. Of course I am looking into every—"

Patty wiped a line of drool from her chin, forced out from the brittle having nearly reached her lips when Charles's angry voice carried through the door. She took a nibble now, as soft as could be, and stood still.

"Kara? Hmm. Her mother might, perhaps. Not without risk, though," he said. "Well, yes, I know that, but I can hardly promulgate the opportunity at hand."

Patty continued to nibble and look around below her, wondering if she could make it back down the stairs without too much creaking. This visit had been another mistake.

Silently she re-sealed the lip of the tub and kneeled down to place it on the doormat. Though would he think this had been an anonymous brittling?

"Terry!" From down in the trees, another man's voice called out, ripping through the silence.

Patty's head spun. The handyman Ian, now naked in reverse in nothing but a tight white tank top and underwear, waved to her with both arms from outside the girls' house. He stopped for a second, then waved again insistently, looking directly at her. Not sure what else to do, Patty raised her hand to him. Maybe she'd go by Terry all summer.

"Good Lord. Let me call you back," Dr. Charles's voice grew louder as he turned right toward the door.

Patty bent down to pick up the tub again. The door opened as she was mid-crouch.

"Peg—Patty! What are you doing here? Who was shouting my wife's name?"

"Great to see you, girl! How long are you staying?" The ancient, nearly nude nut bellowed from beneath the stairs where Dr. Charles and Patty stood.

"Shut up, man!" Someone shouted from the boys' house.

"Ian? Patty?" Charles leaned out the door.

"Patty," Patty confirmed.

"Whatever you say, boss," Ian said, beaming up at them, delighted to see Patty, whoever he thought she was.

"What is everyone doing out of bed?" Charles glowered at her. "Ian, for God's sake, attempt pants!"

Ian saluted them both then waddled back down the stone walkway, his bare legs disappearing beneath the leaves.

"This is for you," Patty said, her heart skittering around like a trapped mouse inside her ribcage. "To say I'm sorry, for everything. My mom made it."

Dr. Charles stared at her, his eyes thinning into a glare that didn't budge as he accepted the butter-smudged tub of treats. "How long have you been out here?"

She turned to leave.

"One moment," he said, lowering his voice. His face slackened as though he'd just stumbled upon a new idea. She braced herself, hoping he didn't suspect that she'd squirreled away a whole other half of the brittle.

"You have cost me my supplies," he reminded her. "Therefore, I'm going to need you to compensate if you wish to remain here. You will be my eyes and ears, yes? A go-between when there's something I must find out or when something must be delivered. As you can see, I am all the way up here," he gestured to the trees. "And it would be helpful to me if, when asked, you're able to fetch things from the lab for me, or even from the site itself. And what did I say was required to work here?"

"SPF 45 plus."

"What else?"

"Discretion."

"That's right. And so?"

She nodded, a wave of relief crashing down upon her to learn that there was a definitive way she could make up for it all and stay. "Definitely. Yeah, yes. I can do that."

"Of course you can. Now, good night."

Without looking behind himself, Charles stepped backwards into his room and closed the door in her face.

Patty walked back down the stairs and suddenly felt struck with sympathy for the celebrants saddled with Charles's supplies when they'd been expecting their . . . items. Maybe the owner of the similar brown suitcase would have a better idea than she did what exactly someone might do with two freshly painted faux discs.

Chapter

3

The next morning, it was eighty-five degrees before sunrise. As Elise hiked up to the excavation site, she could already smell herself. That was a good thing; the clarity of her urine and the potency of her pits were dual proof points of her body's superior efficiency in the heat. The volume of her daily water intake was a point of personal pride, and alternatively one of bafflement; for some reason, despite several annual faintings, no one else here drank like their lives depended on it. Dehydration wasn't about to take her down the way it felled other supposedly seasoned diggers every year. Clear pee and strong sweat (which outcompeted even her illegal-in-the-UK-strength deodorant) meant she was hydrated enough, something the rest of her team was loosey fucking goosey about in the face of danger.

Everyone else drove up in the van with the equipment every morning, and thus Elise preferred to hike. It was the only time she had to be by herself. You'd think being down inside your own dirt trench all day was private enough, but it wasn't. People were always yelling over her across their own trenches, or demanding her help, or even playing word games with each other to which the entire field was subject, and then stopping by on their water breaks as if they hadn't already blown past a lifetime's quota of chitchat. Even when she went down to the orchard to pee (frequently, critically), she heard them blabbering. *God forbid I miss a moment whilst I squat down and urinate!* And down in the village, forget it. It was so small, and the team was too big; it busted at the seams. They did all their meals and all their sleeping together. Even still during their free hours, the insatiable Ugs (or as they referred to themselves, *Undergraduates*) went jogging, played cards, and did yoga together. It was a cult of lunacy, and they genuinely couldn't understand why Elise wasn't just dying to join. The daily lung-strangling hike up and down to the site was her only relief.

She pushed her wraparound sunglasses up onto her head and wiped the sweat out of her eyes. Her blonde-streaked gray braid slapped the bottom of her spine. She was halfway there. Her myriad feline and hieroglyphic tattoos, courtesy of a deranged decade with her Egyptologist ex-husband, appeared inky under a thick layer of moisture, all the more off-putting.

Rooming with her friend Z was a small consolation to her tenth consecutive year living in the girls' house. She was forty-four years old, and this was the only site she worked where she still slept on a cot in a public room. When she rotated to other digs throughout the year—three months apiece in Thessaloniki, Corinth, and Crete, that was her life—she always had her own single, and rightly so. But the Mount Megalopolis excavation seemed to take pride in its summer-camp-style camaraderie, which obliterated privacy, as if the exercise here was a Margaret Mead investigation into the rituals and value systems of twenty-something American maniacs.

Z had become that rarest of people to Elise—a true friend. She'd never met anyone like her before or since. That first summer that she was here, Z had crash-landed at the Mega site in spectacular fashion, arriving high on the horse as beloved Gary's girlfriend before tumbling down into the social trough of despair when she publicly took a baseball bat to his heart. It was here in the trough that Elise had fallen for her friend in what she considered a Shakespearean display of comeuppance. A pointless young man, vicariously aggrieved by Z's romantic choices, Elise guessed, loudly called Z *bitch* as she passed by him one morning in the cafeteria. Without so much as jiggling her watery oat-meal, Z stopped, turned, locked eyes with him, stood perfectly still, and launched her right foot up and into his crotch.

Elise had been stunned. Right before her eyes, there was someone else manifesting the singular wild fantasy Elise had every day. By God, Z just did it! The act we long to do but don't! Elise sat, coffee mug sus-pended mid-sip, and watched her very dreams unfold right there from her usual table of one in the corner. Then suddenly Z walked over and sat down across from her. They'd hardly spoken before and never during meals; Z *usually* held court at the raucous table of Ugs in the center of the room, which included the newly infertile young man. That era was clearly over. Today was the first day of the rest of these bitches' lives.

"Well done," Elise said, barely holding back applause. Charles was nowhere to be seen, and as such Elise was, in theory, the adult on duty. She shook Z's hand.

Z shrugged. "I saw you kick over that construction guy's wheel-barrow when he waved a euro at your belt." Elise nodded, and they sipped their coffees as newfound colleagues who'd long admired each other's work from afar.

After that they played poker together every night, jointly fleecing anyone who tried to join in and then splitting the money. Z regaled her with tales from the horror that Elise understood to be The Real World, a place she had no interest in visiting but was morbidly curious to hear about. Up at the site, Elise taught Z what to look for in the dirt, how to parse the ground for potential discoveries she could call her own, and the correct amount of awe to feel.

This exchange continued when Z left. They stayed in touch through a handful of colorful emails every year, Z's reports a firehose of names, places, and exes that seemed incredibly important but then never came up again. Elise's responses were escapist, if grievance-filled, descrip-tions of her Mediterranean dig work that Z asked legitimately non-bad questions about. They were attracted to the rarity of the exposed rawness in each other. True irreverence was hard to find, and it just seemed so obviously practical; it felt like they'd finally met the only other logical person on the planet. They each tethered the other to worlds they were respectively afraid of participating in fully: Elise denied herself friends, Z denied herself mountains. Elise had missed Z, she admitted begrudgingly, and had been even more head-down with her work after Z left. Having her back in the mix might make the slumber party sleeping arrangements tolerable.

The furthest thing from tolerable was the fact that this year Elise's nemesis, Kara, would be occupying the dig's only single room. This made her seethe. She'd been here twice as long as that witch, and yet.

Charles lived and died by a strict hierarchy. Elise had worked for some colossal buffoons before—especially the developers, the ones who needed to get a third-century Athenian mosaic "outta the way," so they could build a sewer line to move toilet water from a new hotel. But those guys at least treated her like an expert and an equal. Charles's shine toward someone, however, was disproportionate to how much they sweat. He demanded hard work and then looked down on those who did it for him. Consequently, he didn't care whose hands pulled a discovery out of the dirt; it was instead whoever carried the piece across the threshold into the lab who got the glory. As if it hadn't just been perfectly safe, doing just fine, thank you—for *four thousand years* in the ground.

She could find Plato's mummy down there and mouth-to-mouth the guy back to life, but it wouldn't put a framed piece of paper on the wall for her.

It was a particular limbo she lived in. Elise existed in the precise center of the professional archaeological spectrum. Those at the top running the digs were all professors, scholars, and researchers with that obnoxious noodle soup of letters behind their surnames. To them,

Elise was a tragic figure whose promise was cut short, having dropped out of Sheffield due to a workplace romance catastrophe she was loathe to acknowledge to anyone. They couldn't understand how she could stand to tread water in such a sea of disappointment. These arrogant boobs were forever suggesting she get a few more credits, take some standardized tests, and return to school in her forties. Whenever she was huddled around a map or an artifact with people like this and proffered a new trench location or topographical explanation, they looked up at her and slapped her gently on the shoulder.

"Now Elise, that's an excellent idea. See? You do have what it takes. My offer to put in a good word with the dean still stands."

She dreamed of violently murdering them all with the rusty edge of her trowel, every time.

Then at the bottom rung of these digs were the construction workers. Local cash handlers who moved boulders or uprooted trees and spoke the lingua franca of a hand thrust forward holding a pack of cigarettes. Elise spoke fluent Greek, an impressive bilingualism that earned her dealings with the only people on the site who humped the air in their overalls when female excavators passed by to go pee in the woods. One rung above these Grecian emissaries were the Ugs, who were only allowed to shovel out new trenches and sift recent dirt for things previous excavations missed or left behind. A testament to their sophistication was their wild excitement over finding a bunch of British crap. This whole caste thought Elise was an un-fuck-with-able genius.

So she was smack dab in the middle, a lead excavator tasked with the most promising trenches. This required her to work like a dog digging under a fence in the middle of summer, and also like a cancer surgeon, able to identify the centimeter of a piece that protruded from the dirt, surmise and map its surroundings, and then extract it flawlessly.

With one last step over the edge of dry grass ringing the site, Elise climbed up onto the plateau that was the enormous track area. Behind her were a million miles of green, lighting to life as the sun spilled over the far side of the valley. It was silent, and as soon as she'd stood for a moment and wiped the sweat from her upper lip, she turned up the volume on her pocket radio. She was an obsessive soccer follower, and had broken apart and souped up an old radio Ian found to get a station that played the FIFA women's games. The announcer piped in now, her tin-can-ified voice lofted over the grounds by the wind.

The entire excavation rolled out before her, rising gently from the oval, dirt-packed track up into the wide stone bleachers. The bleachers lead back to the processional, up toward the locker rooms. Atop an abrupt, steep hill rose the altar, perched above all the other trenches, all hers.

They were excavating an ancient athletic site where the Greeks had once held the Olympics, before the Olympics were at Olympia. It boiled down to a bunch of creepy toga priests blessing teenage athletes, who competed butt-naked, running around the track with everything flopping everywhere, for everyone to see. The local rich people sat higher up on the stands than the poor people, who clapped and yelled and got wasted and ate ancient corndogs and placed bets on whose junk would cross the finish line first. The altar up top was where they burned goats and idols, to favor certain athletes or anyone else so goat-rich that they could just set one on fire for good luck. The locker rooms were a set of stone cubbies where the coaches and religious officials pregamed by blessing the athletes, undressing them for competition, and showering their naked bods in olive oil. Basically, like sports always do, the games gathered all the jocks together and got them zonked and bumping into each other in various formations, dropping stuff right and left, which was good news for the nerds like them who'd later come to clean it all up.

Elise loved this site. It felt like home to her—her first excavation in Greece, her first one on her own after leaving her ex—and this morning moment alone with it was a salve. It was a set of ruins she saw herself in. She'd been an avid runner her entire adult life, a regimen that hiking supplanted here, and she could feel in her ramming heart every morning the same kind of blazing ache that *they* must have felt, here, then. It made perfect sense to her, pushing your body like that. No one else, not even Charles, knew what this place really was, what it could feel like completely in its full, raw savageness—or knew how much was still untouched, the screams that were still well buried. That all made her fiercely attached to it, and protective.

Her dream was to take over from Charles. Not that he would ever allow that. God forbid someone who'd actually held a shovel, instead of some tweezer dweeb picking paint flecks off some pottery, run the show. But it's what she wanted more than anything, and knew that she deserved.

She saw this site for what it really was. It wasn't some sit-back-and-ponder-the-ancients or quaint-scenes-from-daily-life place, like so many of her other digs were. No. People pulled their hair, screamed and bled, and lost their goddamn minds here. That's what Charles never got. He'd been a competitive runner, so he knew, on some level, what kind of wild energy competition could leave behind in a place, but he was far too buttoned up. He saw a neat progression of sports-as-military-training, ritual, tradition, torch neatly passed.

For men. That's what Elise saw: that men were given the opportunity to scream and bleed and lose their goddamn minds. *Why not us?* It would've changed everything, she believed, if women had been allowed to be disgusting and brutal too. If the spectrum of allowable female behavior had widened that much earlier, where would we be now? Would we be receiving advice to try covering up with a collared shirt if we wanted to be put in charge? Would we have to field the foreman's invitation to meet for a drink to discuss topography? Would we wonder why Gary made more money even though we'd been here twice as long? Or would we be the ones, thanks to a birthright of completely acceptable disgustingness and brutality, to grab, push, insinuate, and subjugate? She had no idea, but she thought about it all the goddamned time.

To Charles, here were the halcyon days of dudes, testosterone's origin story. His life's work was the distillation and elevation of this essential maleness that he deemed very much still essential. Men being men, always and forever, was the message he supplied, and there was no sign of the demand for that drying up. It was quite popular—*he* was quite popular. This place was an absolutely perfect testament to his working worldview.

But not for long.

This year Elise knew its secret.

It came to her in Crete, where she worked the last season. Elise had been digging alongside an excavator and fellow trench hand—sans title—named Deb. She was a lifer who'd stayed on her husband's site after the guy dropped dead of a stroke, shovel in hand. She was about twenty years older than Elise, with a full head of bushy white hair. If Elise had allowed it the relationship would have bordered on maternal, but she didn't.

A few months ago during an early morning over oatmeal, Deb told Elise she'd read something in one of her dusty old academic journals about women competing in pre-Olympic games; there were ancient writings to that end. They were known as the Heraean Games. Women ran around the track, hurled javelins, wrestled, blistered, sweated, panted, and hoisted fists full of flowers over their drenched heads while standing on top of a little podium to the surround sound of cheers.

The Olympics, started by women. Sports, invented by girls.

The thought electrified her. Buried here were the bones of her "ancestors," a word she'd never even used before. It was certainly not a word she associated with her own mother and grandmother, the only family she'd ever known. They were perennially boyfriended women who'd spent thirty-five years apiece working the department store makeup counter, lacquered, dyed, and diet-pilled into anonymity. They had always been mystified by Elise's preference for the outdoors, school, and her own quiet company. Even the other women excavators she met over the years were apart from her, remaining in the field either through marriage or graduate school obligations and unsure what to make of Elise, with her ambition to run a dig with neither credentials nor connections. And then, in the dirt itself, she found again and again evidence of pottery handling and jewelry wearing that rendered girls either domestic or royal. But now, here— suddenly seeming, but really the evidence had been here all along— here once ran the wild bitches, her foremothers. It had taken decades of digging and brushing, of polishing the ground until it became a mirror. There had always been a healthy, professional distance between the work itself, which she was good at, and the meaning of that work, the history it shored up. But not anymore. Now she was unburying herself.

"Isn't that a hoot, Lisey?" Deb had asked, slurping a bowl of watery oats, the standard breakfast of digs the world over. "There's even a list of gals who ran and did the track events. Naked, too! They're ranked: first, second, third, and so on. And no male names on the list. Not one. Says those games were all between the ladies; the men came later. And then I thought, 'You know what, I got to show this to Elise,' because it sure could be. The dates are all lined up, and this could be right near the Mega site. Yes ma'am, seems to be."

Deb slid the paper over the gingham plastic tablecloth to Elise, who flipped over the cover to find that the journal was from the sixties. Not bad. Whichever proto-archaeo-feminist proffered this nugget would have been long gone, but in Elise's line of work, fifty years was a sneeze into the hurricane of time. It was worth digging into.

Deb had giggled. "Heraea, it's called. The Heraean Games," she pointed at the word on the page. "It's like saying 'hell, yeah,' while somebody pinches your tongue." She did this herself a few times.

"Can I take this?" Elise asked.

Deb pushed it further toward her. "Watch out, world. Lise is on the loose."

There was no evidence though. Archaeology alone was where the facts lived; this is why she respected it. No smoke, all fire. Speculation about that far back was just theoretical, and the only real truth—the only realness you could get your arms around to properly believe in—came from the ground. Anything like this journal—descriptions, lists, accounts, anything jotted down on the lying page—was suspect until dug up otherwise. What was real was what you touched. If there wasn't any hard archaeological evidence for The Heraean Games then it didn't mean a thing. It was the ultimate chimera.

And yet. Was it possible?

Charles was dickwashing history.

Of course he was. There was no way he didn't know about a hypothesis like this, he was simply smothering it. He'd built a small empire—bricked and mortared with the tacky teal dust jackets of his lone book and appearances as a featured speaker at club luncheons—on athletic masculinity as a birthright throughout the ages. There was a whole career, persona, and posh suburban house that didn't want the Mega site upended, its skirt blown up. Charles had made a chunk of change erecting this phallus palace, and he would die before admitting it was all built on lies.

Lucky for him, nothing had ever been found to combat his narrative—yet.

Elise's plan was to dig, the only thing she knew how to do, to find the lacunae within the mountain. Because if she did, if she possibly could, if it was down there, she'd expose him. That Chazhole and his protégé Kara had both spent years making Elise feel less-than. It was like they believed she, with her rough, dirty hands, couldn't possibly understand the site or who these buried people were. But now she knew, really knew—girls, girls, girls!—and she hoped to god she'd dig up some kind of piece to help her prove it.

Then they'd put her in charge, they'd have to. It would all finally, correctly, belong to her.

For the first time in her life, she felt like someone down there was calling for her. Someone buried alive—someone like her—calling to be put in her right place.

When she left Crete for the season, she'd tried to slip onto the boat unnoticed, but Deb of course squirreled her way through the damp crowd on the dock and found her. She wrapped her bony arms around Elise's waist and shoved that white Brillo cloud of hair into her face.

Then, with one hand on Elise's shoulder and her other fingers pinching her tongue, the old woman said, "Heraea."

Hell, yeah.

✈

Think about everything that had to happen for you to find me.

All I had to do was wait right here and that was easy enough. But a million little things could've happened to stop you from being there and from finding my story. You're the miraculous one, when you really think about it.

And I know you're thinking, Well, if it weren't me, someone else's brush would've come along and dusted its way down; they always do. But you're wrong. I think you'll find at the end of this that I was, in fact, waiting for you.

Chapter

4

Losing an engagement ring was one of the most understandable mishaps in the world. Surely it happened every single day, one thousand times a day, all over the globe. There were little diamonds wedged into unfindable corners and crevices the earth over. And most of those slipped from the fingers of women doing office work or housework, let alone the rigorous physical labor Kara was doing. Couldn't she just "lose" the ring? And miraculously find it later, of course. It would make perfect sense and be an excellent segue:

"As you know, I can't find my ring. And Gary, well, I'm not sure I *want* to . . . "

"About the missing ring. I didn't even *realize* that I was missing it . . . "

"If we do end up finding the ring, I want *you* to have it . . . "

It would certainly help to strategize. If only Kara could talk to someone about this and brainstorm the breakup, so to speak. But with who? Elise—comical. Charles? Good Lord, no. Discussing the weather stretched the bounds of their professionalism. *There's simply no one else here*, she thought, sitting on the patio surrounded by seven tank-topped, head-bobbing ragamuffins. It would have to be Z and, well, at least she had experience in the field of crushing Gary.

The patio outside the lab was partly shaded at this hour, and Kara sat leaning against one of the squat stone walls with her legs bent. A large black bucket rested between her thighs. Inside was her daily allotment of the previous day's finds. She dunked her arms up to the elbows in the water and rubbed her fingers along the pottery and roof shards, blindly sensing which dirt was willing to slide off.

Half a dozen or so Ugs sat around her doing the same, each lost to the tune of their headphones and each wearing less than the next. A mind-boggling tube top was within sight, next to spaghetti straps already dripping past a set of sunburned shoulders. No fewer than three mens' T-shirts had their sleeves ripped off, revealing an ungodly number of side nipples. A do-rag was among them. She was being forced to examine an appalling display of podiatry thanks to flip-flop abundance, despite her warning to them yesterday about dropping buckets full of sharp objects. Based on the present aesthetic, no doubt a missing toe would be considered chic. Kara had long believed in conveying hierarchy through her sartorial choices; with her white linen wardrobe she was determined, as always, to appropriately look the part. Her wide straw sun hat, flowing button-downs, and classic leather hiking boots with herringbone laces set her emphatically apart from her charges.

She felt clear on how the middle of the conversation with Gary should go; she could very articulately reason her way through *why* they shouldn't get married. But it was the opening salvo that evaded her. Down in the water, against the edge of a roof tile, her disappointingly modest diamond ring caught on the slippery edge; it nearly came off her finger before Kara caught it with her knuckle. See? Just like that.

Now she stood up and walked a loop around the ragtag washers. Buckets were jammed between their legs, mud was caked up to their bare shoulders, and they held hoses that they squirted onto their heads and into each other's mouths like dogs. All of them appeared to be melting, oozing sweat, sunscreen, and wrongful attempts at makeup in the dwindling patio shade. Despite the heat, they seemed to be having the time of their lives. Their little whispers and laughs implied a joyful belief in the work itself that Kara took full credit for instilling in them.

As she walked about, hands clasped behind her back, she winked at every single one of them in a row. It didn't occur to her what this would look like in aggregate.

More than once in Kara's life, someone had stopped her mid-sentence when she was just talking about something she considered totally casual and said, "Honey, it's OK." Her anxiety was often palpable to others, no matter how hard she tried to appear calm and composed in every circumstance. Some people were able to make put-together look effortless, but Kara was not one of them. Knowing this made her aim even more stridently for *easy breezy*. Winking was part of her new personality plan to win friends and influence people; she'd seen Z do this with the Ugs. Correctly executed eye play could be one of the keys to endearing herself to others, something she was beginning to suspect had been a factor in her failed interviews. So far not a single auction house had offered her a spot, and she was starting to panic. Her heart was set on being a preservationist at one of the top houses, Christie's or Sotheby's, and yet neither had taken the bait on her impeccable resume. It was not possible for anyone to come more prepared or better recommended; she had a gnawing feeling that it was a personality fit issue. Likability was at the top of her list to tackle this summer. She would return to the city armed with winningness.

Kara's stepmother Evelyn, the goddess of silk scarves, had assured her this was the missing piece.

"It's not who you know, dear. We know everyone. It's the *mood* one can create. Here," Evelyn said just before Kara left, handing her a discreet, embossed leather pouch containing a dozen tiny, white anti-anxiety pills. Kara's nerves weren't particularly extreme, but Evelyn found stress vulgar, particularly in women, and encouraged Kara to think the same. Why dally and let a doubt fester into full-blown worry? The proper mood, a smooth vantage point from which one could solve one's problems evenly, could be created at once. Kara loved Evelyn more than anyone in the world and relied on her steadfast council for nearly everything in her life. Her parents—both maxed-out, furious finance titans Kara barely saw save for tense ten p.m. dinners—had divorced when Kara was a toddler, and Evelyn had married Kara's father not long after. She then lavished attention on the lonely child, a perfect, tabula rasa baby she'd obtained without having to ruin her figure. She was utterly devoted to Kara and had been the one to cultivate her interest in antiquities in the first place. Evelyn appreciated various pieces for their statement decor and had long encouraged Kara to study the treasures of ancient history. She pushed the girl to strive further than Evelyn had been able to go herself—and to pursue a doctorate in Mediterranean Archaeology to solidify an expertise in this most elegant, timeless, *appropriate* subject matter.

Evelyn would be proud of the structure Kara imposed here, if scandalized by the appearance of its participants. Every single artifact and fragment passed through this place, her pristine temple. She continued walking laps around the patio now, touching up here and there; it was critical for everything to look its best when Charles returned for the midday break. That's when the vans would disgorge the repellant field team with a dozen rubber buckets filled with fragments of cups, plates, roof tiles, coins, utensils, bones, bowls, glass, weapons, you name it, plus rocks, bugs, and trail mix peanuts. Her team removed the dirt and placed the cleaned pieces on the patio to dry, then moved the pieces every few hours to chase the baking heat as the sun crossed over. Once they were bone dry, they'd be categorized and stored. If they found anything that looked promising—an inscription or particular beauty or strangeness, as determined by Kara—she took over cleaning in her VIP bucket or by the light at her desk. The system she'd put in place was, by necessity, foolproof. Her goal was to run this place so well this year that anyone could take it over next year when she was long gone; indeed, she would measure her success by the incompetence of her successor.

The white stone lab building was perched so that it stuck out from the steepest drop marking the base of their village. The bottom of its floor was propped up by splintering wooden stilts, which stood parallel to the walnut trees. "Precarious" was putting it mildly; the stilts appeared like toothpicks compared to the sturdy, hard-barked trunks that had been licked black by recent forest fires. Luckily, the absence of structural soundness wasn't visible from the parking lot or the lab itself; only those who ventured on walks down and around the nearest street were treated to the life-affirming view of the building in which they'd been working. But the stilted position allowed for the best views in the village. The edges of the lab's wide, wraparound patio rose with stone half-walls for sitting or leaning, and the entire valley unfurled below and you could extend your hand out to grab a handful of green, flesh-wrapped walnuts on the nearest, highest branch. You could look down onto the cascade of treetops that waved along the mountain, dashed by white streams of passing sheep or the splash of a cross and then trickled out into the flat expanse below. There the road became clear, a black slither into misnomer Megalopolis; the city from this vantage point was just a yellow-gray thumbprint, alone in the enormous valley that was bowled in by mountains like theirs on all sides.

There were a million more mountain perches just like this one encircling the land, and Kara wondered as many times why these Greeks had chosen to ascend, build, compete, and live here. On a clear day from the top of the altar at the site, the town of Olympia was visible a few peaks over. They too had taken a look around here, after a practice century or so, and thought, *We should upgrade.*

For its part, Megalopolis was famous for two things discovered in tandem in the sixties: while excavating ruins of a fourth-century BC Arcadian theater, archaeologists uncovered lignite coal deposits. The theater was a dime a dozen around here that in fact produced zero dimes for the locals. The deposits, however, became the foundation of the town's economy. Looking down from the dig, the lignite factory was the only other human structure visible in the valley, a belching white dot outside the town. Years ago, when he still harbored any interest in expanding hearts and minds other than his own, Charles dragged the team down to the Arcadian ruins for a poison-gas-scented tour. If you walked among the remains and stood in the middle of the arc where the stage had been, your feet crunching pebbles that had once been rocks beneath the feet of these actors, you could look out at the former portico down a long line of Doric columns. From here the marble stalks lined up perfectly with the smokestacks right behind them, giving the impression of a white pillar lineage that extended forever.

"Aw, can't he hang out with us?" an Ug asked, looking up the hill.

The resident stray, Nuts, barked up there by the houses all morning long. He aimed mostly at the cafeteria, hoping for some pre-lunch scraps. Ursula was known to fling ladlefuls of lentils out the door for him to lick up in the grass. Some archaeologists trained dogs to sniff out ancient human remains as a way of finding burial sites in dense forestation or impenetrable jungles. Nuts's repertoire had him stumbling over a bagged sandwich.

"He's hungry!"

"I bet he's thirsty."

"He just wants a belly rub."

A favorite village pastime was to debate the correct ways to feed and care for dogs without ever doing either for Nuts. Not that he seemed to mind. Nuts waited very politely until later in the season to bite someone.

People didn't often guess that Kara was an athlete herself, but she'd participated in rowing as a coxswain. The position was ideal for her petite frame and excellent sense of giving directions. She'd been completely obsessed with the Olympics and her chosen sport's rich heritage. She hadn't made it even close to competing at that high level—her parents never for a second entertained that route—but the absolute rigor of it captivated her. That's what she loved about these artifacts: they spoke to a consistent practice and devotion that she understood and admired deeply. However, Charles routinely emphasized that, unlike her rowing, the sports they were looking into here had been savage competitions: lung-shattering sprints and relays, grueling long runs at altitude, and the hurling of javelins and discuses that stretched ligaments to snapping. The athletes were filthy—sweating, screaming, blistering, and bleeding. It was nothing at all like her junior varsity experience sitting in the stern of a boat speaking into a headset, zipped into a cozy fleece against the crisp autumn air. Charles's stressing of the savagery at the competition's core, a rugged maleness, prevented Kara from feeling as strong a personal connection to *them*—the Greeks—as she would've liked to. She did think of herself as an athlete, certainly when she was younger, but through Charles's lens was relegated to imagining herself as one of the spectators.

The only downside to being second in line behind the excavators was being at the mercy of those dirt pirates, like Elise. While she'd never crawl into a trench herself, Kara sometimes wished she could have more of a hand in the process, particularly when the pieces she was tasked with restoring had been yanked out of the ground like weeds. She wouldn't trust the field team to pluck her eyebrows.

Case in point, the Victor fiasco.

Can you imagine if, after being down there for four thousand years, the first person you glimpsed on the other side was a cat-tattooed, kneepad-strapped maniac in wraparound sunglasses?

What killed Kara the most was that a discovery like that would've guaranteed her a spot at Christie's. Elise had ruined that for her.

Any minute now the swaggering trench team would be back, and it would be chaos at lunch, and her whole team would be riled up for the afternoon. She snatched the hose from someone's hand to wash up, scrubbing up to the elbow like a surgeon. Then she stepped inside the building to search for the discuses for the hundredth time.

There were two missing, and both bore inscriptions she hadn't even had a chance to fully inspect yet. In the past weeks she'd torn the lab apart and meticulously reconstructed it half a dozen times, knowing for certain the discs were here in this village somewhere—they had to be. On her watch this would not stand. Charles was notoriously disorganized, and even though she'd begged him for years to let her maintain the lab's storage system, only this year had he finally relented. When he'd passed the torch, he made quite the big deal about her shouldering the blame should anything go wrong there. She assured him it wouldn't, and yet here she stood with two pieces unaccounted for.

She knelt before the lowest set of storage drawers for what felt like the millionth time—hope sprang eternal—and began filing through again, slowly, ever so slowly, lifting each piece, unwrapping, and re-cataloging. The search certainly gave her time to think.

It wasn't that she didn't love Gary. Everyone loved Gary. He was one of those people that everyone called "the best."

The problem was that this dusty bowl of weirdos wasn't just the first sentence in the blurb on Gary; it was the whole blurb. The entire thing would be about laser topography at this and other Greek athletic sites, which was fine for him. That's what Charles's blurb was before the 2004 Greek Olympics, and many would consider it a dream blurb. But Kara dreamed of something different. For Kara, this whole five years was just the start of a single second sentence after her education pedigree: *She completed her research at the Megalopolis excavation in Southern Greece as the Preservation Director before going on to* something fabulously impressive. And it builds from there; it becomes one of those blurbs where you have to go back and read the first part again because you'd like to know how someone who could end their blurb with such a bang got their start.

Merging blurbs with Gary was not an option. To her, the stairs at the center of this village were an escalator; to Gary, each step was a tiny seat on which he could stop and watch the world pass by. This had not been clear when they began dating. They'd both been walking up together, rising up, hands clasped. Then he simply paused, smiled, and said, *I love it here, don't you? Look, a Eurasian collared dove!* And that was that; she'd been incapable of prying his foot one inch higher. He took such pleasure in the small things in life that she felt he missed the big things—the things she felt he *should* be getting pleasure from. It frustrated her deeply that she hadn't seen it sooner, before they'd gotten engaged. She was ashamed to find out that her love was conditional, and the conditions had changed.

ON THEIR HIKE UP THE STAIRS TO DINNER THAT NIGHT, CHARLES SIDLED up to Kara at the midpoint, smelling like a damp wool sweater. He whispered in his aspirationally English timbre, "There's something I'd like to discuss with you."

The missing discs. Her stomach plummeted.

She gulped, "Of course!"

"After dinner. Just you," he added, before jogging the remaining steps then slipping through the cafeteria door.

Inside was pandemonium. Ugs socialized at an unbearable decibel and scrounged for food as if they'd all been starved in solitary confinement. One of them had recently uncovered a shabby boom box in the shed and now subjected them all to its one single disco mix cassette at all hours of the day; Charles inconceivably enjoyed this grooving mobius strip of nightmares, and so it remained on. Behind her in line for food was Patty, the infamous, mulleted Ug who'd lost Charles's suitcase and was presently sniffing Kara's hair.

On the buffet table at the back of the room were large trays of purplish gray chicken; Kara took one piece, obscuring the meat with rice. It was a similar offering meal after meal: a fine enough rotation of every dish one could conjure from varying levels of heat unto lentils, poultry, or tomatoes. Much to Evelyn's and her own delight, Kara lost weight every summer.

"Here, have some vegetables dear," Ursula scooped a heap of salad, vinaigretted to death, onto the very edge of Kara's plate. Half of it plopped on the floor for Nuts, who roamed the room snout down.

"Thank you," Kara said. "Where's Ian been? We haven't seen him much."

"He's been wandering off lately," Ursula said and bit her lip. "But I've got my crystals saying he'll be back by nightfall." From her apron pocket she pulled out and held up a well-worn nugget of pink quartz.

Kara executed the correct eye movements to politely end this exchange.

She lingered at the end of the food line with Z, asked if Z would like to sit together, and then steered them as far away as possible from the table where Gary and Elise sat. Gary gave her a confused look; Kara raised her eyebrows in practiced surprise, as if Z were the one dragging her off.

"So," she said, once they were seated and soundly protected by walls of Ug nonsense. "I'm not going to stay with Gary."

Z choked, the rice in her mouth blasting onto Kara's plate. "What?"

Kara placed her fork down, permanently. "It's just not the right relationship for me. I know I shouldn't have said yes. There was just so much momentum though. And just like you, he was my first real boyfriend and so, it just sort of naturally . . . progressed. I'd never felt like that before, a love feeling. I thought, this is what I do next! But now . . . Anyway, I just don't know how to, I guess, remove myself."

"A love feeling. Jesus. Wow, OK. You haven't talked to *him* at all about this? These doubts or whatever?"

"I don't know what to say, or how."

Z sighed and shook her head before continuing to eat while she spoke. "I mean, that I get. It's tough. Well, definitely don't go on a nice long walk in the park the day you do it. I can tell you that. The thing is—and I've been dumped like a million times—you just have to be prepared for the suck. You know?"

Kara nodded and wished she had a notebook in case, at some point, something helpful might be communicated. "Exactly. I'm wondering how I can prepare."

"I'll be totally honest with you Kar: I'm not the right person to ask about this. You remember how he and I broke up, right? I think you were there."

"I do." She did. In fact, she'd been the one to comfort Gary in the aftermath.

It was the stuff of Mega lore. Z and Gary had been the dynamic duo—before Z got otherworldly drunk on the annual beach weekend in Pylos and kissed Ryan, a worker who at present was moving rice, grain by grain, from a pile on his crotch to his mouth.

"Right. So, that's a fun route to go, the old straddle and skedaddle. I both highly recommend it and also don't. It's not really your speed, no offense. But hey, caveat emptor, as these dudes say."

Kara winced for so many reasons. She couldn't believe she was in this situation. Wedding plans were moving slowly, which she attributed to Evelyn's prescient sense of her reluctance. The club had been booked, and crustaceans had been committed to, but losing a deposit would feel almost heroic to her parents—with the stroke of a pen, they could extract their daughter from an unwanted situation. Teva-wearing Gary being completely agreeable to a black-tie wedding had only added to her sadness. He would agree to anything she said. All the little contortions he made to squeeze into Kara's Evelyn-designed box depressed her. She had made none for him and never would.

"Well, thank you, I guess," she concluded with Z.

"Always down to chat. And I won't, you know, say anything until you do whatever it is you're going to do. Here to help, seriously." Z peered over at Kara's plate, her fork hovering. "You gonna finish that?"

THEY ALL WENT OUT TO THE PATIO AFTER THE MEAL, AS ALWAYS, where they sat around the best picnic table to have exactly one beer each. Gary plopped down to Kara's left and slung his arm around her, chatting up Ian about relative wood strengths. As was their habit, Z and Elise played cards. Every single night, Elise showed up to dinner with her hair sopping wet from a shower, dressed in identical clothes to those she wore to work (a cargo short for every occasion). Around her neck, a quarter-sized black boxing glove dangled from a thin gold chain.

Before things went sideways with Victor, Kara had one memorable long talk with Elise. They'd been stuck in the van together on a supply run when an endless stream of sheep held them hostage for an hour, and Kara had learned about the boxing glove. Although Elise hadn't mentioned the necklace specifically, she told Kara matter-of-factly that she'd grown up in rural Henshaw, Hadrian's Wall country. There, she dodged her mother's string of seedy boyfriends by running off a lot out deep into the hills near Vindolanda, the Roman fort ruins where they'd discovered two-thousand-year-old boxing gloves among swords, arrowheads, and tablets documenting life on the northern frontier of Roman Britain. In the summers she sometimes stayed out all night, sleeping among the stones. That's how she'd gotten interested in this work in the first place, as a lone wolf dig team. *Way less lonely, I was, knowing they were there.* Kara had been stunned by this personal response to her mere chitchat with someone she barely knew, but Elise spat it out evenly in no more than three sentences and without a trace of emotion; it was what it was. At the time Kara had stammered a response about being taken to the Met a lot as a child. But ever since then, she'd had the words for her inexpressible feeling on the nights when she was all alone in the lab touching the edge of a coin or a bowl. She was not alone, because *they were there* too.

Playing cards slapped the table as Elise shuffled. She glared over at Kara, probably suspicious of how and why she'd stolen a meal with her only friend here. Kara felt her eyes on her and didn't return her gaze.

The Ugs lounged below them by the old swing set, their glowing bands of tan lines aimed like arrows at one another. Nuts lay in a pool of shadow nearby, obliterating someone's shoe.

The table conversation inevitably turned to the primo topic, Now Canonical Formerly Horrific Injuries. Every season there was a freak accident that no amount of warnings, lectures, training, or first aid kits could prevent. The current safety guidelines in Mega, a place filled with sharp tools, steep hills, precarious boulders, untethered hormones, and a menagerie of poisonous bugs and snakes, could be summed up as que será, será.

One year, someone burned themselves trying to smoke Kalamata tree leaves. One Ug carved Coolio lyrics into a rock and sliced off the tip of his finger. Two kids got bitten in the genitals by the same persistent, perverted snake when they were off in the woods together. Another kid packed forty electric toothbrush head replacements for a three-month stay, buried his stockpile behind the cafeteria (excavation skills inspiring the young minds already), couldn't find the spot in the dark three days later, slipped on some moss, and broke his leg in two places. They never found the dental accessories, though to be fair no one looked that hard. Who knows what the excavation crew in 3610 would think.

Yawns finally circled the table, and Kara felt her chest constrict once people started to leave for bed, one by one. She tightened her ponytail—this always fortified her—then waited out everyone else and slithered her way up to Charles's room, unseen.

"I APOLOGIZE," CHARLES GREETED HER. "PLEASE," HE SAID, GESTURING to an upholstered armchair in the corner.

This miniature, luxurious room was jarringly out of place here. There was a red carpet, excessively tasseled, with curved corners and a long-faded Oriental pattern. The walls were aglow with the soft light of antique brass standing lamps. Stacks of papers, maps, binders, and books snaked around the floor, two of which were piles of only *Running Naked*. Kara assumed they were here to replenish the supply in the lab, should anyone ever take one. A heavy wooden desk faced the wall nearest the bathroom and had an L-shaped fluorescent lamp atop it. The light beamed down upon an array of dusty items mid-inspection, each encased in plastic storage bags and encircled by rubber bands. He even had an old printer, which lent the place an air of technological advancement in comparison to his surroundings. On the top rim of the desk there was also a silver-framed photograph of Charles with his wife, Terry, her hair all sharp brown angles, their elbows locked together in black tie as they hammed for the camera.

Kara had met Terry many times at various faculty soirees and had even been to their home for dinner before. The pottery-forward aesthetic there confirmed that Terry was a kook subdued into suburban acceptability. The woman had undergone a lifelong descent from parent-supported artist to married art teacher to crafty mom, to empty nester art hobbyist, at present. She and Charles both were the kinds of WASPs who at some point had indeed been wealthy, no longer were, and were confounded by it.

The room was filled to the absolute brim, with only a thin, vacant halo around the sturdy wooden bed frame. There was a large satellite picture of Arcadia tacked to the wall and a geological map of the region beside it. In a cavalier miscalculation of safety, a green candle burned on top of the bookstack that stood in as a bedside table. Charles walked over to the desk and pressed play on another boom box, the mere sight of which made Kara wince. Classical music piped in, to her relief, but she knew instantly that he intended to muffle their conversation.

She found a navy blue armchair and sat up as straight as she could, eschewing the ottoman, and smiled at attention. The cushioning felt uncomfortably squishy after spending the last few weeks on stone and picnic benches.

"I hardly mean to be so cloak-and-dagger about all this," he put up both hands, as if something weren't his fault.

"Oh, it's fine! This room is lovely," she said. "Lovely" was a word she'd been taught to deploy strategically when you wanted to convey warmth but had nothing specifically nice to say about the thing at hand. Her parents had used it when she introduced them to Gary.

"Did Terry do all this?" She asked.

"In a manner of speaking. She encourages me to make myself comfortable here." He looked down at the floor. "Perhaps too much."

"Mmm," Kara screwed her smile on tighter.

He looked up and matched her purported emotion. "It's certainly nice after a long day. I do wish we could make you all more comfortable down there."

"Well, I'm loving the single. So thank you again. And Charles, I want to just say first thing: I am very close to finding those two discus fragments. I know it's taken longer than it should, but I'm sure they're there, obviously, after the reorg—"

He huffed a balking cough. "Of course they are! You're in charge now, Kara. This is what you claim to have wanted, full ownership down there. Each piece is your responsibility, and yours alone."

She lowered her head in solemnity, catching an unforgettable glimpse of her boss's laundry pile in the process. When she met his eyes again, she raised her chin to the moment. "I will find them."

"Do."

Silence waffled between them before Kara began, "Well, it's impossible to have a private exchange down there."

"How right," Charles said, as if the burden was on her to steer the conversation in the direction he preferred. "Yes, I'm glad you understand. I'll get right to it then. Kara, I'd like to talk to you about your mother."

"Which one?"

"Oh my. Right, yes, well. Your stepmother, that is."

"Evelyn," Kara confirmed. She felt the slightest pang of disappointment; it was not the first time her stepmother's reputation had superseded hers.

"Yes. I've had the pleasure of meeting her only once, at that function in the city where I spoke."

"The book tour," she said. In Kara's first year working under Charles's tutelage, she'd proudly taken her parents to see him speak at the University Club—an event, much to Evelyn's horror, co-titled with the tome in question and co-hosted with the Athletic Club. The experience confirmed every suspicion she'd ever had about people who admitted to wearing gym shorts.

"Exactly. I've always admired her work. And seeing as next year I'm slated to retire, well, I'm wondering if there's yet another chapter for me along those lines. If there's some way to connect further with her, ah, network. I imagine she deals with quite a few private collectors, and I simply feel that I could be of service—in a consulting capacity. I'm sure she has her hands full and I'm, well, always eager to assist those who care deeply about antiquities."

Kara wasn't surprised that Charles had remembered Evelyn—their name covered enough endowed chairs for that—just that he wanted anything to do with her professionally.

Evelyn was proof that one could replace letters after their name with zeros and be taken very seriously as an amateur scholar by way of avid collector. Over the past twenty-five years she'd become a voracious antiquities patron, middleman, and advisor for all kinds of arrangements in this sphere. It was a highly elevated form of the interior decorating so many of her ilk took up as a pet passion. Rather than upholstery recommendations, might she suggest to her insatiable circle a set of fine classical statuary to flank the fireplace? She knew of just the pair and had the authentication paperwork all drawn up already. Evelyn had an extraordinary eye that Kara admired, and an easy charm she envied.

"That's very sweet of you, but she loves doing it. It makes her so happy to help people find the right thing. Between you and me, I think she gets a little thrill from the commission. It's just fun for her. I'm sure you and Terry will have your hands full in no time, with all your travels. I saw that you all went to the Relais and Châteaux in Deerfield. It's something, isn't it?"

Charles looked ill, dabbing the back of his neck with a handkerchief. "It was, yes. Indeed. Well, now, I'm wondering if I might press you on this."

He lifted his open-faced palms and then put his hands together in a slow, silent clap.

"You see, I feel as though Evelyn's set could benefit immensely from knowing someone like myself. And after I'm finished with teaching, perhaps there could be other opportunities for me: some kind of consulting arrangement, you see. If there is anyone she knows who's interested in this sort of thing," he gestured loosely to the room, the site, the mountain, the planet, "I would love an introduction. It could be, well, a bit of a second wind for us, ah, well, uh, financially." His lips curled around the last word, and his eyes blinked as if the muscles in his face had betrayed him by forming the unsavory syllables.

Kara flinched. She was as shocked as if he'd asked for one of her kidneys. "Oh!" she said. She leaned back into her chair, like she'd been pushed in the chest.

"It would be quite impactful," he added. "Helpful, really. For both Terry and me. Quite necessary actually, that I bring in a bit more money, at this juncture." He twirled his wedding band around his finger and didn't meet her eyes.

Her parents had so ingrained in her the value of never acknowledging "resources," as they called it, that she'd made it to nearly thirty with zero experience with or curiosity on the subject. It simply wasn't wondered about, and by no means pointedly. It was rude, distasteful, and beneath anyone to do so. She'd found the appearance of actual digits and commas anywhere a crass one. And listening to Charles, she found she felt the same now.

"Of course," Kara said, putting on a prim smile. "I can email her right away."

Charles looked up from the floor.

"Call her," she corrected.

"Kara, that would be terrific. I do hope I'm not putting you in any kind of jam." He lifted both his hands up now for a third time, like a stage manager in the rafters held them on a string. "But that's all we're looking for, just a few introductions to keep me in the mix, and working. Contributing. And frankly, I feel that given—" He waved around the room, his kingdom, his life's work stacked among piles of socks. "I've got quite a lot to add to the mix, if I do say so myself. I know this is just the ticket."

"Absolutely."

She bolted up, and Charles extended his hand right away.

"Thank you again," he said, for the first time. He put his palms together and did a little Japanese-style bow. She nearly expected a white wig to hit the floor.

She reached for the doorknob. Charles waited with his hands now clasped behind his back, smiling like he'd just accomplished something big. This notion worried her.

"Good night!" He whispered.

She gave a little wave and stepped back onto the landing. The door closed with a click. For some reason, she pictured Charles behind the door pumping his fists in triumph, like Victor's little raised arms, though she couldn't imagine why. Her boss, a founding father in his field whom she deeply admired and, in many ways, had modeled her early career after had for some reason been reduced to begging. It did not bode well for her own prospects.

Chapter

5

Z needed a moment alone up at the site, and this was the only way to get it.

The squeaks of shifting cots mewed around the communal bedroom, which was still pitch black, lit only by a single candle stub on each windowsill. Z pulled on her skort and laced up her tennis shoes, all the while feeling Elise's eyes on her. Her friend stood in the doorway, silhouetted by the faintest silver in the trees behind her as the sun began to rise. Hands on hips, Elise had been ready to go for five full minutes and would happily leave without her.

Z stood slowly and tiptoed out onto the stairs. "This blows," she whispered. "Do you seriously skip breakfast?"

Elise shoved a granola bar into her ribs, a flavor which Z had already eaten, conservatively, thirty of since arriving. "Woof."

"This is me being nice," Elise reminded her. She trotted down the final stairs and onto the narrow dirt path that led up the mountain.

The hike nearly killed Z; with every vertical step she regretted not just stealing one of the vans. It was still dark, the amber-rimmed charcoal sky surrounded them. Elise marched forward as if the ragged path filled with loose rocks and thorned branches wasn't intent on their demise. The backs of Z's thighs flamed, and a cramp serrated her side. She was torn between the scorching effort of making conversation and the need for anything to take her mind off this misguided death march. The latter won out.

"Kal is totally hot," she huffed, her face purpling. She lifted her hands over her head to unfold any possible square inch of lung left to utilize. Kal was Mega's mayor who stopped by the site weekly, almost exclusively just to see Elise.

"We both know I could run up ahead and leave you here to die," Elise replied.

Z opted not to push. Though she had only a scant collage of Elise's romantic history—if you could call it that—it was dark enough for Z to grasp her reluctance on the topic. Elise's story had been doled out in snippets, each in a cautionary-tale-type response to one of Z's emails about a relationship snafu. Pieced together: Elise had fallen for Seth, one of her college professors, dropped out at his behest, followed him to Egypt, married him for some murky international financial reason, and started working on an excavation in Luxor, where they settled and from which Seth was increasingly absent. Elise put up with this arrangement until she very abruptly didn't (she did not offer Z more specifics on the escalation of his affairs). Elise had described the moment once, memorably and instructively, as *waking the fuck up*. When she told him she wanted to leave him and go finish her degree somewhere, Seth yanked the book she was holding out of her hand and threw it at her head, hard. It was a copy of *Queens of Egypt*—that detail she mentioned. Elise flew to Greece that same night, where a dig colleague knew someone she could work for, and had never left.

"I didn't know about Gary getting engaged, in case you're wondering," Elise said suddenly. "I would've told you. What the hell is he thinking?"

"It's not great," Z wheezed. The sun was up, and it hit the sky running, beaming heat at her back.

"But hey, at least you're having fun here anyway."

Z couldn't possibly hold court on the Gary situation now. "How's your friend Deb?" she heaved. She loved to hear about all the cargo-vested wingnuts that worked on Elise's digs. They were all itinerate like her, roving from excavation to excavation every few years—or in Elise's case, every few months. They were under-degreed shovelheads who snatched years from different centuries and probably knew more than the professors at the universities they contracted for. They spoke in time warps (*What plane are you on to Carthage?*) and reminded Z of human versions of the bottled sand layer art you could buy at a beach shop.

Deb, as Elise described her, was an octogenarian widow who'd spent the last two decades hopping between Greek islands to work seaside digs. After her archaeologist husband kicked the bucket (full of pottery shards), she picked up where he left off and succeeded him. She swam every single morning and showed up at whatever site she was on with her white hair Medusa-d into mythological status. She barely lifted a brush anymore, but it was said she had a preternatural sense of where to open the next trench. Z wanted to be her when she grew up.

Elise turned around for the first time to look back at Z. "Why do you ask?"

Z grunted along the lines of "uhdunho."

"Deb's fine. I might owe her one, actually. She gave me some decent information."

This was Elise-effusive. There was no world in which she would elaborate if not prompted. Prompting itself had limited results. Z was unable to continue holding up her half of the dialogue and focused on breathing.

By the time they reached the site, Z's shins were striped red from the claws of every malicious bush on earth. At the track, a horizontal mercy, she kneeled down and rolled flat onto her back. She closed her eyes.

In the wooze of drifting off she was twenty-one again, a senior in college studying this stuff. (She shouldn't have been surprised; here it was all about time travel.) After taking an intro to archaeology class freshman year to chase a theater guy she quite incorrectly had a crush on, she'd fallen absolutely in love with it. Her mother had been a history buff, and her father was devoted to detective procedurals; her chosen field of study seemed a logical combination. All her classes were held on the second floor of the university's ancient history museum, a city-block-sized institution containing hundreds of thousands of extraordinary global treasures that no one ever saw. The museum was at the far-flung edge of campus, across from the football stadium and formally designated Way Too Far To Walk To. It was a gorgeous, cathedral-like building, a perfect rectangle of ivy-lined brick walls with enormous arched, white-framed windows and a towering, domed rotunda that rose from behind, encircled with intricately patterned brick and stone rings. At ground level, above a handful of white stairs, was a fifteen-foot-tall marble door, which was very likely pilfered from a building somewhere else. Set far back from the street, the gardens out front held elaborate rose-bush mazes and lines of tasteful boxwoods, which flanked a long stone pool, generously goldfished. Two lion heads fountained water onto the reflection of the dome above.

Since Z was there all the time anyway (her parents gave her a bike), her beer-money part-time job was helping out the museum's events team. They threw all kinds of parties for faculty and donors; the place was a flawless anachronism that reminded a certain generation exactly why they ought to mention the school in their will, for nothing short of eternity. Z acted as table-arranger, caterer-wrangler, and additional bartender if it was a particularly parched bunch.

One such evening, she stood behind the bar as a prodigious crowd of alumni listened to a professor's presentation, "An Archaeological History of Japan," a topic they could apparently exhaust before dessert. It was black-tie, and everyone looked richer than usual. Z wore her only long dress, yellow and constricting. The bow-tied presenter stood at a lectern that Z had wheeled out that afternoon. Beside him was a large white poster board resting on an easel, onto which his slideshow was being projected. The audience was riveted as the talk touched upon the preceramic period of seven thousand BC. Every now and then, the jumbotron across the street touched upon buy one, get one free nachos at halftime.

Z zigzagged from behind the bar to the supply closet inside, keeping her portion of the proceedings afloat. She was buoyed by the prospect of the imminent after-party, wherein she and the other student caterers were allowed a ration of the leftover booze as well as use of the projector to watch a movie in the garden.

As the party wound down and professors linked arms with their partners to steady themselves on the cobblestone walkways, Z hauled the projector into place. By this point in the evening her chest and cheeks shone with her efforts. She could hear what her mother would say: *Women don't sweat, they glisten*. A dozen half-consumed bottles of wine stood at attention next to two trays of miniature quiches on the remaining white tablecloth as everything else was cleared away.

Soon it was dark out, and the garden was empty save for a handful of her fellow staffers who were seated patiently before the white easel, having blown through the mini quiche minutes ago. Z flipped the switch on the Toshiba projector, and before a single frame of the promised *Indiana Jones* appeared, smoke slithered from the lens. It spat out a single spark and died. At a speed suggesting they'd expected this, the overworked group loaded the wine bottles into their backpacks, and left.

Z stood alone, holding an orange extension cord in her hand. Then, just as she was wondering how on earth she was supposed to disassemble the giant party tent by herself, she heard footsteps. Walking toward her was a tall man in a perfectly cut tuxedo holding a foil-wrapped hot dog in each hand. He smiled as if they already knew each other; she looked behind herself to see only a squirrel. She returned her eyes to him, and her stomach wobbled. Never had a vision ignited her like this, and she blinked twice to make sure she hadn't been concussed by some errant piece of machinery. The man holstered the two hot dogs into his suit pockets, then pushed back his rowdy hair with one hand and adjusted his glasses with the other. Heat careened inside her chest.

"Shiba strikes again." He lifted up his arms and shook his head.

Z tried to close her mouth. Without another word, he crouched beside the ancient projector and rubbed its top like the head of a sick pet.

"I have to thank you," he said. "I've spent about half of my time in grad school so far fixing this thing. You might've finally killed it." He stood up and extended his hand. "Gary. You want one of these? I figured you didn't get to eat much all night. Only so many mini quiches one woman can survive on."

She cocked her head and accepted the hot dog in lieu of a handshake, unwrapping it immediately. "Zara. This is for me?"

He smiled. "I saw you earlier, zooming around behind the bar. And believe me, I know these guys can't be the best crowd."

"All tweed, no tips." She said with a mouthful.

He nodded, "Too bad about Shiba."

"It belongs in a museum," Z growled in her best Harrison Ford voice.

"That's my favorite line!"

"Duh, it explains everything." She waved her arm toward the gigantic building beside them. "Raison d'être!"

Gary bit his lip. Then he crouched down again, poking and prodding at a few of the old buttons and taking the cord from her hand, plugging it back in. He handed up to her a plastic red button cover with the white *To-* rubbed off by years of fingers. "I don't even know where this goes." Z slipped it into her dress pocket.

After a minute, there was a low rattling noise, and then Ford poured onto the white screen.

"What a guy," she said.

Gary stood and adjusted his tux. Z held up her hand. He brought his palm to hers, then wrapped his fingers in a kind of vertical shake—a downright sensual high five.

"Should've brought more hot dogs," she purred.

An hour later they were in the middle of the film, just the two of them seated side by side in the dark garden, faces lit by the screen, shouting out lines. By the end their limbs were pressed together, her arms inside the sleeves of his borrowed jacket.

As the credits rolled she said, "I want to do this again."

"I'm thinking . . . ten to twelve thousand times more," he suggested. "And I am so glad you're not in my class."

She raised her eyebrows.

"'Introduction to Survey Methods in Greek Topography.'"

"Ooh." She fanned herself.

"Wait till you hear about the dig I'm on. It's for my thesis: a map of burial practices at pre-Olympic athletic ritual sites, baby."

Ten months later, they were in Greece.

Being with him was the easiest thing she'd ever done. During her final year of school, she became aware of a creeping cynicism among her classmates, especially the ones with jobs lined up—a preemptive world weariness. She just wanted to travel for a while after graduation, and they looked at her from on high as if she were stepping out onto a ladder in order to purposefully descend to a lower tax bracket. Z's roommate at the time—on a one-way ticket to a miserable decade on Wall Street herself—told her, at twenty-one, that Z had Peter Pan

Syndrome. But when Z was lying in bed beside Gary, someone who stopped to marvel at everything that flew or crawled by—someone who, like her, lived for the possibilities of lunch, she thought, *Yeah, and it rules.* Every night they spent together felt stuffed with potential. It was above, below, and all around them; together, they multiplied their abilities to exhaust it all.

The dig was certainly a more practical focus than her vague notion to *see the world* for a few months that summer. That's of course not to mention the fact that the university flew her out, put her up, and included a free, fantastic boyfriend.

"Every single summer could be like this," Gary reminded her. "Not a bad way to live." He often touted the merits of graduate school—delayed development and all—but Z pulled against those lines. She was itching to get out of school and move on to what was next in her life, whatever that might be. The fact that she could stay with Gary *and* fly halfway around the world at this juncture was absolutely perfect.

In the middle of that summer, at what neither of them knew to be the apex of their relationship, the two of them slinked up one night and buried that red projector button cap by a cluster of trees near the track. The pointless plastic piece of a machine, made in Japan and used in America to flash movies about fictional archaeologists onto white sheets, made complete sense to them as the enduring totem of their love.

It had thrilled her to think about each morning, as the tires crunched over the gravel on the drive up there together, their fingers jammed together tightly as they sat in the back seat of the van. That sound, a slow murmuring crunch of the van cruising right beside the track, there it was. She could feel the dust inside her nostrils and the crunching grew louder, louder, louder.

"Stop!" Kara screamed.

Z shot up from the waist like Frankenstein Barbie, launching her pink sunglasses onto her feet. The grill of the blue van hummed a yard from her face.

A Greek chorus of *Oh-shit-you-killed-her*s rang from the sliding doors, which unleashed half a dozen Ugs. They surrounded Z, who was still seated and trying to breathe. Gary leapt from the driver's side door. She hadn't been this close to him just yet; she'd been deliberately avoiding that with friendly waves from a distance and promises to *catch up in a second* in order to buy herself a bit more time. He'd been busy himself, absent from meals and volunteering to help Ian fix things around the village. It occurred to her now that he might've been avoiding her too.

Gary and Kara pushed some kids aside and crouched down on either side of her, apologizing and assigning blame. Each of them put a hand on one of Z's shoulders, and then Gary put his other hand on Kara's, a triangle that made her wish the van had kept going.

She rolled over gracefully like a hog, onto all fours, then stood. With hundreds of hours to prepare for this moment, she slapped the back of her skort to clean it off and reintroduced herself to Gary with a cough, "Butt dust."

As the crowd let her eloquence sink in, Gary cleaned his glasses on his T-shirt, lifting up the edge to reveal a marvelous inch of torso that she forced herself to look away from at once.

"I'm fine," Z said quickly. "I hiked up with Elise."

Kara barked a haughty little huff of air.

"Hey, come on," Gary said to Kara. He turned to Z. "You hiked?"

"Grave robbing is my kink. You know that."

"She's funny," Kara said, cocking her head to the side and not smiling.

"I know," said Gary, pushing down the sides of his mouth. "Are you sure you're all right? Ooh, I got you," he said and handed her the same brand of granola bar Elise had an hour ago. He knew her well, but not of late.

"That was crazy," Ryan said, leaving the van minutes after everyone else to check on her. "No offense, but that would've totally fucked up the van." Somehow he was already shirtless and sweating, his toolbelt jangling obscenely around his glistening waist like stripper Bob Vila. "I mean, we only have the two vans, man."

Z hated herself for ever touching this person.

Barely disguising her disgust, Kara ducked back into the driver's seat with a wave, and Gary leaned into the window to kiss her. Z watched as Kara sat perfectly still, withstanding it.

The Ugs disbanded, swapping ideas for the disposal of Z's body had she been properly run over. There were so many ditches here to choose from.

Gary returned to her and lifted an eyebrow. He wore his uniform of performance sports shorts and a souvenir T-shirt, his recent whereabouts mappable through breast-pocket catchphrases. The pack of Greek construction workers plodded by, dragging their shovels. Charles used the men to remove trees, boulders, and sections of the earth that got in his way. Without stopping, one of them said something to Gary, who replied back in a stream of fluent Greek.

"So?" He turned to her. "Any revelations after your near-death experience?"

Z very rarely had anything to lose and now, looking down at her torn skort, calculated that dignity was off the list as well. She sighed.

"I came up to check if Shiba was still there."

He reeled back like he'd been pushed. "Oh." He looked over at the bend in the gravel path that led out from the track, at the patch of scraggly trees. When his eyes came back to hers, she couldn't read them. If he asked her why, she really didn't have a good answer.

"I mean, if it is . . ." she started.

"It belongs in a museum," he finished.

For the first time they properly locked eyes, and both smiled. She stuck out her tongue, even though she had absolutely no idea what kind of ground she was standing on yet.

She'd administered a brusque ending to her longest relationship on the annual beach weekend to Pylos the team took every summer. Gary had sat her down on the balcony of their hotel overlooking the water, sweaty thighs glued to plastic furniture, and told Z he loved her and wanted to be with her forever. In a stupefying display of grace, Z broke up with him on the spot, spiral-panicked about her life being over by twenty-two, got positively hammered, and fled their hotel to go make out with Ryan in the disco-balled hallway of a nearby bar.

Those two men were a testament to the power of time and lasers to bring people together over perceived differences.

Her insides churned, and she swallowed hard. In the immediate days after the beach, Gary hadn't spoken a word to her, icing her out around the village as she begged him to let her apologize. After she left for home they hadn't spoken again, not once in all this time. But right now, in this very moment, his light brown eyes extended their surrounding crinkles like oars in a rough sea. It was possible that he wasn't so mad, that he didn't absolutely hate her, that the intervening years had filled him with bigger and better things to feel.

"Kara!" She blurted out. "Wow. I mean, congratulations. You did it!" It was bizarre to speak to him like nothing more than an old friend, but the alternative seemed even worse.

"Crazy, right? Look at me go. Getting married next year," he said proudly.

Another "Wow!" She hoped her eyes didn't look as crazy as they felt, widening by the minute. She had been pissed at Kara for being with Gary, and now she was pissed at her for leaving him.

"Good. Great. Excellent. Yeah, well, just glad the timing worked out for me this summer. I love it here, you know."

"It's cool, Zar. I know—about the job stuff," he flattened his lips and nodded kindly. So kindly her throat almost caught. "We're lucky to have you back."

She opened her mouth.

"Elise told me. I ask her about you sometimes. Yes, I admit it." He jutted out his neck like a turtle and looked sideways, and it was so weirdly charming on this giant man that she wanted to mount him.

"I'm maybe thinking of going back to school," she said suddenly. "You know, I was always kind of thinking about that."

"Really?" This genuinely seemed to shock him and in fact it shocked her too. She'd never said that out loud before but realized now that it was true somewhere, in between all the in-between stretches she seemed to be accumulating. And why not? Here she was starting over again; she could go nuts and make a wise choice or two. School might be the only way to tie herself to a mast and ignore the siren songs that soundtracked her life. She felt a surprising flood of gratitude that it was him who heard her say it first.

"It's pretty expensive these days," he said.

If you're going to get slapped in the face with bad news, doing it after you've already been slapped like ten times in a row has a powerful numbing effect on the skin.

"Right, totally. Cool. Well, I better get down there," she cocked her head toward the trenches.

"Hey," he said. She'd already turned and pulled the trowel from her belt. "I haven't touched it, so for all I know Shiba's down there. You going to dig it up?"

PROBABLY, YES, SURE, *SOME* KIND OF HISTORICAL RECORD WOULD survive. But she liked to imagine a total annihilation outcome. Only a cataclysmic turn could blow up all the computers and all the books and all the words and leave nothing but objects. In that case, the only way to tell what happened here on planet earth would be to dig for it. Pieces of this, pieces of that, lives, relationships. Pottery for food, strigils for sport, goats for the gods, and plastic Toshiba buttons for love.

Any archaeologist who tells you they haven't buried something like this for themselves is lying.

Now she knew: it was still buried. So if you're measuring by millennia, and you really should be, love was still there for her.

Chapter

6

Here Patty was, standing in the center of the world, the cradle of civilization, the navel of humanity. Her chest puffed out, she failed to hold back a slack-jawed smile and sneaked a look around. They stood in the middle of the oval track interior, which was tufted with scraggly grass and checkered with drying tarps. The track itself was a wide, beige band of packed dirt cratered with shoe prints. Patty bobbed on the balls of her feet at the end of the line of Ugs, all of whom were gathered before Charles, Ryan, and Z, who were presenting something called "dig etiquette." Patty looked to her right: the full excavation ascended in a gentle grade from the stone bleachers to the processional to the locker room, then all the way up to the altar. Elise was at the top, the size of a bug from here, and hacking away at something; Patty could faintly hear the clinks and clanks carried on the wind. She pursed her lips and watched Elise for a longing moment. Gary was out working too, standing on one foot beside his laser-making machine and untangling his legs from a too-long line of measuring tape.

Patty returned her gaze forward and looked past her instructors out into the valley. It was just after sunrise, and orange peeled over the mountains on the far side; the greens on neighboring hills were just ripening to life. She was astonished: Not only was the landscape out of this world, but it meant something. What that was exactly, Charles was explaining.

"Now, I know this is difficult to imagine, but great men once stood here," he said.

One of the Ugs raised a hand and proceeded without being called on. "When is the beach weekend?"

"I will consider answering questions at the end," Charles said. "Now, as I was saying, I am not here to instruct you on tool use—that is the purview of Zara and Ryan. Zara, please hold up your trowel."

She held up a brush.

"Zara!"

Z pinched at the armpits of her tank top and puffed out her chest to ham for the crowd. She wore one of her usual skorts, which she flipped up with abandon. The inside shorts pockets bulged sideways with the pebbled spandex of loose peanuts that she kept in reserve. Her tank top was the latest in a seemingly endless supply that featured the name of a concert or band, none of which Patty had ever heard of.

Finally Z lifted up a small gardening shovel, a device familiar to Patty. She winked at the group just as Ryan did too; he'd been batting lashes with various members of the audience this whole time.

"This will be your primary appendage. Now Ryan, please hold up the sifter."

"Oh, that's in the van." He nodded. Z bent down and picked it up from its resting place next to their feet. "Whoa," Ryan said.

"This too, your instructors have already begun to familiarize you with," Charles said. "I will say nothing more on the labor portion, except to warn you that we will bill you should you break any tools."

Patty made a mental note. Charles went on. "My goal today is to convey to you the greater meaning of your work here so that you might view your toil within a richer historical context."

On cue, one of the Ugs sat down on the ground, settling in. The rest of them looked at him, then around at each other, made the unspoken assessment together that Charles couldn't fire the entire team, and sat down too.

"Now, see, this is precisely the point I'm attempting to make. Comfort was anathema to the great men who performed here. Indeed, when you are exerting yourself in the trenches and thinking to yourself, *My, I am parched, I am in need of a spa, I am weary,* then I implore you to picture the exceptional athletes, the men who push, push, pushed themselves right here on this very track! That pushing is the bedrock of our collective legacy of man's struggle for accomplishment, which we still revere today in our wider world of sport. And you, by being here, are tiny pebbles in that stream. As history flows over you, you are doing your part to smooth its way along."

Patty alone was rapt. Her hand shot up before she could stop it. When Charles dragged his eyes over to her, she shrank down. "Sorry, but, just wondering, what about the girl athletes?"

He delivered her another withering look. "As I believe we all know, in this magnificent era women did not participate in sport."

Patty's shoulders slumped. Another Ug's voice piped up behind her. "Excuse me? Someone told me there's a party in the city we go to? And isn't there a Field Day?"

"Incorrect." Charles gritted his teeth. "*We* do not attend this party. That is my annual fete. And Field Day is not for another six weeks."

A collective groan.

"Oh, I have one," Ryan said, raising his hand. "Thought about this a few months ago and I just remembered. Have we ever found some skis? Because that would mean this was also the Winter Olympics."

Charles's knuckles whitened around the edges of his clipboard. "Zara, you may proceed. I assume you've already made a list of assignments."

"Better. All right, team, get up." She waved, and the group staggered onto their feet. "Girls here, guys there. We're going to run two laps around this track, and whoever finishes first in each group gets to choose whether they're digging or sifting. Whoever comes in last has to stake out the pee tree."

Yesterday morning they'd undergone a parallel training outside the lab. Kara had done most of the talking and passed out pamphlets with Charles's face on one of the glossy panels above a blurb describing his career. Patty slipped it into her luggage to show her parents, who'd expressed concerns over Charles being some kind of international swindler who lured young women into labor camps. Patty struggled to clarify the difference for them.

At this presentation Charles mentioned to them that, should they want to purchase a copy of his book, he was offering a ten-percent discount for the summer. But Patty, however tempted, wanted to save every dime of her small stipend. She would sock it away and add to it throughout the school year, so that next summer she could add a week to whatever summer job she chose and go travel somewhere new. She was a traveler now.

The suitcase incident had done serious damage to Patty's standing in the Ug group, dented to begin with by Patty's tiresome questions about exchanging cash (they wouldn't need any), checking in for their flight home (over two months away), and whether anyone had thought about making a Greek cheese called Boba Feta. The nail in her social coffin, however, seemed to be her genuine interest in the dig, a dynamic that perplexed her. Every time she thought she'd found a clear bonding moment, like the time they found a snake and Patty picked it up (they'd always kept snakes as pets at home) and wondered aloud if the same kinds of snakes had existed here in ancient times, she was immediately skewered with a cynicism she'd previously only seen in television villains. She felt like she couldn't do anything right. The girls openly pitied her for being so sincere, as if it was just sad how completely she was missing the point of all this. The boys, thank God, weren't interested in her at all. Together they were far more interested in one another than their surroundings, which Patty simply could not understand. Greece was spectacular.

This left her to seek companionship one rung above her station. A few times when Elise was busy, Z played cards with Patty. And after making the mistake of asking Gary what exactly it was that he did, Patty had been subject to nightly laser lectures for a week.

Once at the lab, when Patty lifted a drying pottery shard to inspect it, she released a loud *Wow* upon noticing a clear signature carved into the blue paint.

"I was the same way," Kara said, gliding closer. "That's how it gets you." She tapped her heart and beckoned Patty inside as the other Ugs turned up the boom box volume. "Not everyone understands," she added.

Inside, Patty knelt beside Kara at the base of a gigantic tower of plastic storage containers. Kara pulled open a few drawers at the bottom and carefully lifted out more fragments with writing on them.

"I would show you the discs," Kara sighed. "But—I can't believe I'm saying this—I can't find them anywhere. They'll turn up; I just need to reorganize. Maybe you can help me!"

Task-based bonding was an unforeseen downside of befriending her superiors.

"I'm pretty sure Charles had some discs in his luggage," Patty offered.

Kara laughed. "Right, maybe he made some copies." She held a piece of pottery in one white-gloved hand, and in the other showed Patty a laminated picture of a large, shallow bowl set atop a tiny stand. "This is called a *kylix*. It's for wine, and where we get the word chalice."

"Did they drink before they ran? Or after?"

"Both," Kara answered. Her eyes went wide with a maternal smile as if they were in on something fun together. Patty felt a warm, snuggly rush flood her chest.

As Patty was about to pull open a drawer herself, a loud *Ahem* punctured the moment.

"Kara," Charles bellowed from the doorway. "I doubt that's a fruitful use of our limited time, don't you?"

✈

Don't worry, I've got all the time in the world.

Chapter

7

The next day, as Elise was sinking down into her trench at the altar at the top of the site, the van pulled up and the doors slid open. Z waved both hands up at her.

"Elise!" she shouted. Elise gave her a deterrent nod, then strapped on her kneepads. Every single night so far, the two of them had spent at least two hours talking: during dinner, card games, and even in the once peaceful moments before bed.

Hey. Z would roll over in her squeaky cot and whisper to her right in the moment when everyone else had finally piped down. She asked Elise about Heraklion, her apartment in Crete, the Thessaloniki subway tunnel excavation—anything to parse the details of every dispatch Z had received over the years. This was not Elise's idea of bedtime conversation, nor was any conversation at all. But Z considered every moment fair game for chat. She'd forgotten how relentless friendship was.

It was clear Z had come back, in large part, for another crack at Gary. With that plan thwarted, she was forced to aim all her attention at the work. Elise believed this was for the best and told her so at every opportunity. Despite her line of work, Elise was remarkably uninterested in peoples' pasts, her own least of all. She advised Z daily to look up and out and listen to no one but herself.

Once everyone was in place in their trenches, at ground level or below, they couldn't see her at all. But Elise was able to see everything from atop her dusty panopticon. She watched now as the last litter of Ugs spilled out from the second van and trudged to their places. Newbies were mostly relegated to the processional walkway, the stretch between the locker rooms and the track. That's where ancient fans would have dropped their meats-on-sticks or pocket change while they drank, ate, cheered, and jeered as the athletes made their way down to compete. Wine barf turned to sacred dust by the passage of time.

It was north of ninety degrees now, and her knees started farting. Her legs were slick with sweat front to back, making the kneepads slippery. The dirt and perspiration slipped and slid against the rubber, making flatulent sounds every time she moved an inch.

On all fours, she scanned the thirty square feet before her where she was spending the summer. Bumps big and small—promises galore—textured the miniature landscape. Trowel in hand, in glove, she hit the ground running.

Give it to me, she thought.

The last big find she'd had was Victor, the biggest find of all time as far as the Mega site was concerned. It had been an unmitigated disaster, the line that defined her time here: Before Victor, After Victor. She had trusted Kara to handle the next step once he'd been removed from the ground—that wasn't going to happen again.

Victor popped up at the end of a long, dry stretch three years ago. It was a searingly hot day, and she was here in this very same dirt, down on all fours with the stretch of exposed skin between her shorts and shirt sizzling like a strip of bacon. She expected nothing; the year before had been fruitless, and the past few months had coughed up coin after coin, useless tender she was sick of. Nothing indicated that she should keep digging in this one spot. She should stop—professionally, she knew that. Charles told her, *Enough. Tarp it and call it quits. Measure out the next section.* But for some reason she did not stop. Even now when she thought back on it, she couldn't quite place the feeling that drew her hand down toward the ground. Again and again, the nose of the trowel had magnetized toward the earth's core. *Go, go, go*, it said.

And then, there he was. Her wide bristle brush swept across the dirt, and she gasped. Her fingertips slowly approached the ground and met fingertips. Up from the earth, poking through like a stem seeking the sun—a hand. A tiny, perfect white hand sticking up out of planet earth, waving to Elise. *Hey.*

Extracting this piece from the ground was the hardest work of her career, especially considering the shockingly unhelpful audience of ig-norami leaning over and nut-burping in her ear the whole time. Charles made the helpful choice to stand behind her and conduct his own mirrored hand symphony above Elise's head, with commentary. She worked with every fiber to painstakingly, gruelingly remove each millimeter of this person from the ground over the course of weeks, ignoring her surroundings, focusing her heart on him, Victor, com-pletely. Abundant didn't even begin to describe her level of careful with this thing—there was no question that the removal process was textbook, better than textbook. It was a pristine job of a pristine piece, her finest hour.

Victor was their biggest discovery in decades: museum-quality, Met-ready, the find of a lifetime. It was unquestionably the find of Elise's life. After years of fragments and pieces, here was a fully formed, foot-long statue. It looked just like one of us, if one were a freak who liked to play frisbee in the buff.

The little person was an athlete, muscular and lean, with arms raised in an *It's good!* parallel, elbows bent at ninety degrees. The left hand gripped a discus the size of a quarter. It was a chalky white marble with delicate features and a blank expression on its small face; a golden laurel wreath crown rested on its head. Elise was not a gasper, but when she made it down that far, brushed the dust from the top of the head, and saw the perfectly carved miniature gold leaves, it took her breath away. The body and legs were curved with smooth muscles, and at the groin was a noncommittal jumble that hinted at haphazard modesty.

More proud than she'd ever been, smiling more than she'd ever allowed herself to, she delivered Victor to Kara with the grace of handling a newborn. The two women locked eyes above Victor as he lay on Kara's desk, perfect, waiting to be cleaned. Elise had never made that much sustained and loaded eye contact with anyone, but for a fleeting moment she felt a current surge between them, vibrating with *Dear God, look at us, stringing together the limbs of civilization, and holy shit, we are humans alive on this earth touching humans alive on this earth four thousand years ago, and it is astonishing.* Both women teared up at this moment, but neither would ever admit to that.

A few weeks passed, during which Elise actually sat with her peers at lunch and dinner for the first time, recapping again and again her extraction highlight reel. Kara, Gary, Ryan, and even Charles egged her on, aggrandizing their memories of small moments they'd witnessed during the process, asking Elise about her strategy at the time, and claiming they knew all along that something of this magnitude was possible here. A new giddiness balled up tightly inside her chest. She even allowed herself to hope that after this remarkable accomplishment, she'd be given the chief role she deserved, finally in charge of the dig now that Charles had clearly been surpassed by his staff.

But naturally, no.

One morning after she'd finally gotten back into a rhythm with the rest of her work, Charles climbed to the altar and stood with his hands on his hips. He didn't even wait for her to pause what she was doing and meet his eye before he spoke.

In two words he kicked over her delicate stack of possibilities. "Victor's gone. The earthquake—he, well, his display was shattered. It was—he—was shattered."

She wrapped her arms around her chest. A wave of nausea rose up within her, and for a moment she felt she might be sick into her trench. Then just as quickly the wave retreated, leaving her feeling hollow inside.

Elise blinked and tried to swallow, but her throat felt clogged with sand. "What are you talking about?" That little earthquake was nothing. It was routine earth maintenance; they'd barely felt it here. "No. No, that's not what happens."

"It pains me to say this," Charles grimaced, "But I believe he was damaged to begin with."

She flung out her arms. "Doc! You saw me. You've got to be shitting me—"

He held up a hand. "Elise. Remain professional, please. I was with you here, I know. We were shipmates, side by side at the helm for the removal."

"Right. And weren't you with Kara? Weren't you next to her in the lab?" Her volume rose with every word.

Charles extended his pointer finger and thumb, like he was measuring an inch of the air between them, and then he turned his wrist to the left, dialing her down. She plotted his death.

"No," he lowered his voice. "Kara wanted to work alone, for her concentration. She insisted, and I entrusted her to do so. Although apparently there were cracks, from what I could see when I completed the packing, the stone had been quite aggressively scrubbed. Too forcefully, in my opinion. Pressed."

"Pressed?!" Now she was yelling.

You didn't press. There was no pressing. Pressing was for entitled halfwits who thought they'd take a crack, literally, at sprucing up a four-thousand-year-old piece when no one asked them to. No pressing, no scraping, no scrubbing. Depending on what you had for lunch, you didn't so much as pass gas in the same room as a thing like that. To say that ancient material is sensitive to pressure was like saying a hamster is sensitive to blenders.

"What in the bloody fuck, Charles? Are you kidding me right now? She cracked him! No wonder it crumbled. Jesus Christ! I mean that's what happened, right? It was *her!*" Her eyes burned with the strength it took to remain dry, her throat clenched like a fist.

THAT WAS THREE SUMMERS AGO. ELISE HADN'T SPOKEN A WORD TO Kara since, and never would again as long as she lived. Before Victor-gate, the two of them had been friendly enough—as friendly as Elise was with anyone, which wasn't saying much. But there had been waves exchanged, professional courtesies and consultations galore, and the occasional group beer. They were pleasant colleagues. There had never been anything deeper between them, save for one single flicker of con-nection that tethered both their souls at the same time to the space-time-civilization continuum. But now, with this news, Kara was despicable trash, Elise's top enemy on a lifelong list. She'd ruined everything.

It seemed the feeling was mutual. The glares they shared in public were withering, and they'd both avoided being alone together for years now, even for a moment. Elise had no idea what Kara had to be so pissed about, and Kara had never even come close to an apology—not that Elise would've accepted one.

Elise would dig up something else to call her own if it was the last thing she ever did. She would blow this place wide open and kick every last one of them off this mountain—physically, if need be. She opened her mouth as if to air out a stench. The memory tasted rotten: her fin-est, greatest hour *pressed* into oblivion. Victor would still be here if not for that selfish, arrogant, entitled, careless little—

"Yo, Elise dawg! Arf, arf!"

Every single morning, Ryan greeted her like this as if to coax her into homicide. In their own version of a ceremonial flag raising, Ryan did as he was doing now and removed his shirt, tying it around his head like a Floridian keffiyeh. His year-after-year employment on this site was one of Elise's first clues that Charles was intentionally surrounding himself with idiots. She ignored him.

Her resentment of Ryan stemmed from his proximity to her on the professional spectrum, and she loathed the idea that anyone here might conflate or connect them. Using the pittance Charles paid him here— Ryan was Charles's wife Terry's nephew, or some such related person who required hiring—he used the off season to migrate from beach to beach around the world. Only a man of this resourcefulness would choose to designate the remaining eight months of a year "off." The idea that Elise was one vacation season away from being seen as Ryan would keep her working until she dropped dead, right into a ready-made, six-by-six trench.

A FEW PRODUCTIVE HOURS LATER, WHILE EVERYONE ELSE TOOK THEIR water breaks and fingered around for M&M globs in the corners of trail mix bags, a small white car pulled up onto the track area behind the vans.

Kal stepped out and lit a cigarette, tossing the match as if it had rained here even once in the past three months. He wore a white linen button-down shirt with athletic shorts and sandals. His beard had filled out since last year and was combed; his wild hair was now tied back into a bun which, including the glasses, made him look borderline professional. A professional *what*, exactly, was anyone's guess. He gave a thumbs up to no one, or all of them, and started walking up the grass toward Charles, high fiving each bewildered, peanut-drooling Ug he passed.

Everything one needed to know about the small valley town of Megalopolis was that the mayor, Kal Loukanis, was missing a tooth. Not one of the front ones, but a visible molar. He was undeniably good looking, with a year-round golden tan, soft-looking dark hair pulled into a ponytail, and a quintessential nose that felt immediately familiar to those first laying eyes on him, having seen it countless times before on Greek statues the world over. He was proud of this feature and often attempted to position himself in profile when he first met someone.

It wasn't clear whether Megalopolis's political structure officially included the position of mayor, but Kal used the term liberally and spent enough time sparring with various regulators over schemes du jour that it could've amounted to that—election by attrition. He was the local multi-hyphenate, always pitching the dig team on grand plans he had for Mega and claiming at the end of every season that next year they wouldn't even recognize the place, so improved would it be with a new town square, public pool, schoolyard, playground, or large business headquarters. Elise thought he should start with himself—be the dentistry you want to see in the world. He appeared at either the site or village at least once a week bearing bizarre gifts, like a case of two hundred royal-blue hats that just said "Birthday" on the brim. Kal often trotted out the US excavation team at local community functions as an example of the kind of business, scholarship, and industry that his town could attract: twenty dirt-caked nerds with tan lines above their butt cracks from hunching over in the sun all day.

He was ruthlessly positive, and it drove Elise insane how much she liked him. She suspected that he didn't care for Charles too much, and she enjoyed watching him pretend otherwise. The two men stood across from each other now, shoulder slapping and performing chat as if they were old chums—not men with wildly different lives who were trapped together for a few moments a year on a far-flung mountain, so that one could dig up the ancestral remains of the other.

They parted, and Kal immediately turned up to the altar.

"Elitsa! Yassas, Elitsa!" He yelled. "How was the winter? My friend tells me you were in Pylaia!" Everyone on the site could hear him and looked up at her.

He started climbing up the steep hill; halfway he realized, as all visitors did, that the grade necessitated two hands, so he put the cigarette in his mouth and bear crawled the rest of the way, his black and white ponytail bobbing up and down.

Soon enough he towered over her, hands on hips to jut out his broad chest, winded but still smoking. Ash trickled into his fire-hazard chest hair. "You know, I have my family in Pylaia," he said, wiping his brow. "I was born very close to there, by the port."

"I missed that historical plaque. You okay?"

He waved her off and pushed up his sleeves to reveal a deeper gilding across the skin of his arms than she remembered. "Extremely beautiful there, no? Elitsa, you know I know beautiful when I see it."

"Kal." She stood up, crossed her arms, and suppressed a smile. This summer she was focused on the job more than ever, and so she was determined to nip in the bud whatever it was that always crackled between them. It had been nine months since she'd seen him last and to her horror, the crackling had resumed immediately, with a vengeance. His woozying scent hit her all at once, the same as ever, as if he'd taken a blowtorch to a lemon and then rubbed it all over his body. It made her skin feel like it was levitating, and she crossed her arms tighter as if to hold it down. Her lips were not cooperating at all, and her cheeks ached from trying to keep them in place. There had only been one other time in her life when she'd felt a physical, chemical pull this hard, and that had ended so disastrously, so dangerously, that she refused to even entertain this one. In every way she was safer alone. Kal began stretching, as if the crawl up had reminded him of latent muscles. As he stuck out his left foot and bent forward over his thigh, she forced herself to drag her eyes away and gaze chastely out over the mountains.

He continued, "Chuck, you know, he does not appreciate you. I tell him, 'You have the most talented person working for you here.' Everyone who does the digs with you, they say she is the best in business. And the other people like Chuck, the bosses in the other sites, all over Greece, they come to me and say, 'How do I get Elitsa to come work for me? She is so smart, and she is no trouble, and everyone respects her.' I always say, 'Trust me, Elitsa doesn't do the thing she does not want to do. Never. If she comes to you, she comes to you, but I cannot make it happen. Trust me.'"

She reached over, plucking his cigarette from his lips and taking a drag. A sickening thrill wrapped its fingers around her spine at the thought of her lips touching where his had just been.

When she gave it back, she made sure not to touch his hand. "You wrap up the tourist center while I was gone?" she asked.

For years now Mega had been attempting the world record for slowest, smallest construction project. A minuscule tourist center, highlighting the area's proportional archaeological contributions, had long been in the works to attract visitors. They broke ground ten years ago and had several holes in the earth and one inexplicable Poseidon fountain to show for it; the project was Kal's baby, the crown jewel of all his big promises.

"This year," he said. He rubbed his fingers together in the universal gesture of someone who doesn't have money.

"Great, I keep my promises," she said. So confident was Elise that the Mega Kentro tou Tourismos would never exist, she'd made an earnest guarantee to Kal that she would run it when it did. She meant it. It was like promising to give him a shout out on the jumbotron when the WNBA drafted her. Sure.

"That is why I do it—for you. To trap you here with me all year long. No more all this time apart. Nine months is too long you have been away."

Elise rolled her eyes, and Kal leaned in with a smile to drink it up. This little play they were putting on for each other—had been performing for years—gave her a feeling as close to giddiness as she'd ever had. She needed to tamp it down.

"What was Charles whacking off about down there?"

Kal's eyebrows inched closer together, shadowing his eyes. "I don't know," he said, unconvincingly. "He has some ideas for me. You know, we work together."

"No, you don't."

He stood up straighter. "I know a lot of people, a lot of important people." He cocked his chin, as if he'd impressed himself with this point. "So he wants to know the people I know, of course. Everyone does. That is my job, putting people together. That is how I got the new bus stop! And of course, everyone knows that I know you, Elitsa, greatest archaeologist in the world. How about that? You are good for my reputation."

She waited.

"Come on, why do you need to be the Elitsa politsa? It's been all this winter, and finally here we are."

She looked down the hill at Charles. He was wearing a pith helmet like an old-timey, racist dingbat. She wanted to strangle him.

Kal must've seen the longing on her face. He lowered his voice, "OK. He just says something about, Do you know someone who is—what is the word, who keeps many things, all the same—"

"A collector?"

"Yes. He asks, do I know someone like this."

"What does he care? Wait, do you?" It wasn't the right question, but she found herself ravenous to know whether Kal spent his time with people like that, people with at least the patina of sophistication.

"My aunt, yes. She collects the birds. All over the whole room, they cover the walls, the wings and feathers—and I don't know, you know, if they are dead when she gets them. I never ask."

He lowered his voice. "Please don't say that I say anything to you. I know you will not. You know I coach girls' soccer team, and we play up here sometimes, and I don't want a trouble with that. They love playing on the track. Let's pretend that we laugh now—" Kal exploded into a full-throttled guffaw. "This way he thinks we are just having fun, you and me. No secrets!" He cackled.

"Birds."

"The little black eyes—they haunt me! Ha! Ha! Ha!" He projection-barked down the hill, toward Charles.

Assured of his cover, he reeled back his display and pulled out his phone. "Listen. I want to show you something I saw yesterday. One of the top persons from the factory, I go to him to ask for money for the Kentro tou Tourismos, and I see this at his house. I thought, Elitsa will know what this is. Look."

He scooted over so close to her that the warm skin on the sides of their arms touched. Shoulder pressed to hers, Kal shaded the screen for her. A cloud of smoke passed over it, making the image all the spookier.

Immediately, Elise yanked the phone from his hand. She unpinched her fingers to zoom in and see closer.

Good Lord.

It was a metal discus, about a foot wide and broken down the middle, the greenish-silver surface worn. The left side was perfectly rounded and thin; Elise could nearly feel her finger tracing the hard, smooth edge. The other side had been sharply cleaved, leaving the silhouette of a lightning bolt—she felt like one was striking her now. In the center, barely legible, there was a letter inscribed.

"Eta," Elise breathed. The feeling in her fingers vanished. She was looking at a stolen artifact.

"Yes! That is what I saw too," Kal beamed. Clearly she was on to something, which meant he'd been on to something.

He smiled at her as if they were talking about a dog picture, as if they weren't talking about loot—pilfered, filched, snatched, perhaps from this very mountain and forked over to whichever factory executive goon down in the valley had bargained for it. But bargained with who? When? Her eyelashes grazed the screen, but it wasn't a quality photo by any means. There was a hamburger plopped next to the thing and the reflection of a singing competition on TV in the glass table's glare. But the piece itself was unmistakable, or an extraordinary replica. The only question was whether it was one of theirs. One of *hers*, she thought.

She'd been so focused on the ground in front of her, she hadn't imagined a piece of evidence—evidence of *something*, surely—would come to her on a silver, telephone-shaped platter.

"How do you say in English?" Kal asked, looking over at her and smiling coyly, obliviously.

His arm was still warm against hers, and the mix of feelings flowing about her limbs was highly confusing. On the one hand, the familiar desire to punch something; on the other, a new desire to remain in contact with Kal's hairy forearm. She stiffened between these two urges.

Even the smallest discovered fragments were carted off to Big Universities and Important Museums in airtight plastic sarcophagus boxes handled with gloves. It had to be a knockoff, didn't it? She badly wanted it to be; the idea of one of her pieces being in someone's house made her sick. But there was a small sliver of her that gloated in a sing-songy voice, *Charles is in trouble*. And isn't that what she wanted?

Or better yet, Kara. She was the one who handled the pieces once they were out of the ground. She would've been the last one to see this thing. This was on her.

"H," she answered. She squinted at the screen. Were they even missing a discus? She had no idea what went on in the lab these days, made it a point not to. The bifurcation of lab and field, Kara and Elise, was total. Even overhearing the Ugs talk about Kara's organization and plans and systems there made her livid, since all the tight-assery in the world hadn't saved Victor. But her nemesis was wound so tightly that it didn't seem possible for someone to extract so much as a paperclip from that place. The whole thing was far-fetched. Kal probably didn't know what he was talking about.

"*Ayee-chuh*," Kal confirmed.

"You didn't show this to Charles," she stated.

Kal glanced down at Charles, then back to Elise. Using the inside crook of his elbow, he wiped the sweat from his face up onto the top of his head and sighed. "I have a big feeling," he began, lowering his voice even though no one could hear a thing up there, "Charles does not believe in the Kentro." He gave a serious shrug and pursed his lips, as if this were shocking news. Indeed, Charles mocked Kal weekly for his plans to build a small museum here; he thought it was ridiculous and that bus stops were more than the town deserved.

"Years and years I ask him to work with me to get some things like this," he shook the phone, indicating the piece in question. "And still I have only an ice cream machine. It is an incredible machine, Elise! Delicious treats! But, you know, he does not believe like you. You are the only one who asks about the Kentro. You are the only one who says, 'Kal, when you finish the Museo, I will be there, I am here to help you.' Only you. And so I think," he leaned in conspiratorially, "If we work together, maybe we could get this for the Museo. But if I tell Charles, he will go move it back to America, and we will never see it again. Yes?"

"You're right," she said. *We,* she thought.

Kal grinned. "Now we have a secret together."

Again he ran a hand over the top of his hair, smoothing sweat down onto the ponytail. Goddamn, a good ponytail did something to her. She couldn't help herself. Even now she felt the tiniest of stirrings, right now inside the first bud of what was almost certain to blossom into a catastrophe.

Kal put his hand on top of hers on top of the shovel and squeezed it. He was right. Whatever that disc was, she wasn't going to tell Charles about it either, she decided. This could be it, the lever she needed to catapult the dicks off this mountain.

"See you for lunch. I miss what Miss Ursula can cook up for me. Nine months is too long without my best friends!" He gestured toward the dirtballs working downhill, clamped the cigarette between his lips, and went down the grass on his backside. In front of his car a few of the Greek workers waited for him, and he distributed cigarettes accordingly.

She'd no sooner crouched back into the trench and resumed digging when she heard it.

"Ahem."

Charles's face appeared above her in his problematic hat, the long string to which dangled down into her face, fishing for resentful subordinates. His camping pants and sun-shielding shirt were pristine. Even though he'd spent decades in the field, every year it looked like he'd just walked into J. Peterman and said, *One of everything, please.*

"Yes," she said, to fend him off. "The tarps are secure. I checked last night. I'm going to do the new tarps with all of them this year."

"Well, we'll see about that. Hang on now, did you come up here yesterday, after what we discussed?"

"I did." They'd discussed her not coming up here.

"Elise." He flipped up the tinted lenses on his sunglasses to intimidate her—into an admission, apology, or prescription eyewear. If he had any idea how often she came up here by herself, his eyes would pop out of his head, bounce down the hill, and plop into a bucket.

Sensing that remorse was neither forthcoming nor in existence, Charles sighed. Elise was in no mood to appease him, less so now than ever. The back of her mind swam with how in the hell she was supposed to find out more about those discs without tipping off anyone here.

"Z's got them under quite the spell." He gestured to the group of Ugs Z was now regaling with peanut tosses. Why Charles was keen to plumb the depths of the oaf moat surrounding him was a mystery to her. These kids would breezily admit they couldn't find the Mediterranean on a map.

He waved toward the parking lot like royalty. "This is our year, Elise. I know what the surveying says, but do you think there's the chance for another Victor here? You've got something of a connection to the land. What does your gut say? It would just be magnificent to find a few more gems like that, some real showstoppers, you know. How about opening a few more trenches toward the east?"

Elise grunted and clenched her fists at her sides at his suggestion of her taking on hundreds of hours of additional work.

He cleared his throat.

"And now, what were you and Kal getting on about? He always asks me about you, you know. Did I mention that he sent me an email this past winter to ask if you were coming back this year? I told him, 'Well, of course. She's my right-hand man.'"

Elise doubted that response very much. "E-mail?" She couldn't imagine Kal in proximity to a computer. He existed only outside, beneath a tree, climbing a hill, shading his eyes from the sun.

"That's what you were gabbing about?" Charles pushed.

"He killed some people and just asked, you know, if we're not gonna use all of these," she gestured to the row of rectangular trenches below them.

"Elise. You're testing my lines," he said. "And I wish I knew why."

"You want to open more trenches, be my guest," she tossed her trowel up in the air, and Charles fumbled to catch it without slicing open a palm.

"I won't be having any more of this ballyhoo. I simply want to encourage you to work up to your full potential, so that we may find something big. Together. We need to keep the hatches battened this year, Elise."

When Charles wanted to be finished having a conversation, he used words indecipherable to those who didn't sail. It worked.

"Victor number two could very well be waiting. And between you and me, we'll keep it as far away from you-know-who as possible." He tilted his head toward the road leading to the village, to the lab. "Now, back to work." He turned and crab-walked his way down the slope, unfortunately safely.

She looked down the hill and spotted Kal as he was getting back into his car. He was already looking up at her, and their eyes locked. He jiggled his phone and winked at her.

Elise crouched onto her haunches and surveyed the dirt before her, willing another tiny white hand to reach up through the wild and crazy crust and point a perfect stone finger right at her heart. She would take that hand in hers and never, ever, through a million years and a million earthquakes, ever let go.

Chapter

8

Six years ago, Z was on her hands and knees checking to see if an ancient priest had dropped anything from his toga pocket. Now a half decade, four jobs, and eight boyfriends later, she was on her hands and knees checking to see if, when the priest had dropped anything from his pocket, it bounced.

She was crouched down inside a probe trench, an eight-foot-deep, four-foot-wide rectangle meant as an exploration—and tangentially, a meditation—on one's own death. If the lasers said so, the excavators dug one extra-deep trench like this to see if it was worth digging more in the vicinity. She could stand up on the floor down there and still have plenty of space overhead, or raise her arms and just reach her fingertips aboveground. But mostly she was in the tabletop position, kneeled on all fours and surrounded by enormous walls of wet black dirt, cool, dark, and surreal.

Apparently they'd closed up this trench a while ago, but since someone experienced was back, Elise opened it up again to give it one more season to cough something up. Z was flattered to learn that she was considered professionally experienced in anything. Elise and Charles could have had her up there with the Ugs, ripping out weeds or marking out new trench locations and shoveling out the impossible first few feet. In archaeological lexicon, this type of work was known as *bullshit*.

But there was nothing like this. Squatting in the mud was filling her with a staggering sense of possibility. Here at the bottom of a pit, Z felt revived. The physicality of it all energized her with a much-needed sense of control. *She* was in charge of what happened down here; the pace and style of digging and brushing was up to her. Sweat pooled in pockets of fat and flesh that hadn't felt used in years, and her muscles were blissfully sore. It had been a long time since she'd felt this good.

Surprisingly, the trowel felt natural in her hand, considering the last tool she'd held was a nail file. Despite all the years since Z had done this kind of work—work that required famously meticulous care—Elise had simply walked her over to the trench, clipped a tool belt around her waist, and grumbled something like, *You know what to do*. And shockingly, Z found that she did. Inch by careful inch, she was easily swept back into the flow, her arms remembering precisely how to peel back the eons. If Z had done this sooner, just retreating to Mega after previous breakups, she would've avoided years of binge drinking, blind dates, double dates, pity dates, the unfortunate Brazilian, the disastrous Texan, the surprising Canadian, and perhaps the entire tree-carving incident.

She'd messed it all up before, salting this very earth when she'd broken up with Gary and making it so that she couldn't come back to keep doing the work she liked. Even in the moments when she'd thought about returning to Greece, she nixed the idea: too embarrassing, too much of a retreat. And yet, as her life in the city increasingly qualified as an embarrassing retreat from success, the idea had seemed more and more reasonable. What a stroke of genius to return to the beginning—to set the bone right this time, so it could heal.

Never mind that she'd flown to Greece with Gary's torso top of mind. She could—she *would* prove that she could start off with the wrong intentions and still make it right. This moment was her chance, by God, to finally cleave man from progress. She could do it; she had to. It would help if she could find something in this trench, a big something she could hold in her hands and hoist over her head, so she could convincingly say, *This belongs to me. I did this*. A discovery like that could make the past few years seem just a necessary intermission for her to come back here, stronger. She could be what she was beginning to believe she was meant to be all along: a single, middling archaeological assistant.

The work was just as exhausting as she remembered. Despite its grandiose possibilities, it was highly repetitive, slow, and—down inside the deepest trench—lonely. No matter how many snack breaks she took or how hard she tried to keep her mind on its new, higher plane, she still had hours to parse the Gary roller coaster. First, *Game on. Here I come, baby. Summertime, fun time.* Next, *Great, cool, stellar. He's actually getting married to the lamest person I've ever met.* Then, *False alarm: in fact, he* will *be available again. Only sad that this time his imminent ex thinks we're best friends, and I can't even warn him.* Jesus, people, was it so much to ask for one summer of zero responsibility, disappointments, or consequences?

She needed to "focus on work," a phrase she'd never tried before.

The north wall of her new cubicle was a rainbow of stratigraphy, a layer cake of history. The very top levels were grayish fresh ground, followed by darker and darker dirt, from milk chocolate to black coffee, then a paper-thin yellow line that was a bug tunnel, then a thick red streak of pottery that was probably a Roman roof, then a gray stone layer that was probably something, then a bright green streak which was almost definitely something else. Halfway down, the lines shifted from horizontal to diagonal, recording an earthquake. It was so beautiful, a wall whose historical dimensions were five years by five thousand.

"Well, well, well," a voice called above her. "Someone's been totally avoiding me, man."

Z looked up, which was no small feat. It required her to lie down flat on her back at the bottom of a dirt hole, where she folded her arms behind her head like a corpse on vacation.

Oh, right, the other person she'd been dodging, the fulcrum upon whom her original bad decision had pivoted. "Ryan, I'm not avoiding you," Z lied. He was a walking reminder of who she used to be and had an annoying suspicion she still was.

"Huh?" His shirt was off and wrapped around his head and ears, just as she'd left him years ago, an animatronic hunk who'd been un-plugged, placed in storage, and now dusted off and turned back on. He looked like he'd wandered off the set of a rap video and into a landscap-ing gig. His hair was buzzed, and his baggy shorts hung below a tool belt, which had to be chafing his abdomen, Z imagined, but it certainly didn't seem to bother him. It was depressing to see that his looks had just hardened in the best way possible, every angle of his face and body crystallizing effortlessly into permanent generic handsomeness. It was comforting to know deep down that over time, sadly, cheekbones that thirsty sucked a brain stem dry.

"I did move to New York," she continued. "If that's what you mean."

"No, not avoiding me in like, life. I mean here. You haven't even come over and been like, 'Hey Ryan, how's life?'"

He sat on the edge of the trench and dangled his boots down inside, exposing his anklet that matched his bracelet and necklace—the man had never met a puka shell he didn't like. Charles had once framed Ryan's role here in a "temporary helping hand" light, and maybe since this was a place where years didn't amount to much, it made sense that he was still employed. Certainly those ancient freaky priests would approve of him.

"Totally fair. How is life? How's it been here?" she asked. "I mean, it looks rad."

"Man, you're looking at it," he spread his arms wide, and all she could see between them was the sky. Impressive. "You heard we got the new lidar machine now."

"Hadn't heard that. Sounds exciting though," she said, having com-pletely forgotten what lidar was or were. In spite of all the survey team shop talk she'd been privy to back then—Gary and Ryan were in charge of the lasers—it still conjured up images of a cat chasing a red dot on the wall.

This style of conversation kept happening to her; everyone she'd talked to just picked up in medias res, as if they'd left off with her minutes ago and not years, as if they'd been interrupted by a phone call and not a half decade of debacles. They seemed to feel that they still knew her, which of course they didn't. They knew the fresh-from-college wild child she'd once been but had now, surely, grown out of. But whatever had happened to her beyond here didn't seem to matter; the changing years meant nothing to them. This conceit of erasure was delightful to live in.

"Cracks this baby wide open," he continued. "Uncle Charlie doesn't even know it yet. Plus, I got a drone last year. It is so sick. I had it down in Costa Rica for the off-season. Yeah, I went to Costa Rica."

She forgot that Ryan described his fall, winter, and spring this way: a bold vision. "Cool."

"Extremely cool," he corrected. "They've got some pretty amazing cerveza down there. Oh! And these cute little monkeys that'll just like, come over and start hanging out with you for no reason."

"What's that like?"

A pair of glasses suddenly dropped onto Z's stomach. Another face appeared above her, squinting after them and blocking her sun.

"Whoops," said Gary. "I can't really move until I get those." He was frozen blind at the trench edge with both hands fully extended in front of him.

"You need a croakie, boss," Ryan said, taking the glasses from Z then handing them up to Gary. "They're these straps that stick onto your sunglasses and then wrap around your neck, so you don't lose 'em. You know what, damn, bet they'd work for regular glasses too."

"Can you check on the water supply?" Gary asked. Ryan gave a thumbs up and walked off in the opposite direction of the water supply.

"Come on down, Stevie Wonder," Z said.

Gary nearly running her over in a van was the best reunion with an ex she'd ever had. It brought the right amount of guilt into the mix, placing her on more even footing.

He lowered himself into the trench. She loved to clock the ways he was the same. There were lines shadowed on his outstretched arms that she didn't recognize—muscles, evidently, though his body still mostly retained its appealing layer of chub across his tall frame. His soft baritone voice always teetered on the edge of a laugh regardless of subject matter, which made every conversation feel vaguely fun. He was so calm, genuine, and completely at ease with being a magnificent dork. Plus, he smelled like fresh cotton sheets left out in a pine forest to dry.

When he reached the bottom of the trench, he carefully set his feet in the cleared section of the ground, where he wouldn't step on anything she was working on. He wiped his hands on his Zagorakis soccer jersey and removed his bucket hat.

"Great news," he began. "The freezer broke. We have to eat like, two hundred chicken drumsticks tonight."

"Outstanding," she agreed. "What happened to the freezer?"

"An Ug jammed an ice pop into the outlet."

"Excellent."

Gary leaned closer to her. "So, I wanted to ask you something."

Her stomach swerved. He was going to ask her about Kara. He was going to ask her about their breakup. He was going to ask her if she still loved him.

"I know this sounds a little crazy, but I'm thinking I might come up here a few nights. Sneak up, you know. I want to get a few more measurements from the burial grounds."

"Oh," she exhaled. "Spooky."

"I need somebody to help me out, and I know you've been up here at night before."

"We came up together, Gar Bear."

"Well, yeah," he emitted a deep belly giggle, which provoked in Z a passing vision of Kara's body hurtling down the mountain—but in like a quick-death, out-of-her-misery, everyone's-okay-with-it kind of way.

"And I don't care about pissing off Charles," Z added.

"Never have, never will."

She lifted her chin with a smug little wiggle. Her fearlessness in the face of authority was the trait she was most proud of. It had gotten her nowhere in life, but she liked it about herself too much to let it go despite mounting evidence that some healthy fear might work wonders for her resume. There were plenty of things she was afraid of, all of which wcrc variations on being alone: spending too much time by herself, being single, missing out on group events, everyone who loved her dying. She considered this the correct fear in life; her priorities were the only ones *in* whack, she believed, and so no, she couldn't possibly muster much stress over a tense exchange with old Chaz. It just didn't rank. She had a radical notion of consequences— that there usually weren't any, and if there were, they didn't matter much—cultivated by a life in which nothing particularly bad had ever happened to her.

"Obviously, I'm in. What's the doc hiding up there?"

He ran his hands over his hair and threaded his fingers together behind his neck. "Bones. It's the only place we ever found human remains up here, but as soon as we started to find stuff, he made us close up. Even though he knows I need more measurements. We did get some bone samples, but he said he didn't want to get into a 'sticky wicket' with the Greek Orthodox Church over remains. So he just shut it down."

"Charles is in touch with those people?"

"I doubt it, seems like baloney to me. Anyway, I don't even care about the bones. He and Kara already mailed them off to Dr. Chen. I just need to get the topographic measurements down, like, yesterday. I am trying to not be a student for the rest of my life. So, up we go."

AFTER Z SPENT AN HOUR MOVING A LAYER OF ROCKS, HER SHOULDERS throbbed. She decided it was time for a break. The sun had already arced overhead, and the walls wafted with the preserved heat. Too tired to deal with the ladder, she heaved herself over to the other side of the trench. Immediately, something jabbed the edge of her butt.

"Ow!" Had she left another chip clip in her back pocket?

She turned onto her hands and knees to look down and instinctively pulled the trowel from her belt loop. She pressed its nose into the ground where she'd just been sitting, and the small shovel scraped against something hard. *Oops.* It was a thin mound of dirt in an unusual crescent shape, and she leaned her face closer to see if she could make out anything else. The dirt was too thick. She pressed her trowel in again, to the side, to try and break the ground free around it. She forgot all about her aching shoulders. In theory she should've been moving more slowly, but as the days passed and she hadn't scraped against so much as a roof tile she'd begun to act faster, taking a more carefree approach, shall we say, to the art at hand. But remembering her training—one hour, five years ago, of Charles gesturing with his hands in a stir-the-pot, dance-like motion to dig *around* and not *into* any object of interest—she scraped away the surrounding inches near whatever this was for a few long minutes.

Finally, she pulled the trowel back and laid it down beside her knee. With her gloves on, she gently wiped away the topmost layer of dirt, then peeled the gloves off to get a better feel. Whatever it was looked like a half circle with a thin edge, and it was some kind of metal. Elise had been right: this hunk of earth wasn't done coughing up goodies after all.

There was a magic feeling—a shiver up her spine—being the first person in several civilizations to lay eyes on something, to collapse the gap of thousands of years with a single finger grazing the object. There was them, eternally, and then suddenly, there was Z. There was no way to not be an absolute cornball about it; it was just plain awesome. She'd been enamored with this feeling once before and afraid she might never have it again. This was raising the dead. It didn't get any more metal than that.

And the greatest part of all—she could stop working. Elise had told her in no uncertain terms, *If you even think you've found something, if you even think you might find something, stop. Remove yourself from the trench immediately. Your very bodily presence in the trench threatens its contents. I wouldn't trust you to floss corn out of my teeth. Don't touch anything. Just come and get me right away.*

Aye-aye.

It was the hottest part of the afternoon by then, well over a hundred degrees out, so hot that every cloud had floated as far away as possible from the maniacal sun. First, Z climbed the ladder up and out of the trench, then somehow managed to haul her roiling body up to the altar to tell Elise the good news: she'd be quitting for the day.

Water break included, it took a full twenty minutes to go from the bottom of the trench to the top of the altar, for the love of god. At last, she stood there panting and making a real show of it, hands on knee-pads, bent over at the hips, a cul-de-sac of sweat at her groin. Though she'd been blaming the altitude, it was more so the return of exercise to her life that made her feel like hurling constantly.

Elise gnawed her lower lip in concentration; she was very close to extricating one side of a charred goat skull. These freaks had major boners for torching goats.

Between breaths, Z huffed out, "I think, maybe, there's, something, down there."

"That's the idea," Elise said, not lifting her eyes from the bleating socket.

"No. I mean like, something-something. It's metal, in like a semi-circle."

Elise's head flew up, her eyes thwapping Z's face. She dropped her brush, unfurled her stance, and stood in one quick, fluid motion. Fitness, Z marveled.

"You're serious right now?"

Z pointed to the visible puddles of sweat gaining ground along her chest and crotch. "You know I wouldn't drag my ass up here if I didn't have to. You told me to come get you, and here I am, getting you. You're welcome."

Elise pulled a tiny notebook out of her cargo pocket. "Where? And how'd you uncover it?"

"Southeast corner. And by conducting excellent archaeological work, if you must know."

Elise glared.

"I sat on it. But it's fine, probably. Isn't this just going to be a German beer bottle, or shell casing or something? Yah?"

"No, not in the probe trench. Too deep." Elise looked nervous, jumpy even. "Shit, I wish I'd found it."

"Found what?"

She didn't answer, just kept jotting down notes in her pad and grumbling to herself.

"Do you have any granola bars left? I'm starving. Ooh, can I have some of this?" Z picked up Elise's water jug and drank it without waiting for an answer, then wiped her mouth on her wrist, streaking dirt across her chin.

"OK, listen. Don't go back down there," Elise warned.

"Shucks. If you say so."

"I'm going to stay and go in there after everyone's down for dinner. And do not, under any circumstances—I don't care if Gary bribes you with his body—do not mention this to anyone. Not one word."

Z pulled the elastic on the back of Elise's kneepads and let it slap.

"I'm serious, Z. Do not say anything, especially to Charles. Don't even look at him."

"Chill, woman. My life's purpose is avoiding talking to men over fifty." Z leaned over to peer inside Elise's trench and see what she was working so diligently on. "Look at you, Vincent van Goat."

"You're fired."

Z gave a thumbs up, then sat down on the grass to start worming her way down the hill. She'd never seen Elise so worked up before. It was kind of thrilling.

At the side of her trench at ground level, Z's rubber bucket contained a handful of strigils, pottery pieces, and some rocks and turds she kept in there just to fuck with Princess Kara. She picked it up now and dragged it over to the track, where they'd load it into the van later. Also, she was supposed to be checking on the Ugs this whole time.

"Hands!" She shouted.

All of them raised their right wrists, around which they'd tied pieces of bright yellow tape, making it so much easier to find them.

"Way to stay alive. Any M&Ms left?" One of them wordlessly fished out a bag from his pocket and foisted it over. She chain-snacked like this from one conscripted pocket to the next. She'd already told the girls how to pee in the woods without spraying it on their shoes—what more wisdom could they want from her?

"All of those—" Z said, finishing off the last of someone's peanuts. She pointed to a row of Styrofoam gallon jugs of water. "Need to be empty by the end of the day. If they're not, I'm going to line you guys up for a chugging contest. And let me be clear: one of you will puke."

Invaluable life lessons received, they each collected their water and trudged back to the trenches, dragging their shovels behind them. Ancient coins and corndogs awaited.

"Z?" One of the girls, Patty (the one with a truly impressive mullet and baggy basketball shorts), piped up. If Z were in any position at all to take someone under her wing, this chick would be the one. As it stood, Z was on the lookout for a warm and dry spot to crawl under herself.

"What's up?"

"Is this," Patty looked around her to make sure no one could hear, then whispered, "A bone?" She opened her palm to reveal a small white cylinder.

Now here was a teachable moment. Z had been bringing this one up at parties for years. "Watch this," she said.

She stuck out her tongue and popped the white thing onto it. It slid off. Patty was agape.

"Bones are porous; they stick to your tongue. Rocks just slide off, slippery." Elise had taught her that.

"Whoa," Patty marveled. Then she licked the rock herself, to corroborate the historical record. Z grimaced, having just put the thing in her own mouth, but all right.

Patty unzipped her fanny pack and paused as she was about to place the rock inside. Genuine worry flickered across her face. "Am I allowed to keep this? Wait, was I allowed to lick it?"

Something about the questions poured a warmth into Z's chest. This girl was lost in ways that hadn't even occurred to Z. Patty needed her, probably like Z had needed Elise. She opened her mouth to lob a joke about who was allowed to lick what around here, but stopped herself.

"For sure," she said. "Technically, you're not supposed to take any-thing from the site out of the country. It's all considered cultural prop-erty, even really tiny stuff. But I'm pretty sure you can sneak a rock. I actually took a little baggie of dirt, and I keep it in my apartment in a mason jar. People always ask about it."

"I'm going to do that," Patty said.

"Just sift it really well first," Z advised. *Had she ever advised anyone on anything before? What a rush! Was she the smartest person in the world?*

Patty nodded solemnly, accepting the advice like it was valuable, worth hearing, like she was grateful to be on the receiving end of it. Z wondered whether this strange satisfaction she was experiencing was that of doing her job well and enjoying it.

She walked down and took a seat on the wide stone bleachers, which had the best view on site. Gary and Ryan were hunched over shoulder to shoulder above the yellow tripod screen down in the middle of the track. Ryan was making an orange laser bounce off the rearview mir-rors of the van and onto people's butts, unbeknownst to them. His first victim was Charles, who was talking to the overalled Greeks and trying to bridge the cultural divide by waving his arms around like one of those used car lot pump-up balloon creatures.

Suddenly, Charles turned and walked toward Z.

She waved and muttered *Go away* through clenched teeth.

"Zara! How are you?" Charles began their mandatory conversa-tion as he approached. "I don't feel as though I've properly welcomed you back."

"Thank you."

"Welcome."

". . . Thank you."

"You're very welcome."

He was a human learn-a-language tape in which his half of the dia-logue was perfect and unadjustable. Whether a second party could keep up was not a concern. He said what he wanted to say, topics were extremely limited, and the participation of another party was optional. From what Z remembered, the man bulldozed through life this way, a Bobcat driver in plaid pants bloviating in Anglo patois.

"Anything of note down there so far?"

Without missing a beat, she answered, "Nope." She didn't have to look up to feel Elise staring down at them, and thought that to look up at her now might give something away. She had no idea why Elise wanted to keep this particular discovery to herself, but understood why anyone would want to avoid Charles's insufferable series of check-ins, report-tos, and circle-backs.

"Mmm. It makes sense. I'm sorry we've saddled you with this trench. Elise is convinced for some reason that it has more to give. But, between you and me," he said, doing nothing with his voice to create privacy, "She does not have the formal training, as you know, to make decisions like that. She doesn't know any better. But with you coming back into the fold, I thought why not. We'll appease Elise, and you can watch the kids while you're at it. Two birds, one stone indeed!" He laughed.

"Wow."

"I remember so vividly the last time you were here because I'd just returned from a speaking engagement in Malta," he said, breaking his own record for quickest redirection of the conversation back to himself. "Speaking of speaking, aha! I thought you might tell the young ones about the time we watched the videos. Do you remember? That was quite the affair."

She remembered. And she'd known it was just a matter of time until Charles brought it up.

On a handful of nights, the whole group would gather around the lab patio, pass around tubes of Papadopoulos cookies, and listen to a lecture by one of the experts in residence—any researcher who had come to stay with them for a stretch. There was the visiting geologist who scared the shit out of them by going over the history of violent earthquakes in the region and how, time-wise, they were definitely overdue for a doozy. There'd been a botanist who projected, based on seed residue, that the mountain they were working on had once been a veritable acid trip of flowers. And lastly there was an archaeo-blood expert, whose presentation on scraping DNA residue was wildly boring but provoked a fascinating round of questions from the Ugs on how to cover up a murder.

For Charles's night of lecture, he chose from his crowded quiver to discuss the history of Charles. He touched for five minutes on ancient athletic artifacts of the Mediterranean, which covered a span of fourteen hundred years, then rolled right into an hour on his glory days as an NBC sports guest commentator. Those glory days had spanned a total of six weeks. When Athens hosted the 2004 Olympics, he'd been asked to join the network as a resident ancient sports expert, tasked with popping in between heats to provide fun facts to American audiences about the origins of the games. As he eagerly told anyone he so much as walked past, it was the job he was born to do. His niche knowledge was at last called for and worth something, and he enjoyed his brief ride on the gravy train immensely, having never worked outside of academia. This brief bout of celebrity boosted him up to and among the kind of people who regularly appeared on the air during the games, from athletes to heads of state to newscasters; not a day went by when Charles didn't mention one of these people by their first name, prompting someone—anyone—to ask who he was talking about. His six weeks of intermittent, mostly dull television appearances propelled him onto the speaker circuit for a time as well; Charles's presentations aimed to rally salesmen and middlemen into achieving their true greatness by pondering the ancient art of running extremely fast. On the lecture night he'd made Gary haul out a projector, which blasted video clips onto the stone wall of Charles on various

news programs, quipping with blondes and Bobs about togas and
standing behind podiums in stuffy conference rooms talking about
the legacy of nipple chafing.

"I've got a face for radio these days, I'm afraid. I've been inter-
viewed on satellite radio quite a lot lately. You know what's always
topical—athletics!"

The kind of people who were into sports had probably never uttered the word "athletics" once in their lives, but sure. Z had said so
little by this point in the conversation she was certain it had to die out
soon for lack of oxygen, but as usual she was wrong.

"I've got an idea. How about you join us for the Mega party this
year? They're giving me an award," he preened.

Each year, the executives who owned the lignite factory in
Megalopolis hosted a gigantic, formal soiree to honor Charles for his
cultural contributions to the city. This was surely a misguided PR exercise. Insofar as anyone who was paying attention could tell, Charles
hadn't contributed much beyond a jobs program for American college
kids. He'd used the meager findings here not to help Kal start a local
museum, but rather to buttress his own archaic reputation back at the
university. The only glamorous piece he'd ever found—that statue—
was long gone at the bottom of a dust bin now. But this party was stuff
of Mega legend, and Z had attended last time she was here, even though
Ugs weren't allowed to go. She'd weaseled her way in as grad-student
Gary's girlfriend. It hadn't even occurred to her that she wouldn't be
going this year, but Charles never missed an opportunity to be viewed
as gracious. The party was held in one of the seal clubber's freakishly
fancy homes, and it boasted both a baklava buffet and an open bar.
Plus, everyone left the excavators alone and just circled Charles like
flies. Z couldn't wait. She'd packed an inappropriate dress specifically
for the occasion.

"Totally! Never turn down a party. What's your award for?" Z asked.

Charles's head slid backwards, his chins tripling. From this neck stance his head vibrated, and his eyebrows rippled like waves. It seemed this simple question had caused a system malfunction.

"What is it for?" He scoffed.

He reacted as if anyone who had to ask a question like that obviously didn't understand who they were dealing with: someone who could potentially receive an award of any kind at any time. Now he pursed his lips and squinted at her, unsure how a yo-yo of this magnitude had been permitted within ten feet of a Great Man like himself.

"I mean, sweet, congrats!"

Now he raised his chin and replaced his hat, which had been dangling down his back by an adjustable string, onto his head, making himself as tall as possible.

"Yes, I've got quite the speech prepared for the party. Then you can hear all about the forty years of my life I have devoted to the vital preservation of sport. Now, really, you haven't encountered anything in the trench so far? If you do, you must come to me right away and straight away. I know you've had certain . . . allegiances and dalliances here over the years, but I don't need to remind you that you do not work for Gary. You certainly do not work for Elise. You work for me. You all do."

She froze. Her entire body wanted to turn around and look back at the trench behind her. A long-dormant protective instinct flooded her. Suddenly she felt like the earth couldn't shelter the things lodged inside of it as well as it needed to. As soon as the dirt lost its grip, that was it.

She remembered one of the first things she'd learned in class once she'd started studying this stuff, a rubric that stuck with her all these years as she repeatedly molded the unwieldy blobs of her own life into presentable little sculptures.

The first story is told when the item is placed down for the last time—that is the truth. The second story is time. The third story is told when someone finds the item, and that is rarely the truth at all.

Chapter

9

The sun was setting in all its summer slowness, and Elise was by herself up at the site, her favorite way to be. She came up here at this hour at least once a week for both the sunset and a break from the incessant imbecility. But tonight she was here to work because of three magic words: someone found something.

She tried to let it go that she hadn't laid eyes on it first. At least it had been Z. She leaned back against a tree and waited tensely until she could be sure she was truly alone. Sure enough, a moment later she heard the approaching crunch of many quick footsteps across the gravel. Like he did every day before dinner, Charles came jogging up the road in his green short shorts and tank top, his skinny knees bobbing up and down like a sporty praying mantis on its last legs. Trailing him were eight deranged acolytes, all with identical headbands on, as if they'd pow-wowed and together decided, *We just aren't insufferable enough.* They jogged diagonally through the track and onto the gray, rocky trail that wound up through the hills. They didn't see her among the orchard shadows, and fifteen minutes later they were jogging back the way they came, soaking wet. One of them was limping after a likely tango with a loose rock. Somehow Charles corralled a group like this to run with him every year, and invariably there was an inaugural round of ralphing once summer fitness dreams greeted the altitude. His main reason for leading a team of incomprehensibly eager joggers was for a captive audience, to regale them weekly with another chapter of how he parlayed his college track star glory days into the impossible dream: an academic career in sports! This is something Elise had heard him describe without irony on multiple occasions, and every year's gullible batch lapped it up. Charles was always doing this, asking people to correct their vision of him. There were things to admire about the man—his teaching ability, Greek proficiency, an encyclopedic knowledge of amphora—but those weren't the things that he wanted to be admired for.

Once the footsteps had retreated, Elise walked to Z's trench and descended. When she reached the bottom of the ladder, she hung on a moment to assess where it was safe to place her knees, lest she replicate Z's faulty discovery tactics, then crouched down onto a clear spot.

There it was. It was no more than two inches long, a raised half-moon of dirt. Z had done a good job here keeping the trench clean, and the piece, whatever it was, stood out perfectly from a flat area that had been well brushed. It's possible there were other things buried nearby—there usually were—and Elise would find out. There was still enough light down there to see the slight curve of the piece, forming a flattened *U*. In no time at all she would find out what the full shape was.

She removed her gloves and touched it. It was still coated in a thick layer of dirt, but as soon as her finger reached the edge, she could feel that it had to be metal. Gently she swept the pad of her finger across the top: once, twice, then again. Then she picked up a soft-bristled toothbrush and did the same, ever so delicately loosening the dirt. Finally, a soft gold hue nuzzled up through the dust. She gasped, and her heart swamped with neon-red blood so fast she thought her chest might explode. She picked up the pace. With a hard-bristled brush, she swept around next to the mound to see what it might connect to, and how far down and around. She brushed like this, steadily, for an hour.

The dirt slowly piled beside her, and at last she could see that the shape extended into a complete circle. It was hard to say how far it went down, or what the rest of the circle connected to. But it wasn't a bowl or a cup; no one would've eaten or slurped out of this. It was too delicate.

It grew darker down there as the sun set lower, and her eyes were starting to strain. Again, she removed her glove and softly placed her finger along the edge. A drop of sweat slid down the curve of her neck and dripped onto the ground beside the glove. She shivered.

Holy shit.

What kind of idiot was she for not packing her headlamp? She needed to be up here all night. Every night. She peeled off her bandana and placed it flat on top of what little was exposed, then carefully laid a layer of dirt on top of that, hiding and protecting it for the time being.

In a daze, she climbed back up the ladder and sat on the edge of the trench, her heart swimming laps in an Olympic pool of adrenaline. Her stomach churned, and she inhaled her plastic-wrapped dinner of melted protein bar, the calories instantly quickening her heartbeat still further in a heady mix of fear and elation. As she chewed, she kept looking down into the trench, just to make sure nothing had moved, as if the golden circle might pop up, shake off the dirt like a dog, and trot away.

This was it. Her life wasn't at all where it should have been and she had the cat tats to prove it. But this little hunk of gold just might be able to vaunt her to where she belonged.

She turned the protein bar wrapper inside out and ravenously licked the gooey remains.

The coal-belching factory down in the valley made for surreal, chemical-fueled sunsets that heavily suggested human history indeed had its limits here on earth. The air turned green and purple in places, the clouds slipping and sliding into greasy prisms out onto an oil slick floating between earth and sky. It was nature unhinged, and perfect for this ferocious moment. Elise especially loved that no one else was up here to see it: the sky erupted wildly for her alone.

She stared off into the distance, losing all sense of time, until a tiny white car pulled up on the track. Kal.

He got out, cracked a beer with a satisfying clack-hiss, and scooted onto the hood to watch the wild light mushroom over the valley. She watched him do absolutely nothing at all; he sat perfectly still and moved only to bend his elbow and slightly recline his head as he took a sip. After each one he returned his face toward the orange spectacular. He came up here to see this, alone, just like she did.

"Hey!" Elise called and began walking down the hill.

Kal spit out some beer and swung his head around to see her approaching.

"Ah, yassas! Ooh, you scare me. Come sit," he said and tried to recover the beer on his chin. "What are you doing here?"

"I work here," she stopped in front of him. "What about you? I didn't know you came here without us."

For a moment he looked sheepish but quickly recovered. "I have key to the city," he said.

"The city," she air quoted, "is an hour away." Yet again the muscles in her lower cheeks worked hard to exert pressure on the far edges of her lips. Part of her wanted to hide all this from him and not let him in on her private hype; this was all hers, and she'd waited for it. The other part wanted to grab his hand and run together over to the trench, so she could show him everything. She honestly couldn't say right now which was the correct instinct. It felt like gold dust might start spraying out of her pores.

He slid down the hood and went over to the passenger side. He ducked his upper half in through the open window, returning with two more beers and a walkie-talkie.

"For you."

She paused before sliding her butt onto the hood and accepting his offerings, hoping she could keep it together long enough for a drink.

Hopefully it would calm her down some. A walkie-talkie was something she'd asked Charles for before, but which he hadn't granted, reserving a monopoly on contact with the outside world in case of emergency. She wondered if Kal had been saving it for her.

"I know you need one of these. You are right, it is important for the safety. And, better, you can talk to me this way. I will listen for when you call: nighttime, daytime, any time."

They clinked beers. "*Efcharistó*," she said. They drank in silence for a moment and let the sky terrify them. It was taking all her strength not to turn around every few seconds and check on the trench, as if it would fill itself in unsupervised.

"No practice today," he said. "Normally I am with the girls now. You know I am the soccer coach. The child of my sister . . . niece. My niece's team, I am in charge of. She is ten years old, but the next Messi, I am sure. I love being the coach, did I tell you?"

She nodded. "I remember. You know I played, and basketball too."

"Oh, I think you were good player. Strong Elitsa. Maybe would be good for the girls to meet you."

"I was good," she admitted, fondly remembering elbows to faces. "So, what's up with the museum? Give me the latest." The beer was already loosening the tight fingers of adrenaline around her shoulders. She leaned back onto the hood.

As Kal spoke of construction costs, she relaxed and tried to imagine the place. A gargantuan Poseidon fountain. A wall of bowl, roof, and goat skull fragments encased in Plexiglas. Without any big-ticket items, a coherent concept was a pipe dream. They would need the ice cream machines he'd purchased to bribe people into visiting.

"Elitsa, can you get it back?" He asked, jerking her back to the fore. "The discus." He placed his beer down between his thighs, then pulled on the loose band holding back his hair until it released, dropping the frazzled strands just above his shoulders. With both hands he contained the mass and lifted his elbows to secure it in a neat bun. She watched a tiny muscle ripple across the back of his arm as his fingers wrapped and tied.

"I'm working on it," she said, tapping the neck of the beer bottle onto the side of her head, which about summed up her strategy so far. The gold circle had so completely T-boned her in the brain, she'd momentarily forgotten all about the previous week's calamity. As far as working went, she hadn't done a thing but stew, paralyzed by her inability to ask either of the people who'd actually knew something. And now this.

Kal put his hand on top of hers, for the second time that week, and squeezed it. She slowly turned her hand over and pressed her palm into his, mixing their fingers for the first time. He beamed.

"Will you please come with me to the party for Charles?" He asked. "Be my date to the big party? Come on."

The big party. Z was already aflutter with anticipation for it, and from what she claimed, so was Kara. It was the event of the season—literally, the only one—but Elise had never been. Kara and Gary were always there, and Charles had begrudgingly invited her every year, if only to produce a decent showing of his team, but she'd never acquiesced. It would've required her to dress up, drive an hour down the mountain, chitchat with earth-destroying strangers, and subsequently, specifically, not smash them over the heads with their own wine bottles. It was a big to-do, and she was a big do-not. Kara came home every year ranting and raving about the dresses, décor, and desserts, but it was hard to tell if the soiree was genuinely fabulous or whether there was, as they say, no sauce like hunger. Beyond the bleak applause circling a sheet cake for someone's birthday every few months, she couldn't remember the last time she'd been to what anyone would call a party.

She was curious; she had to admit it, having spent a decade of summers here and never once attending this seminal annual event that Gary once claimed was "nutso." But no. She just couldn't bring herself to do it.

"I'm not going to that," she said and let go of his hand. "Not my speed."

His face fell slowly, until it bounced back up into a reluctant nod. "I bet if you come, I get all the money for the Kentro. Just throwing to me. The world-famous Elitsa. OK, maybe just Greece-famous."

She slid down off the front of the hood. She felt her guard creeping back up after being struck with a hard ask so suddenly—after these years of performative flirting, these cautious steps. She looked back up at the trench and felt her skin nearly moving up there without her, willing to drag her bones and muscles behind it just to get her back inside, back down into the dirt.

There was a headlamp on the floor of Kal's car. "Hey, can I borrow that?"

He bent inside and fished it out for her. "For the night soccer practice," he said, twirling it around on his finger before handing it over. "I give you a ride back down to the village now."

"No. I'm going to stay up for a bit."

"I stay with you."

She smiled and shook her head. "No."

He looked stricken. "OK. If you change your mind . . ." Kal picked up his walkie-talkie and waved it. "I listen for you, always."

HOURS PASSED, THE KINDS OF HOURS THAT MAPPED TO YEARS. HOURS that meant it was the middle of the night—well past dinner, well past bedtime, well past sanity, well into the next day, decade, or century. But you're hardly concerned with hours and days at a time like this.

Because this is it.

First things first, there's no pulling. And you don't dig down; you dig around. You need as much room sideways as you do on the top, and don't forget the bottom. The last thing you want is to lift and feel the bottom part of the thing pop off in the dirt. There's no telling how wet it is down there. A foot of dirt contains climate multitudes from dust to mud, and you have no idea what's going to slide right out and what the earth is going to clutch onto for dear life. You just build a block of dirt, in the center of which is your diamond, and work in from there. Under normal circumstances you'd bring the whole block into the lab, but that's not happening this time, *fílos*. This one you have to get a good look at right here, right now in its entirety.

It's the end of the middle of the night, a night at the end of what feels like a year because time is confusing as hell in the trenches, and you haven't slept, and you don't remember, and you're more than reasonably delirious, but you're so close now. Only a few more centimeters until you make the switch from trowel to brush, and that's when you start holding your breath.

Here's the secret the brush reveals to you: below the gold rim are the curved sides of a cup. From the bottom of the cup extends a sturdy stem. At the base is a thick square stand. You are looking at a gold trophy.

That's the silhouetted gist of it, and you're gasping for air when it comes into full view. Instead of feeling sated, you're starving because there's even more to see.

The brush is moving, and you have no idea how because it feels completely separate from your hand. It's so dark and so cool down here, and you could just sleep. You could just roll over a little bit to the right and lie down, and tomorrow you'd wake up and already be right here at the office, and that could be kind of nice. There's a bug crawling on your shin, all six shiny legs on yours, and it doesn't even matter. You can't feel a thing anymore; the brush just keeps moving, up and down and up and down and side to side and side to side. Soon it's brushing up on the surface of the cup—gently, gently, gently—it's slowed itself without you even realizing it. You've never brushed like this before because it's not your job. You're not the delicate one; your hands are rough, but this time is very different. You have to know what's beneath, and you have to know now, before anyone else knows. The headlamp lights the way, a tunnel of white that leads into a dream, maybe. Your eyes flutter, and you could just close your eyes, and right there, there's the beginning of a sweet dream. Your heart is wide open, and your eyes are pounding, and what you're seeing is a clear inscription on the gold cup, beautifully carved onto the trophy, beaming up through a zillion eons of dirt and straight into your chest.

Ἡραία

Or, as an old woman pinching her tongue might pronounce it: *hell, yeah.*

✦

It's disorienting on both sides of the equation. I've been down here four thousand years, and the first person I glimpse on the other side is a cat-tattooed, kneepad-strapped maniac in a headlamp. I would say, imagine my surprise, *but as I mentioned, I've been waiting just for you.*

Chapter

10

"I think someone took them," Kara said. Her fingers fiddled anxiously with the hem of her pink, sweat-wicking workout shirt, the one she'd saved for a hike like this one. In the early days of their relationship, she and Gary took these walks all the time; extra exercise was the only way to get any kind of privacy. But they hardly had the same effect anymore. Being alone with Gary washed Kara in guilt, and now, given the urgency of the lost discs and Charles's fishy appeals, it seemed impossible she'd ever relax again. And now Z had joined them for this walk, at Gary's behest.

Kara's stress over the lost discuses had reached an internal fever pitch. She hadn't intended to mention her search to anyone—hadn't intended for the search to last long enough to even be mentionable—but it had been weeks now, and no matter how many times she turned the lab inside out, they refused to appear. They'd never lost so much as a paint chip before, and yet here she was, finally solely responsible for keeping track of things, and a find of that magnitude goes missing. Charles had been famously disorganized, performing the perfect picture of a professor too preoccupied by his lofty ideas to trouble with storage units, file cabinets, and the spreadsheets it required to keep tabs on all their finds. When Kara took over, she'd come early and spent weeks just getting from zero to one in terms of a basic filing system. But after all was said and done and accounted for, those two discuses simply weren't there.

"What if one of the Ugs stole them? Brass balls," Z said. At first, Z's joining them on the hike had seemed like a blessing. Gary was visibly delighted that the three of them were such pals; but the mood, for Kara at least, soured when she couldn't stop feeling guilty about the whole thing. Having Z there just reminded her of the company she was soon to be in—the company of those who'd broken Gary's heart.

"No way. Have you checked the storage shed?" Gary asked. "Charles probably stuck them there at the end of last year. Remember? It was that big rush to wrap up at the end. That kid broke his foot, and we had to roll out a day early to take him to the hospital," Gary said. "So annoying. I forgot my mouthguard and ground my teeth the whole flight back."

Kara clenched her jaw. It had been a mistake to tell these two about her issues at the lab. She was supposed to be a duck on a pond, webbed toes frantically but invisibly paddling, gliding flawlessly on top. That's how she thought of herself, but she just couldn't help it. She needed assistance if they were ever going to recover these things; every time she mentioned it to Charles, he grew more and more distant, washing his hands from the stink of her mismanagement. If she couldn't find them, she could kiss Christie's goodbye.

The three of them stopped to wait patiently on the steep face of the back side of the mountain. In this direction what lay before them was an endless sea of emerald hills rising and rolling in hues of green she was envious of, appearing so lush relative to the other side of the mountain's scorched sage. From this vista it made perfect sense that human beings would have wanted to spend their lives here. There were ample pockets of shade, and the wind rushed around them with the faintest possible hint of salt from an impossibly faraway shore. A narrow, sporadically graveled hiking path led away from their excavation and wound through these hills all the way to Sparta, dozens of miles away. Legend had it that one year Charles led a group of students on this very hike, making it only halfway prior to mutiny. Various alleged reasons for this rebellion included the the narrow, foot-wide path (with stones making surprise appearances to twist ankles), the difficulty of finding water springs, and a roving terror-zoo of snakes, spiders, and scorpions. It reminded the participants that the city of Marathon gave its name to a journey at the end of which someone died. The trail was not, in fact, intended for humans at all, but sheep.

The three of them were seated on an accommodating pile of rocks experiencing this hold up. A seemingly endless stream of shaggy sheep crossed in front of them, baah-ing away with the faint chime of a bell or two ringing among them. The shepherd, an elderly woman wielding a neon-orange plastic walking stick, trudged behind.

Last year she and Gary took walks like this a few evenings a week, a mile or so all the way up to the tiny, one-room white church at the second bend in the path. There was always a candle lit there. She'd been falling in friendship with him back then, when they were just getting started, impressed by his steady commitment to his field of study and his reputation as one of Charles's smartest students. Kara was also flattered that he—widely considered the second-ranked hunk of the bunch—was interested in her. It was true that she'd never felt fireworks or butterflies, exactly. Rather, it felt like she'd finally handed off to someone a very large, heavy object. It felt delicious to relax, a state she'd heard so much about and yet been incapable of experiencing herself. To have moments during each day to dip into a warm pool of *not trying* felt blissful, rapturous, and indeed sinful. He lived like this every day! It had dazzled her. It made her sad (how the buffet tables had turned) to think how far he'd fallen in her estimation simply by staying his same, wonderful self.

THE ANIMALS ALL HEADED FOR A DRINK AT THE SAME BUBBLING SPRING where Gary went to refill his water bottle. He walked over to wait in line for his turn, giving Kara the chance to ask Z why, exactly, she'd joined them on this walk. It seemed the woman was incapable of not participating.

"He asked me to come! What am I gonna say—no?"

"It is an option."

"Hey, I thought I was doing you a favor. You don't want to be alone with him anyway, right? Oh wait, crap, was this the breakup walk?"

"Shh! No. It was supposed to be, you know, a state of the union, if you will."

"I won't. Just rip the Band-Aid off, dude. You're making it way worse. And this?" She gestured to the mountains, sun, or general pleasantness. "Making *memories* right before you drop the bomb? That's brutal."

Z was right. Kara's focus on ending her engagement had wavered in light of recent events. The point of this summer had been to cruise through, shedding the weight of this place and all of its attempts to hold her back, but lately she found herself in need of Gary—his reassurance, his comfort, his steady sameness. Her unsettling conversations with Charles had put her on edge. She needed to talk to Evelyn and collect herself.

Gary was uniquely able to talk her off the ledges she constantly found herself up on. He recognized and understood her anxieties, mostly work-related, and had a way of methodically unspooling them that left her calmer. He'd adapted this method over their time together; at first, he simply encouraged her to look at the bigger picture. *It's not all about work!* But he quickly learned that for Kara, her career was the biggest picture, and she needed specific, detailed reassurances that she was approaching it correctly. Would another partner ever be able to do that for her? It made her heart shrink to think *maybe not.* Though yes, it was wrong to prolong things now that her mind was made up, she'd been reaching for his hand lately, scooching over closer to him, and relaxing into his touch. It was weak of her and added another toxic splash of guilt to the mix every time. But she needed it—she really did, lately—and she'd hoped this morning that a long Gary walk would be just the ticket to temporarily calm her nerves and remind her of her core mission. It wasn't fair to him, no, to make him play this role against himself, calming her so that she could fortify herself enough to leave him—and yet. Telling Z had been the right move to hold her accountable.

"You haven't said anything to him, have you?" Kara asked.

"Nope. Look at that guy. You think I'm going out of my way to harsh that vibe?"

Gary crouched down and let one of the baby sheep drink water from his cupped hand. Then he took off his glasses and put them on the lamb's face.

"Sheepers peepers!" He yelled over. Z and Kara both smiled like mothers at a playground.

"Believe it or not, I haven't hit 'break off engagement' on my you-fucked-up bingo card yet. That's all yours. And are you sure? I mean, come on. People would kill to marry old sheep peeps here."

The way Z was staring at him indicated she might well be one of them.

"What about you?" Kara asked, swiveling to look Z squarely in the face. She could picture it clearly, all of a sudden and with a sickening flip in her stomach. Both of them had an undeniable fun streak, and Z probably accepted Gary's goofiness—even liked it—while Kara herself was routinely embarrassed by it. And Z would probably benefit from Gary's steadiness, a sturdy person in her life to inspire any kind of commitment to anything; he was someone for her to aspire to be. The longer Kara dwelled on this previously hypothetical concept of someone else dating Gary someday, her ribs felt like fingers squeezing the air from her lungs.

With one hand, Z pulled out the waistband of her shorts, and with the other she flapped a stream of breeze into her nether regions. It did trouble Kara somewhat that her betrothed might prefer . . . this.

"Pfft," Z burbled unconvincingly. "Been there, boned that. No, no, no, no. Please. Plus, you know, I'm supposed to be getting over someone else at the moment, still recovering. No, I'm just focused on doing me. Self-discovery time." Her fanning continued.

Kara sighed. Her stomach was in knots. "I just . . . it's hard for me to even think about *this*"—Kara motioned at Gary, who now stood in the middle of the flock dodging the shepherd lady's orange stick, which she used as a violent extension of her lively hand gestures—"until I find those discs. The last thing I want to do is ask the Ugs about it. Do you know who some of their parents are? I cannot be accusing them of stealing."

Z chomped into her beef jerky stick. "Was there anything special about them?"

"Every single piece is special."

"Thank you, Mr. Rogers. I mean do they look any different? Or are we just talking hunks of round metal like all the other ones?"

"There's an inscription, *H*, apparently, according to the file. It's the only one with that kind of marking that's even clear. On the others you can't really make anything out."

"*H*. I got it; trays for hotdogs."

Kara closed her eyes. Her brain was in active triage. She hadn't even brought up the Charles conversation and didn't dare to with these two, but it lazed in the back of her mind like a sleeping monster.

"Why don't you ask Elise?"

Kara's eyes popped open. "Why would I do that?"

"Um, because she works here? She knows a shit ton more than I do about it, which you know, and yet here you are asking me. *Me*," she pointed the beef stick at her chest for emphasis.

"You're my friend," Kara ventured as if throwing a knife into the air, unsure if she'd catch it handle-side down.

"Well, yeah," Z confirmed, and Kara smiled for the first time that day. "But if you actually want to figure this out, that woman doesn't miss a beat. Also, if one of the Ugs really took it, or somebody else did, she could make them fess up like that." Z snapped her fingers loudly, and a jumpy sheep flinched.

"And give her one more reason to say how terrible I am at my job."

"You two suck," Z said, and Kara thought she sensed a hint of affection that made the corners of her lips curl up ever so slightly.

The sheep were finally thinning out, and Gary ambled back over. "That lady has lived," he said. He leaned down and kissed Kara on the cheek.

"I'll help you look, babe." He placed his palm on the back of her neck, and she nuzzled into it like a chastened dog. Z glared at her.

WHEN THEY RETURNED TO THE VILLAGE, KARA USED THE EMERGENCY landline on the side of the road to call her stepmother. Charles was desperate for money, and she was desperate to understand why.

Maybe Evelyn would even have some bright idea from a thousand miles away about where to look for the missing discuses. She'd conjured up rarer artifacts with fewer leads before.

"Hello?" Evelyn's voice came in clear as a bell from Manhattan.

Kara stood up straight. If anyone's skills extended to discerning posture from the tenor of a voice, her stepmother's did.

"Evelyn, it's me," Kara said.

"Well, well, we're just leaving the Club right now. Oh, by the way, I meant to tell you that we're absolutely going with the Hinckley room for your reception. It has two bars, one at either end, which is essential. Even with champagne circulating, you absolutely need two bars. Nothing is more uncomfortable than having to wait in line for a drink at a wedding; you never know who you'll get stuck talking to, and it could be an eternity. Don't get me started on Sandra Callahan, the second

Nelson nuptials, single bar line, 1998. I am scarred to this day by how much I was forced to learn from that woman about some crustacean charity. They're going to outlive us! They're sea dinosaurs, for God's sake! Anyway, did you know the Swan room only has one bar? It creates such a bottleneck, no matter what they tell you—and they always try to tell you."

"Mmm." Kara knew better than to commit to an opinion at this juncture, let alone about an event she was about to call off.

Evelyn's trick was to appear clear, to sound as though she was speaking very explicitly, and yet every word contained letters that spelled out a code. She relished watching how people unraveled it, or if they could at all. Nothing, in fact, was ever obvious, and this was most apparent in her home. Every item in every room at Evelyn's and Kara's father's apartment was a test within a trap, and once guests left, they were subject in absentia to a grading based on what exactly they had decoded and how well. Washing their hands with the proper bathroom napkins among the choices of cotton, paper, and linen; complimenting the catering versus the cooking out of dozens of mixed dishes; never acknowledging the existence of smell; choosing the correct conversation topic out of literally anything in the universe. Evelyn was less interested in people who missed the mark completely; they weren't worth the study. But those who tried—especially those who came close, revealing their studies by deploying the word "divine," for example—were her favorite to excoriate.

"I need to ask you something," Kara said and glanced around to make sure she was alone. "It has to do with Charles, my boss—"

"I know who Charles is, dear. And he's not your boss, particularly. I'd prefer you to describe him as your professor or colleague."

"All right. Well, as a matter of fact, he'd like to talk to you."

"Me?" Evelyn made a dainty scoff.

For a moment Kara felt a thrill at the possibility of speaking to Evelyn as an equal—a peer in her field, on a business call, making an arrangement. "He's hoping to expand his network. Oddly enough, he specifically asked to meet you and, I guess, anyone you might know who's interested in these kinds of artifacts. For some, well, *consulting* was the word he used."

Now that she was saying this out loud, she realized that she wasn't exactly sure what Charles wanted from her at all. He seemed to think that simply connecting with Evelyn's friends would somehow remunerate him.

She stated in conclusion, "He needs a bit more income, apparently."

The line fell silent.

"Hello?"

Finally she heard a laugh on the other end.

"I'm sorry. I was chuckling to myself. You know, these calls always catch me by surprise even though they certainly shouldn't. Charles, though, I did not predict I'd receive one about him. I assumed he was one of the good ones. How naive we are."

"Good how?"

"Pure as the driven snow, academia unto itself, professorial until the end. But you'd be surprised how many of these arrangements I'm privy to. A piece here, a piece there—you'll see, and of course I, of all people, know what wasn't included in the most recent auction. They're coming every so often, discreetly, directly from the sites themselves. Greece is rare, I'll grant him that. It's very bold. More often, naturally, I'm offered pieces of questionable provenance from India and the Middle East. But I think there's a taste for it these days, sadly. Some people want to feel a more authentic connection, perhaps. But Charles—my, my."

"What are you talking about?"

"Kara dear, please. Your tone. You'd barely believe some of the predicaments I've heard about, these out of the blue sales people would like to make. One moment it's a priceless piece that's been in the family since Scotland, and the next it's, 'Can you wire it directly to Carter & Weiss?' Once one's become accustomed, I suppose. He was on television at one point, yes? I'm assuming that well's rather dried up."

"What?"

"Excuse me."

"Excuse me?"

"Oh, Kara. If I had a nickel for every vase or statuette of tasteless origins . . . Well, I do have those nickels. How tacky he's mixed you up in this. I had heard rumors, I'll grant you that."

Kara's stomach took a nosedive. "Wait, hold on. Just wait please. You're actually saying Charles is selling artifacts from our dig? For . . . money?"

"He's certainly trying, it seems to me. Though, as I said, it's quite difficult to cross the pond. He'd have better luck locally, though it goes without saying he should hardly be doing this at all."

"Yes!" Kara screamed. A streak of rage soared through her as it occurred to her that Charles assumed she wouldn't say a word about this to anyone else here. He presumed she'd be comfortable with this line of inquiry, even perhaps familiar with it, when she very much was not. Not at all! That, or he was cavalierly willing to besmirch her reputation by association.

"Oh, darling. It sounds like he's quite desperate." Evelyn sounded gleeful.

Kara closed her eyes, massaged her temples, and breathed in through her nose, out through her mouth, as instructed by the person who was presently causing her stress.

"Evelyn," Kara said as sweetly and as evenly as she could. "It's not anything like that. Not in the slightest. This is Charles's entire life; he would never. Or it's all for a friend—it could be that," she added, eager to steer the conversation to a shore, any shore.

"Haven't you ever called someone and said, 'I have *a friend* looking for the best lip lift in the city'?"

Kara sank her shoulders and closed her eyes again. "How could you not tell me there were rumors like this about Charles?"

"You should be thanking me! I've done my best to quash every one, for your sake. Particularly this year you've got enough on your plate. You're a bride!"

This would've been the moment to mention that her plate was emptying by the minute. No job on the horizon and soon enough, no fiancé. She had to get off the phone.

"Thank you," Kara said this firmly, as a prompt. It was how Evelyn liked for her to end all of their conversations.

"Of course. Well, yes, I may very well hear of something for this *consulting*, as we're calling it. One never knows. I personally have no interest in sports paraphernalia, as you know."

"It is not sports paraphernalia," Kara said with the flat tone of someone who's pointlessly made this correction many times before. "It is ancient history."

"I'll see what I can find. Perhaps there's someone else on earth interested in the athletics of it all. Miracles never cease. Tell Chaz to keep his chin up, or should I say, above *water*," she said, not unmenacingly. "Ta ta!"

"Love you," Kara mumbled and clicked the yellow phone back onto the rusting receiver.

She retrieved one of Evelyn's tiny pills from inside her pocket, one she'd stashed there in case the Gary state of the union had gone particularly sideways. She slugged from her water bottle and lay down on the grass.

THE NEXT FEW DAYS WERE SPENT AVOIDING CHARLES AT ALL COSTS and preparing for her guest. Each season the entire team went to the beach at Pylos for one long weekend of break; this year, keen to avoid a romantic seaside trip with her fiancé, Kara was relieved to learn that the first visiting researcher was arriving a week early. She couldn't very well leave him in the village alone.

Dr. Louis Chen appeared a few days before the long weekend, a six-and-a-half-foot-tall archaeogeneticist from Minnesota who spent a few days in the village every year to collect new samples. He likely wouldn't leave the confines of the lab once, yet he wore a wide-brimmed hat, cargo pants, hiking boots, and a sunproof button-down.

"My brother-in-law got melanoma from working near a window at Los Alamos," he explained. "Where can I put the centrifuges?"

Dr. Chen spent his days spinning scrapings from pottery shards around in the centrifuges, which hurled out blood and human DNA material for him to take back in vials to the university. The archaeologists lamented how little of themselves these people left behind, while Chen marveled at how much remained. Once, it turned out a hairbrush they'd been preserving was really a knife; another time, a perfume bottle was actually filled with poison; there even turned out to be a fair amount of blood from multiple sources in a serving bowl. He frightened them and made them feel naive.

"When all you have is blood, everything looks like a machete," he'd say.

Spending three days alone on the mountain with this man wasn't how she pictured her one weekend off. But it was better than the alternative.

"I really am sorry. But obviously we can't just leave him alone here with Ursula and Ian," she explained to Gary when she broke the news about not joining him at the beach. He stood in the middle of the boys' room, rolling up his bathing suits to fit into his backpack. He liked to pack early and re-pack often.

"Do you think you need a new suit for every day?" she commented before thinking.

He glared up at her and didn't respond. Having her single room had ironically placed them into a summer of chastity, which she guessed accounted for the bulk of his disappointment right now. Charles had given her the room under strict rules that it not be used for "fraternization" since she and Gary were still unmarried. Upon hearing this, Gary had joked that they should just go to the court-house so they could room together; Kara had laughed so hard that Gary asked if she was all right. It was just the most absurd thing she'd ever heard. She was an adamant rule follower, as he knew, and she would not allow Gary to visit for more than a few minutes. When he insisted on popping in, she kept the door propped open and loudly greeted anyone who passed by.

"I'm just going to say it: I feel like you didn't really want to come this year, which sucks," Gary aggressively zipped an outside pocket.

Out of habit she nervously rubbed her ring finger, which was bare, the ring safely stashed in the lab drawer. This was a strong opening volley, and for a single second her stomach was weightless inside her body. She thought, *Do it. Say it. Now.*

But she didn't. Not in here.

It reeked of sweat and cured meats, and her eyes darted all over in an effort to avoid connecting specific garments with corresponding smells. She wouldn't be able to look one of her employees in the eye knowing that his were the shorts responsible for bologna cologne. This room made the girls' house feel like The Pierre. Gary's little cot corner was tidy, and he even had an adorable foot-tall bedside table made of books. Even though he had nothing to do with it, she couldn't help but think less of him simply for tolerating this squalor night after night.

"I'll miss you," she said, meaning it quite a lot. She couldn't bring herself to share with him what was going on with Charles. In general she preferred to settle problems alone, and in this case it was an unbearable thought to add to his troubles, whether he knew of them all or not.

The next day she briefed Dr. Chen on the site progress, including which trenches were open or closed for business at the moment, and which Gary had his sights on to laser into next.

"Oh. You never went back inside the burial site?" he asked. Like her, he had a blinding light strapped to his head to better inspect his pieces as they chatted, so they never faced each other directly.

"No, Charles closed it. There was some local issue. You know how it is, Dr. Chen. Of course with the remains, locals are so sensitive."

"Story of my life. I said to a colleague once, 'It's a toga guy, people, not your grandmother's corpse.'"

Kara looked at him and, realizing that a joke had occurred, laughed. "Yes! Right. Well, we got plenty of samples the first time around, the ones we sent to you. Did you end up including those bones in your journal article on athletic durability? You could tell all kinds of markers from those, I thought—even gender. I enjoyed that piece, by the way."

"No. Never got 'em. They got lost in the mail, see."

Kara's hand slipped. "Excuse me?"

"Oh yeah. Statistically, it makes sense, you know. Do you know how many packages get lost every year? It's a lot. My wife lost her luggage on our trip to Cabo. It cost a fortune at the gift shop to get all new bikinis and then, what do you know, it was sitting on our porch under a foot of snow when we got back. And, you know, even with the high-end carriers we use for the real big-ticket items, you can't trust the mail.

Better to carry it on a plane in your lap if you mean it. They paid out the insurance, Charles said though, real generous. So, there's that. Surprised he didn't want to go back in there though—go get the rest just so you guys would have some kind of record of the human remains, you see."

Kara stared straight ahead. "Charles never told me that, um, that they went missing, or, got lost. Does Gary know?"

Kara spun to face Chen directly, and he winced in the headlight.

"Sorry," she fumbled to click it off, her hand shaking. *The bones, the only bones they had found up there, were gone?*

"Oh, I don't know," he said, then smiled big. "Hey, how is Gary? He's the best."

✈

I know it seems impossible that all these pieces could come together into a clear picture. Moving through time—more of it than you can even imagine—is one thing, sure, but space, that's something else. I was used to going down, down, down, fractions of earth at a time, a bug's width of decades, the same home sweet home vertical column. That is until every so often (my version of every so often, your version of once in a generation), the ground would shake off the day, a big belly rumble of the plates way farther down than me, and it would shift me over sideways a little bit, a few inches, a few feet if it was really a doozy. That's basically how these pieces of me stayed hidden all these years; the earthquakes had my back. They pushed me here and there, helping me bob and weave until the moment was right. It's all about timing.

And the timing is good right now. You've come at the perfect slice of it, when the fairer half is finally up here working on digs. Technology is pretty sharp, but not too sharp that anyone with a laser could find me, so it still takes some old-fashioned know-how. Even so, I had to wait for the right combination: the first set of fingers to graze me, the second set to lift me out of there, and the final fingers to clean off the dirt so I could breathe again.

But even once you find all the pieces that add up to me, the thing is it's still incomplete. Incomplete is the name of the game, unfortunately. There's only flotsam and jetsam here and no shipwreck; the shipwreck is something you have to tell yourself. You'll have to take some leaps to put it together, and listen—people get it wrong, mostly because they make those leaps and turn those corners with their own baggage, using their own thread to stitch things together. Trust me, I've almost been sewn together in Latin, Imperial, and Reich style, everything except what I really am.

If I were going to put it nicely, I'd say something like, When you're an archaeogeneticist, everything looks like a machete. *Or I could say,* If you've got a machete, everything can be cut to look exactly like you want it to.

Part
Two

Chapter

11

Charles had Patty reporting back to him daily, giving her frequent opportunities to regale him with who had crushes on whom, who was thinking of switching their major, and who had their period. He cut her short every time, claiming that was not *what he was looking for.* But every time he pulled her aside, she felt a tremendous pressure to give him something—anything!—lest she slip from his precarious good graces.

The back of her neck was badly sunburned; every inch of red, exposed skin was coated in sweat then dirt. The nonstop sweat-dust-slime mix had even reached the inside of her shorts and made her itch all over down there. On the ride back just now, she'd sat on top of her rough work gloves and kind of subtly grinded on them for some relief.

Kara stepped out of the lab at the exact time Patty started up the steps. There was no way now to avoid walking together. Kara was so beautiful to begin with and comparatively non-disgusting on top of that, the only one of them who still looked applicable to the real world. Patty was always trying to avoid being within a few feet of her; it was just too hormonally overwhelming. She didn't have a proper crush on Kara exactly. There was no way to even get a foothold; it would be like falling for a doll, but it was thrilling to be near her. One time in line for lunch Patty stood behind her, just sniffing her hair—it was so pleasant—and Kara had turned around to ask if she needed a Claritin. They'd since bonded over having allergies, so Patty hoped that wasn't one of those conditions that required a lot of details to lie about.

In her exhaustion she gurgled a greeting. She was keen to inspire a monologue and knew that wasn't difficult to achieve with Kara. "How was . . . today?" she managed.

"Well, no luck with the missing discs yet. But the visitors are here, and you're going to die," she began. In her current state Patty feared this to be close at hand.

"We've got Dr. Chen." Kara continued, "He's here now, while the rest of you are going to the beach. His whole thing is, something *may look* like a drinking cup, but it's actually full of blood. Fascinating. Then my absolute favorite, Dr. Newkirk, Trudy, the archaeobotanist, she's coming later. Based only on seed residue, she maps out what the landscape would've been: plants and bushes and fruit trees, bees and pollination patterns. Hey, I bet she could tell us what kind of things they were all allergic to, like us!"

How was that possible? They just covered a world of literal ground, and now Patty still had to come up with something to say about allergies.

"Oh, there's Charles," Kara whispered, then bolted ahead into the cafeteria before he came any closer.

"Patty? A word," he said, beckoning her with a bony finger.

She looked longingly through the cafeteria doors at the young men and women partaking in a Bacchanalian feast of grilled cheese and Gatorade, before reluctantly following Charles around back. Here in the shadows Ryan sat on a large rock, tossing repeatedly into the air what appeared to be an electric toothbrush head, his wrist ajangle with puka shells. Charles put his hands on his hips and started in.

"All right, team," he said. Patty quickly looked around, and it seemed that she was, in fact, somehow, on this team. "What have you seen of Elise? She's been somewhat squirrelly with me lately. See if you can play the fool up there and figure out what she's really working on in her trench."

Ryan saluted then began a solo on the air guitar.

"Elise," Patty confirmed.

"She is abrasive, yes, I know."

Patty grinned. She'd spent the past weeks trying to figure out new ways to be anywhere near Elise. It was her she thought about the most. "I have to talk to her?"

"Yes, Patty, you do. You are on a scholarship at our fine institution, are you not?"

"Yes," she gulped.

"Sweet, for what?" Ryan asked. "For the money or like, sports?"

"Basketball assistant," she cupped her hand and whispered, so that maybe Charles wouldn't hear.

"Ryan, please. You are excused."

Ryan left to partake in what Patty could only assume was the greatest lunch of all time. Her stomach rumbled.

"I would not want for anything to happen to your scholarship," Charles continued. "So yes, if I have asked you to do something specific, I mean it sincerely. And there's no need for you to question me, particularly when you have yet to provide me with any information of value."

Patty nodded tightly. Being this close to him still awed and terrified her. "Except I have kitchen duty this afternoon."

Charles sighed loudly. They rotated so that one Ug was always down in the village each day, helping Ursula with food prep, laundry, and any other miscellaneous task required to keep two dozen American complaints to a minimum.

"Fine," he said. Of all things on site, the kitchen duty calendar was sacred and impenetrable, even to him. "Just keep in mind that I am your professor and can neglect to give you credit for this work study unit, or for anything else for that matter, at any time."

ELISE SAT AT THE END OF THE FARTHEST TABLE WITH NO ONE ELSE around her. Her eyes were ringed with dark circles; it looked as though she hadn't slept in days. Patty perked up and went to sit down beside her with a heaping plate.

"I'm really good with wheelbarrows," she said as a flock of rice took flight from the side of her mouth. "That's why Charles hired me."

Elise stared at her. Finally, she yawned, covering her mouth with a beautifully calloused hand. Her jet-black bandana was pushed on top of her forehead, holding her hair back, and the triangle end stood straight up. Every single thing about her was cool.

Patty tried again, attempting casualness. "So, where were you last night?" she asked. She'd looked for her at lights-out.

"Nowhere," Elise said. "And don't ask that."

Patty was desperate to keep this conversation going. It was critical to her real summer mission. Her first year of college hadn't gone exactly as planned when it came to finding out who she might like to date, which had been a primary motivator for leaving home in the first place. There was very little in the way of exploration. Her jam-packed days juggling classes and two jobs, scrambling between the basketball locker room and the student health office, didn't leave her with many hours—and so she eschewed those long, lazy stretches of *hanging out* in favor of concentrated party time. She hadn't made many friends, nothing like her high school teammates, beyond her roommate Mahira, who rarely left their room. Patty had glommed on to various friends of the basketball players, the ones who hung around outside the locker room and who eventually invited her to events where she knew no one; everyone was older, and somehow she could never find in the crowd the one person who'd sort of invited her. Rather than finding a wholesome and open space to meet and greet a wide variety of nice people, she encountered extremes at these mobbed events. One end of the room was populated by alcoholic nymphomaniacs, loud girls in crop tops and skirts who occasionally wore overalls in such a way that completely redefined the genre for Patty, and they discussed being so drunk that they couldn't remember which body-spray-soaked sheets they'd woken up in that morning. At the other end were couches full of silent, serious clusters locked in conversation who never returned her smile. Those were the girls in loose slacks who Patty later saw around campus carrying the right, great-looking jackets for the right temperatures—something Patty, always either sweating or freezing, could never figure out. She'd heard them discuss being so stoned they couldn't remember if they were wearing someone else's bra accidentally. It seemed like an unimaginable luxury to be having so much fun that you forgot you had a defining sexual experience, let alone with someone who had cracked the jacket math. Where were all the personalities in between? Alcohol helped of course—it propelled her to dance, sometimes, with the group of loud ones or take a seat on the couch beside the cold ones—but by the end of the night all had one by one disappeared into rooms and activities Patty could still only imagine.

There were moments, of course, when one woman or another held her gaze for a second or grazed her back side. Patty, however, was equal parts thrilled and terrified by this. She wanted to take a next step, but she would've liked that next step to be going out for a sandwich and a Coke and getting to know the person, not just running into a stranger's room to . . . who knows what. It felt overwhelmingly fast to her, and she was afraid of making a mistake, acting on a wrong impression and severing the delicate thread that gave her any lifeline to parties at all. It was less wholesome than she'd hoped, a thought that embarrassed her. Of course these women were beyond sandwiches.

This summer she was determined to act. She would do it on her own terms, and she would know for sure. This also had an added benefit: when, if ever, she mentioned anything about her preferences to her parents, in twenty to thirty years, they could just blame Europe.

Elise looked up at Patty for a long moment, then over at the raucous table full of the rest of the Ugs, assessing her place in the scheme of things. She asked, "We're on the same team here, right?"

Patty felt she might faint. "God, I hope so."

"So if you ever hear anything from Charles—if he ever says anything that sounds off to you, or just downright fucking weird, no matter who he's talking to—would you come tell me? I can't stay on top of all his crap, and it'd be good to have some extra eyes and ears on him. He's not the easiest boss, right? Especially if you ever hear him talk about some artifact, new find, or that sort of thing, just come find me. Stays between us."

Patty audibly gulped cheese. It was more than she'd ever heard Elise say before. With that, Elise stood and picked up her tray, leaving Patty alone, nodding, saying *Yes* she would, and therefore lying to this woman she was completely enthralled by.

That afternoon Ursula tasked her with washing half the sheets for the week. Patty hauled a pink plastic kiddie pool up from the shed and carried it over to the picnic tables by the Mythos mural in the shade. The spout of the hose plopped down inside. She let the pool fill up with cold water, sprinkled in the neon blue laundry detergent powder, and then added the first heap of pillowcases. Seated on the nearest bench, she used her bare feet to slosh the fabrics all around in the chilly bubbles.

"While you're at it," Ursula waddled over and tossed in a pile of her and Ian's clothes to the water. She sat down next to Patty and patted her on the knee, then pulled a partly melted Popsicle out of her apron pocket and handed it over. Patty was sick of grape by this point but couldn't bring herself to turn Ursula down, so she unwrapped the ice pop and ate it anyway.

Ian walked over and didn't break stride; already barefoot, he just stepped right into the pool. "Allow me." He hiked up his shorts, which were already mid-thigh, and stomped around to assist the suds.

Once everything was good and soaped, Patty tipped the pool over toward a corresponding blotch of dead grass. Ursula explained the fundamentals of crystals and palm reading while they rinsed and hung things to dry, and Ian told her about how the two of them traveled all over the world like this to different sites (Mexico, Thailand, Jordan), working as a team from dig to dig, era to era.

Patty picked up a pair of Ian's cleaned shorts to wring out. They felt unusually heavy, weighed down by something.

"Oh, no! You left something in your pocket, Ian," Patty said.

Her hand dug into the sopping pocket and pulled out a red roof tile—like one of the dozens they had drying down by the lab.

Patty gasped. She jammed her hand into the second pocket and pulled out another one.

"Oh, Ian," Ursula inhaled. "Oh my, oh dear," she turned to Patty. "He's going to put those right back where they came from. Aren't you, Ian?"

Ian pushed his bushy eyebrows together as if that was the dumbest suggestion he'd ever heard. "Of course I am. I know exactly how to set this whole place straight, right as rain." He pointed to his forehead, then snatched the two tiles from Patty's hands, shoving them into his current, dry pockets.

That night after dinner, Patty was the one who pulled Charles aside. This alone titillated. Here at last was a nugget she could offer up as penance for past performance; finally, something concrete to fulfill at least one of her espionage duties. A clear crime was afoot, and she had all the clues: it was the handyman, at the laundry pool, with the tiles.

Chapter

12

"You're putting that thing in your backpack?" Z hissed at Elise. It was the darkest, deepest part of the night, and the two of them were crouched down at the black hole bottom of her trench.

"Shh! Shut up!" Elise said, "That's what this is for." She held up an Arsenal WFC 1992 Champions crewneck sweatshirt that would be tasked with protecting a four-thousand-year-old trophy.

Z's eyes widened. "What in the actual hell are you up to, woman?"

Before they were interrupted, Z and Gary had been alone together up at the burial grounds all night. It was the farthest ridge at the edge of the excavation, beyond the locker-room ruins, and it felt like they were the last two people on earth up there, huddled in the only pool of light for miles. They were painstakingly lasering away and recording topographies, which turned out to be less romantic than it sounded. Gary was up here to map the spot that Charles had shut down, where they'd uncovered bone samples—the only remains ever found.

The task gave them a tremendous amount of time to talk, all by themselves, and she was relieved at how easy it felt. They started comparing notes on all the dreams and plans they'd had years ago—for him to get a dog and hike the Appalachian trail with it, for her to visit and eat at every ballpark on the east coast—and how far off course they'd veered. For hours she held one of those clipboards with the dangly pen, jotting down numbers and swatting bugs she'd never seen before, but it was some of the most fun she'd had all summer. Gary was a reliable dog sitter for his friends and had done a series of day hikes. She'd only made it to three parks so far. Every time the conversation approached the topic of breakups—not infrequently as she recounted her twenties—she skimped on the specifics with a quick, *so that one was over*, and moved on to make him laugh with her next misadventure.

During one hour they grazed hands inside a bag of tzatziki-flavored potato chips. During the next, he lifted his shirt to wipe sweat from his face, then placed his fingertips on her hips to tell her exactly where to stand. By the third hour the hairs on Z's skin all stood at attention. In circles she reminded herself, *he is engaged, as soon as he is not engaged he will need time, you are also supposed to need time, you're focused on work, but you came here for him, he is engaged . . .*

It didn't work. She was back. She was twenty-two again and all alone in the dark with Gary, who seemed to be having the time of his life too. Of course, a midnight laser mission *would* be the time of his life. They were forming a friendship again—that's what this was—but it was inextricable from the attraction she felt for him. She knew she should be keeping her distance, building on whatever they were starting again here, but she didn't want to. She wanted more.

Just when she thought she couldn't take it anymore—her body was about to burst with a torrent of apologies and overtures and confessions, ideally culminating in Gary embracing her here in what was essentially a cemetery—a blinding smell made her reel back. The object of her misplaced affection accounted for the lust-vanquishing fart with a giggle and the phrase "Beans, baby!"

Thank God.

The site glowed at night beneath the moon, dotted with wobbling black pools of shadows from the few trees swaying in the wind and with matte-black rectangles of trenches. A preposterous sea of stars shimmered in pale green thanks to the coal-gauzed air. It was eerily still out there once the breeze died down, with strange, faint animal noises that didn't sound nearly far enough away. Gary had mixed up some numbers and was on a serious streak at the moment to double check his calculations. He concentrated down at his notebook for several long minutes while Z looked out across the excavation, absorbing the quiet. A velvet stillness draped over the stones. Then, from the blackest darkness of the hills, a voice yelled out.

"Z!"

She jumped three feet, and her mind touched the void.

Gary poked his head up from the lidar contraption, eyebrows bent in a V. "Was that Elise?"

He shrugged and, somehow undisturbed by the idea of a third party being up here the entire time without them knowing, resumed whatever in Euclid's name it was that he was doing.

Once her flesh reattached to her bones, Z strapped her headlamp on and walked over to see her friend. Nothing was more on brand than for Elise to be by herself at the bottom of a hole in the middle of the night. Z climbed down the ladder and sat on the trench floor across from her; Elise was crossed-legged with her back leaning up against a wall. In her lap, on top of a pit-stained sweatshirt with a soccer cartoon, lay a golden trophy, the top of which looked like it might feel very familiar indeed to one of Z's butt cheeks.

"What in the King Tut fuck is that? Wait. No. That's what I sat on?!"

It turned out that little piece of metal she'd twerked onto down here had turned out to be a full-on, intact trophy from around 2500 BC with a clear inscription on it: Ἡραία. It was this priceless, potentially history-affirming or -altering nugget that Elise was presently attempting to smuggle off the site in her backpack.

"You can't just take that! Have you lost it? How the hell am I the responsible one here?"

Elise silenced her and explained everything in a rushed hush, from the journal of Deb's she'd read in Crete that first told her about the games, to what the hell Heraea meant, to the disc pics on Kal's phone.

Finally, she arrived at the entire man-washing of history going on here—the pièce de résistance and coup de grâce.

"Hold the phone," Z said and raised her hand into a Y shape, casting a phone puppet onto the wall in front of her. They'd each twisted their headlamps diagonally onto the sides of their heads. "We are missing two discs right now, from the lab."

"What?" Elise said at full volume.

"Shh, yourself! Yes! If you don't talk to anybody, you don't know anything, bozo. Thank God I'm here for you, lubing up the information superhighway. Kara's been looking for two discs ever since I got here. That's probably them!"

"Christ. How do we know she didn't smuggle them out of here herself?"

Z bulged out her eyes and looked at the backpack.

"This is different!"

"Have you met Kara?" Z asked. "That girl doesn't even turn right on red. She's been losing her mind trying to find those things. You need to talk to her like, tomorrow, or else I'm going to tell her this, and I do *not* feel like it. You have to. I love you, but you have no idea what you're talking about. As much as he totally blows, Charles is a very big deal dude. He could royally fuck you over. As in, you'd-never-work-ever-again-level fuckery. And it's not like you've got a bunch of goodwill built up."

"I have worked for him for ten years!"

"You think he cares?"

"She's worse!"

Z put her palms together. "One, she is not that bad. I don't even really get why you hate her so much. And two, you cannot handle this solo. He will end you if you swing for him. I asked him about that award, and he almost slapped me. You saw. He's the most defensive man alive. He'll flick you off this mountain like a bug."

"Are you kidding? She's the one who'd end me; she hates me! She'd

go straight to her mommy's friend at Interpol or something and have
me thrown in jail. She'd love that."

"She wouldn't do that. Too awkward, probably. Trust me, she's
got . . . her hands full. She's about to—"

"Z?" Gary called across the field.

Z made a peace sign, flipped it horizontally, and pointed it as men-
acingly as possible at her own eyes and then at Elise's. Then she righted
her headlamp and climbed up and out of the trench. Her pulse raced.
What a thrill to find out someone's significantly crazier than you first
thought they were.

She returned to her post beside Gary. Her heart played her ribs like
a glockenspiel. It wasn't fair to say that she was *very good* at this job, but
she didn't think she was bad enough to nearly crack a priceless ancient
artifact with her ass.

Gary handed her one end of a measuring tape. "She's not going to
say anything to Kara, right?"

"What?!"

"About me being up here like this?"

"Oh! Ha! No, you know they don't talk. She's just cleaning up my mess;
I was totally hacking away at the wrong wall this whole time. Whoops."

"It sucks what happened between them. I tried to stay out of it. It's
seriously bad blood. But you like Kara. You guys have been hanging out
a lot. She's cool, right?"

Z took a deep breath and tried to calm herself down. *One disaster at
a time*, her life motto.

Cool? No. But she could see the version of Gary that made sense
with Kara. He was grown up. He was still a student, just like he'd been
back then, which gave Z a false sense that he was still the same person. But in fact, just by doing the same thing he'd always done, he had
completely eclipsed her. He was about to have a doctorate. He was
borderline *esteemed*. And Kara, of course, was the VitaMix to Z's

Jimmy Buffett Margaritaville margarita machine. Gary had moved on to live in a world among those people who claimed the machine was "so loud," and who asked "why does it light up," and did it require "that song" every time they got a refill?—overall, people who couldn't fundamentally grasp that the volume has to default that high to hear it during a party over the crushing of ice. Gary had outgrown her in a lot of ways, and it made this connection she felt between them feel all the more powerful, immovable as it was.

Her head swam.

"Yeah, she's great. But, you know, she's a little uptight, maybe she doesn't let you be you. It's not too late to spread your wings, see what else is out there, just like you were saying, you've been here so long, you can always go live your own journey." Rattled, she was now just sputtering vague, nonsensical breakup platitudes that confused both of them.

"Did you just say the word journey? What did Elise do to you down there? You all right?"

"It's just, there are other people out there, in life, or in a different life, in the world, on various journeys."

He looked at her as she looked down at the ground, and then he removed his glasses and sighed. She had no idea what was coming.

"I'm sorry," he said. "Yeah, I really should've told you about her before you got here. But I didn't want to presume that you even cared, I guess. And you know, I didn't know what it was going to be like between us. I mean, it's been . . ."

"Gary. I obviously care. A lot."

"Yeah," he coughed. "Well, the way we left off I can't say that was a clear takeaway."

Now is our chance, she thought. "I'm so sorry," she said.

He nodded, and then with one long step closed the distance between them and wrapped his arms around her in a hug. Z's hands gripped his back, and the side of her face pressed into his chest. The smell of his sweat and woodland laundry flooded her nostrils, and she squeezed him tighter. He let go and stepped back, then he clapped once.

"All right. We both got our sorrys out of the way. What did that take us, a month?"

"We're idiots."

"Always been our thing. I'm glad you came back." He held her gaze for a long moment. "Right," he said loudly. "Well, let me just get another sample bag and we can get out of here. Way past my bedtime."

He walked over to the other side of the hollowed-out rectangle in the ground in front of them and crouched down. He dug around for a while, eventually scooping dirt and bone detritus into a plastic storage bag and then sealing it shut. Z stared at the tops of his shoulders while he worked, paralyzed by which disaster exactly she should grapple with. This always happened to her; multiple things were always going wrong at once, and she always picked the wrong one to fix first.

"Gary, I have to tell you something. Kara's—"

Boomp! Boomp! Boomp!

Elise appeared out of the darkness and tapped her boot on the hard packed dirt at the rectangle's edge. Chunks of dirt fell from the sides.

"These trenches suck," she said.

"I know," Gary replied. He zipped his backpack closed with the sample inside. "Remember, we never reinforced them. Charles just had us throw a tarp over."

"What've you got in there?" Elise asked.

"A nice bone stew, house special. What about you?" He jutted his chin at her backpack.

"Not in a million years." She clicked on her headlamp, then

cocked her head sideways, beckoning them to follow her down the mountain.

THE NEXT DAY Z CONTINUED HER EXCITING NEW WORK IN MANAGEMENT, a welcome distraction from thinking about either Gary or Elise for a brief moment. So far she'd come up with several sophisticated systems that kept her on top of the staff.

"One!"

"Two"

"Three!"

The Ugs marched past her, counting off their numbered selves as they'd been told. They made it up through *seven* before there was a pause.

"Kevin!" One of them prodded.

"Eight!" Kevin yelled. This one was halfway up the hill to the altar, pushing a wheelbarrow up there for some unknown reason. He was pitched forward so far that his body was parallel to the ground, his back flat and arms fully extended, elbows locked in. His knees were the only things that bent, and they pressed as hard as they could with tiny, wrenching steps upward, pushing this thing up the impossible slope. Everyone turned in his direction to watch for a few minutes, snacking on their peanuts. When he finally made it to the top, they all clapped. He waved, spent.

Elise's head popped up atop the ladder from Z's trench at the sound of applause. She cupped her hands around the sides of her mouth to inquire, "What the hell are you doing?"

Eight just stared down at her, depleted. Then he looked around the altar to make sure Elise didn't also happen to be there. His only instruction had been to bring her a wheelbarrow.

"Switch!" Z yelled. The Ugs looked at each other and launched into synchronized rock, paper, scissors. A moment later, Patty slid her sunglasses on and began ascending the hill while the others high-fived behind her. The original pusher crawled down on his butt, replaced.

"Great teamwork, team!" Z said. She was helping Elise dig farther, faster down into her trench, as scrupulously, speedily, and secretly as possible, in case there was anything else around where the trophy had been. Using a rope and a bucket, they were dumbwaitering dirt from the bottom of the trench up to the ground floor. Elise wanted to make this a quick check before she relinquished the trench back to Z. Today Charles was down at the lab, giving them a wide berth.

Ryan ambled over with his thumbs in his belt loops, pulling down his pants to a level barely north of predatory.

"Shouldn't you be surveying something?" Z asked, accepting the wheelbarrow from Patty. She held out her hand, and Patty parted with her trail-mix tithe.

"Did you know, *survey* means *serve* in French," he said. He hubba hubba'd his eyebrows at Z and Patty.

Then he leaned down to get a look inside the trench. "Yo, you've been down there a while, Greecey Lisey. What's going on in there? What's the deal?" He crouched next to the edge, his butt crack antenna at attention. "Something cool? You wanna maybe let me come down there and check it out?"

He looked back at Patty and winked. He'd never expressed any interest in what was inside any trench before, and the three women glanced around at each other in a triangle of vague suspicion and cluelessness.

"I'm cleaning up Z's shitty work, what do you think? Now get your slimy nips out of my face and scram," Elise said.

"Whoa," he put his hands up as though it would betray his principles to accept such a deal. "Dude, I'm just curious," he said. "Taking an interest, you know? Because like, I'm interested in things."

Elise tilted her head, as if unsure what to make of him for a moment.

"If I hear that you've even attempted to exercise your curiosity down here, or up there," she said as she jutted her chin toward the altar, "I will vaporize your nut sack."

He narrowed his blue eyes in an attempt at menace. "Get in line."

Z couldn't peel her mind from the trophy. What other exquisite marvels had she been one gas pass away from over the course of her life without even knowing it? It made her think of herself as something dangerous; all her carelessness was represented in this one plop-down, that if plopped too hard could've been the end of a line. What she was doing mattered! And not just to her, but to Elise, Kara, and her righteous ancestral bitches. Now she could picture herself throwing a softball to them. *This whole thing, this whole time,* Elise had said, *it was us.* Z couldn't quite wrap her mind around it. She'd come here to reset something for herself, but now it was clear she'd be correcting a much larger mistake.

Gary told her they didn't have to go up to the site at night anymore. He'd gotten everything he needed: his measurements, her apology. Even though she knew they wouldn't be up there all summer together, she was still disappointed. Last night felt more like a fresh start than the end of something, and now they'd return to crowded dinners and group hangs that prevented her from asking him, *Do you ever think about their feet, like how gnarly and messed up the soles of their feet were from running barefoot? Do you think there was ever some kind of murder plot that they covered up by having someone get accidentally javelined in the face?* Getting him alone had always been a safe space for these persistent curiosities of hers. He had a way of making everything she said feel important, as if she were neither eccentric nor erratic but onto something. He believed in her, cheesily enough, and she'd forgotten just how much it changed everything to feel like a Serious Person.

When the excavators returned from the afternoon shift, the lab team had monumental news to report. The fielders were wholly unprepared for the shock that came with an update of this magnitude, and the commotion at dinner was like nothing Z had ever seen before—as if someone had taken the knob on the door and turned the volume inside all the way up.

Charles was allowing them the use of Gary's personal laptop to experience The Internet.

There was exactly one old yellow cable with connectivity, and one desperate, enterprising Ug had plumbed the depths of the massive plastic pyramid in the corner of the lab to uncover a long entombed dongle that made it work.

"He's a legend!" A voice rose from the crowd at the discoverer's table.

The Ugs had been reserving their brainpower for just such an occasion. With levels of speed and organization that would impress the Navy, they created a bulletproof system to charter their course of attack, allotting each member of their unit exactly ten minutes apiece online using a sign-up sheet Scotch-taped to the front door of the lab.

As dinner ended there was pandemonium during the sign-up process, and finally Charles stepped in and put a curfew on the whole thing. But after the rest of them had long gone to bed, dreaming not of buried treasure but of emails, Z found herself walking down the stairs beneath the canopy of trees to the small stone building.

Kara kept the place freakishly clean. She was constantly wielding her tiny, prized handheld vacuum and busting dust everywhere. Tough on grime. It looked like someone could perform surgery on any surface; Z guessed that was what was happening, technically, looking at these pieces under microscopes and cleaning off every last speck of the planet from which they came.

The windows were open, having surrendered to the intrusive leaves; every now and then a gust of wind would swoop across the orchard, and a branch would wail on the outside wall, pulverizing a dangling walnut like a gunshot. They were all used to the sound by now. She was by herself in there and felt eerily more alone than she was comfortable with. She would have preferred coffee-shop-level privacy for this reckoning of *checking in*, a dreadful concept that made her want to remain checked out for the rest of her life.

Seated at the one table Kara allowed Ugs to touch, Z clicked into her email and found nothing important—just promotional nonsense, from juice cleanse to contact lens, and not a single word from the last boyfriend at bat. Her mom had written a cheery note to ask how everything was going and, by way of news from home, provided a detailed paragraph about a stranger's vacation (her parents co-owned a travel agency in Portland specializing in tours for seniors). Her mom's email also included a stock photo of the Acropolis as some kind of reminder to Z in case of concussion. Z was an only child who could do no wrong, and she painted with a broad brush when it came to filling them in about her life. They were under the vague impression things were probably going well enough, that she'd met their requirement of staying more or less afloat in the shallow end of the corporate pool. Keen as they were for her to join the family business, they'd encouraged her to return home from her trip with plenty of recommendations they could pass along to their clients. She replied to confirm she was alive and used a lot of exclamation points.

These were the artifacts of her life, and they were bleak. There was a flurry of automated rejections from companies she'd sent perfunctory job applications to before she left, as well as a smattering of party and long-weekend invitations. She replied to a few as proof of life— *xoxo*s into the abyss—signed out of her account, and teared up for the first time since she arrived.

The door creaked open.

"Oh!" Dr. Chen stepped into the lab and stopped cold.

"Shit, sorry," Z said. She lifted up her shirt to wipe her face, flashing him.

Again, "Oh!"

"I'm fine," she spoke for herself.

She snapped the laptop shut and stood up, knocking over her chair. Kara walked in behind him.

"Z!"

"I'm leaving," Z said.

"I'm leaving," Dr. Chen said at the same time. He beat Z to the door then audibly bolted up the stairs away from her.

"Wait," Z said, perking up immediately. "Were you and Doc Chen . . . headed to the bone zone? Karaaaaaa."

"Zara! Oh my God!"

"I don't know! You're leaving Gary. Maybe he's why. I mean, he's hot, like in a George Takei way."

Kara took a long, deep breath, one of those ones Z kept meaning to take for years now. "No," she intoned. "If you must know, I was going to ask him something about Charles, in private, but, now . . ." she closed her eyes, then collected herself enough to ask, "Are you all right?"

"Me? I'm fine. Sure. I checked my email and, yikes. It depressed the hell out of me, that's it. Just not sure what I'm doing here, exactly."

"You're in charge of the Ugs," Kara answered matter-of-factly. "And they love you."

Z could tell this application of fact was Kara's way of comforting her. She didn't say anything.

Kara sighed deeply and nodded (like they were in any conceivable way simpatico). "I get it, though." She launched into one of those humble brag complaint monologues about jobs, money, and apartments. Her problems sounded awesome.

"Ow!" A grumble burst from the patio, trailing the unmistakable sound of foot versus bucket.

Elise opened the door and froze.

Kara's spine grew two inches, and her chin returned to its rightful latitude.

"Of course," Elise muttered.

Z's eyes toggled between these two ludicrous women. Here was her moment. There was no way for her contribution this summer to be anything but this. It was about bringing two different people together at last. It was about holding hands: one rough palm, one smooth. It was about building a bridge between two far shores, so that the journey was gentler.

Wait. No. It was about smashing two separate atoms together hard enough that the right kind of bomb went off on this place.

Chapter

13

It was possible that an Arsenal WFC 1992 Champions crewneck sweatshirt wasn't going to cut it in terms of correctly protecting the priceless. Elise had brought the trophy-laden backpack down to the lab to improve her storage situation.

Ever since she'd removed it from the trench, Elise felt as though she'd surgically removed her own heart from her chest and was just toting it around town in a blood-soaked bag that anyone could snatch or destroy at any moment. The ground was so safe, she'd always believed, yet she'd had to get the trophy out of there. If Charles caught wind that something was down there, as he was likely to, he would've gotten his dirty little hands on it, she just knew. It was safer somehow—maybe, possibly, hopefully—with her.

With the sudden onset of computer night, Mardi Gras for morons, she assumed the lab would merely contain a drooling, blue-light-hypnotized Ug who she could kick out with a few choice words and/or actual kicks. But of course not. That would be too easy.

"Elise," Z said. She handed over a coffee mug full of ancient ouzo she'd just found in the back of the closet. Elise's eyes burned just being near it. Kara picked up the other mug and immediately took a big swig, coughing as she lowered it.

Z continued, "I'm glad you're here. You've got to tell her. Now."

"Tell me what?" Kara asked.

Z opened her eyes wide and nodded toward the backpack.

"There's something in there," Kara showed off her peerless detective skills.

"It's none of your bloody business."

Z reached for the backpack, and Elise lunged in front of her. "OK!"

It had been years since Elise had even been in the same room alone with Kara. Once, maybe twice in a mutual, furious silence. Just smelling the lab now made her livid, the scent of industrial-grade cleaning supplies mingling with a vanilla-scented candle that probably cost more than her room in Crete for a month. Elise blew it out.

"That was uncalled for," Z said.

Elise held up her hands then clenched them into fists. "Look. I'm not dying to have this conversation."

"Do you need something? Can I assist you with something?" Kara dared to go saccharine.

"No," Elise said. "I found something. And I need you to look at it, and I need you to promise me that you will not tell Charles. Can you manage to do that?"

"Eliiiiiise," Kara whined, as if the alcohol were already getting to her, her eyebrows arching toward a surprising level of actual human concern.

"She won't," Z assured. "Right, Kara? You're cool now."

Kara froze, then nodded without conviction and sipped again from her coffee mug.

Elise tried to breathe. Because for God's sake, Z was right. This was it; it was now that this, whatever this might turn into, had to happen. There was no one else—and that's what a weird amount of history comes down to. If Elise wanted to topple Charles, she had to go through Kara: his mentee, his right hand, the one with the fancy degree and connections who could legitimize this—who could legitimize *her*.

On the big table Elise gently removed what was in her backpack.

Kara stood behind her; even feeling this woman's body heat was making her insane. From within a Nissos beer T-shirt, Elise pulled out a blue journal, the cover sun-faded and frayed, and carefully flipped to a page that she'd marked with a brochure for Crete four-wheeler tours.

"Oh. That's not what I thought you were going to show her," Z sounded disappointed.

Elise stepped backwards and gestured to the journal page with an open palm. Kara sighed as if this were all a real waste of her precious time and leaned down to read it.

Then her hand flew to her mouth. "Oh my God. Where did you get this? Wait, I think I've heard about this before. It's a rumor, but I didn't know there was a journal piece." She flipped to the front page to examine the source.

"You're welcome."

Z elbowed her in the ribs.

"There's nothing to it though," Kara said, scanning the pages. "It's just a theory. There's never been any evidence, even here on the page, so it's not taken very seriously. By serious people. I mean, it's exciting, the idea of it, women running the show here, but without any physical, archaeological evidence it doesn't mean anything. You know that, right?"

She went on, delivering a condescending lesson on how science works, bitchsplaining archaeology to someone who'd spent two decades in the field.

All the while Elise placed the sweatshirt down beside the journal and began carefully unwrapping it. Her heart clobbered her ribs. She felt as if she were exposing a child to open flame. Beneath the now seminal soccer cartoon, a glimmer of gold shone at the arrival of light as soon as she pulled back the fabric, and there it was for her enemy to see.

Ἡραία

Kara gasped, and her throat caught.

"Elise," she choked. She gripped the back of a chair to steady herself.

Having laid the trophy and her whole heart out on the table, Elise started pacing. Kara looked stunned, pale.

"Bananas, right?!" Z bounced up and down on the balls of her feet and suggested refills.

Afraid her nemesis might attempt to ruin this magical moment, Elise started spewing facts. "Trench six, I've got the stratigraphy documented. North side facing, eight-by-twelve perimeter and proximity to two roof pieces from the fourteenth set from last year. Not including a real piece of shit centipede like you wouldn't believe. Z saw it first, and I've been going up at night ever since."

To her credit Kara was able to insert her eyeballs back into their sockets, wash her hands, and pull on her blue plastic gloves in a matter of seconds. As she picked up the piece and moved it onto her desk beneath the white inspection light, Elise locked the door and blocked it with a chair.

"No. I can't believe it," Kara whispered as she sat down before the trophy, her eyes filling up with tears beneath her safety goggles.

Z winked over at Elise, who allowed herself to grin. The fact that Kara hadn't immediately kicked her in the vag and ran for the emergency phone boded well, or so she thought.

"Wait. We have to tell Charles," Kara said, suddenly turning in her chair. "Tonight. Right now. I have to go, I can't be here, in the same room, with this, with you!"

Elise stood firm in front of the door.

"He's lying. He is lying to you, Kara. And to me, and to everyone else. This whole thing is a scam. They were girls, Kara, and he's lied about it all along because of his stupid book and his speaking engagements and his—" she paused in disgust "'brand.'" Elise had never even said that word before and hated it. "He's been shoving everything into this little box, and the truth is right here. He's wrong! I'm right! You ought to be right too!"

"This is exactly why we need to talk to him. He'll be able to explain. I'm sure he's aware of all this, and there's got to be some explanation. I'm sure there is, and we're just getting far out over our skis right now."

"Don't rich-person-sport-talk at me. He doesn't explain. He just gets rid of everything that doesn't fit his little narrative. Are you hearing me?"

"But wait, there's more," Z said. "Show her the other thing. This you're going to like, trust me."

"There's more?"

Elise fished out her phone from her cargo pocket and held it up with the photos of the discus Kal had showed her. "Missing anything?"

Kara yelped. She snatched the phone from her hand. "Where did you get this? Tell me right now. Elise, if you took this—"

"Calm down. Kal showed me. He says this is in some house down in the valley, near where that big party is."

"No! No, no, no, no, no. This is too much. I just, all these rumors she said were out there, but I didn't—"

"What rumors?"

"I really shouldn't get into it," Kara squirmed. She did that thing with tightening her ponytail that made Elise want to chop it off while Kara was sleeping.

Elise clapped once, hard. "The cat shat the bag. Come on."

Kara swallowed. "Well, if you must know, he's low on resources," she said to the floor. "He asked me for some introductions, or to ask my stepmother to make some. Apparently he and his wife, Terry, are in an unsavory situation, financially, at the moment. Obviously, please don't repeat any of this."

"Jesus Christ! So he's not just changing the record, he's selling stuff off! He needs the money, and our discs are suddenly in some dude's house? That's not unsavory. That's illegal, Kara, and he's got you on the hook with this. All of us."

Z shrugged. "I've been on worse hooks."

"He's selling this stuff to cover his ass and pad his plaid wallet. We've got to find a whistle and blow the shit out of it! Doesn't this piss you off?"

The edges of Kara's eyes remained flat and unreadable. Elise had the feeling the woman would never even admit to knowing what piss was. "Now, we don't know that. There's no way Charles would risk losing his entire life just to make . . . money." Kara's lips curled at the word.

"Are you kidding me? No. This is him *preserving* his entire life. He can't let it come out that it's always been women here. Now his awful book about how dudes invented sports so they could crush us for the rest of time is a heaping load of crap. He does this, and he stays afloat and gets to keep living in his creepy Louis Leakey costume."

Kara took her turn pacing. "Now, all right, I'll grant you that it does seem like he willfully ignored some key findings, and maybe massaged some things. Certain finds have possibly fallen through the cracks, but we have no idea what he'd say about this trophy—none. This would be a complete paradigm shift for this place. He might be overjoyed. You might be promoted!"

Elise groaned.

"I'm serious, Elise. You don't have any proof that it's actually stealing, or that there's a connection here. This is all total conjecture."

"Conjecture? Hello? These pictures? Our find's in some dude's living room. And this conversation that Patty heard, I'm telling you—"

Kara scoffed. "A picture on a phone? And what, now we're suddenly taking Ug gossip as gospel?"

"Kara, come on," Z said.

"Z, I told you. She will never come through for us," Elise stated.

Kara protested. "My entire career is wrapped up in this. If we confront him, he could destroy me. You can just go hop on some other dig, but not me. I've poured years into this one place."

"You don't think he could destroy me? You've got more options than the stock exchange. He could make two calls, and I'd never dig again; he could get me banned from ever eating a gyro. But if he's doing this, we have to tell someone. Chen, Trudy, whoever, someone."

"It's pretty fucked up, Kar," Z chimed in. "Any way you slice it. He's bro-washing the whole story, erasing these chicks and what actually happened here, and on top of that, he's making money off of it, using all this work *you're* doing and pocketing it. I mean, you're the most by-the-book person I know, and you're cool with that? You're just going to let this slide? Don't you want those discs back at least?"

Kara stared down at the trophy for a long moment, and Elise watched her. Her face drank in what this thing was through waves of pure awe and then, correctly, anger. They locked eyes finally. It had been a long time since they really looked at each other. Two women trying their hardest, competitors in the arena, just like *them*.

"You think he'd sell this?" She whimpered.

"I know he would. And you do too. You said it yourself. If you're saying he needs the cash, this is—"

"The holy grail," Kara nodded. "And his last season to get something like it."

"Bingo," Z said. "Some guy who thinks it says *Alpha Beta Reebok* would pay a fortune for it. Charles would never let the real story get out; it blows up his whole dumb book, his career, his whole chauvinist life. He'd hide it or destroy it, like he did with Victor."

Kara's head spun toward her. "He wasn't the one who destroyed Victor, Z. I'm sorry, but that was *her*." She pointed a rigid finger at Elise.

"Me?! You're out of your mind. You sat right there and tried to practically CPR the thing so hard you cracked him!"

"You wiggled!"

"You pressed!"

"Guys?"

They both looked over at Z. She was standing on top of a chair, pawing around inside a corner of the ceiling. "Gary and I used to stash stuff here. Look—"

She pulled out a plastic bag of dirt and bone fragments that Gary had collected from the burial grounds, climbed down from the chair, and handed it to Kara.

"Ask Dr. Chen to do his blood work stuff on this. You told me he never got the other bones, right? See if he can test them now."

"That's a good idea." Kara squinted at Z, skeptical of her ability to produce that kind of idea.

"You're not going to, like, narc on us while we're at the beach, right?" Z asked.

Kara spun on Elise, "You're still going to the beach?"

"That's where he'll be, princess. And I'm going to the party too, the circle jerk where you all tell Charles what a standup guy he is. I'm not letting him out of my sight."

"I am so amped for the party. Remember that Nia Vardalos ice sculpture they made for us?" Z said. She picked up the fancy camera from the table and snapped a picture of Kara examining the trophy. "Also, now you have to be cool—legally." Kara balked.

"Listen," Elise said. "When both Chen and that botanist loon are all here together, that's when we confront him. He won't give enough of a shit if only you and I say something. It doesn't matter that we've worked for him for ten years; he'd punt us like a ball. We need people on his level to know, best of all, right? That's how this whole thing comes undone."

"The shame game," Z confirmed.

Elise had never really spoken to any of those visiting scholars. They usually embodied peak condescension, hence needing her majesty here to bridge the divide. At the moment, Kara looked like she was about to throw up. *No doubt this was the biggest dilemma she'd ever faced in her adorable little life.*

"Earth to Kara?" Elise said.

She remained silent and stared down at the pristine floor with unblinking eyes. Suddenly, she lifted her head, raised her chin high, and adjusted the collar on her shirt. The muscles in her face had tightened back to the place they'd been when Elise had first walked into the room. There was no trace of any of the words they'd spoken or heard.

She looked Elise dead in the eyes, and before Kara even opened her mouth Elise knew it had been a huge mistake to tell her.

"You shouldn't have stolen this trophy, Elise. That was wrong. I need to think about this, about telling Charles," Kara said.

For the second time in her life, with a perfect piece laid out between the two of them, Elise saw her future flash before her eyes.

➤➤

Imagine, I almost remained buried alive. This trench was one heartbreak away from never seeing the light of day again. One of you, flung all the way across an ocean, sat on me, and now here we are, talking about a revolution.

Chapter

14

The timing of the beach weekend could not have been worse. Just as Z thought she'd semi-successfully brokered a kind of peace, Kara and Elise had retreated to their separate camps, wound up and pissed off all over again. She wasn't sure how to bring them back together now; Charles had pitted them against each other so effectively with the whole Victor debacle.

Getting them back together now would require a miracle.

The party was only days away, as soon as they returned from the weekend trip. Then Kal was going to introduce them to the man who owned the discuses.

A few days seaside would give her and Elise some time to brainstorm their confrontation strategy for the party. Elise's knee-jerk plan was to knee the jerk in the nuts. Z favored more restraint, a more-flies-with-honey approach, the honey in this case being a plate of kebabs which she herself, for example, would be helpless against. Either way, they had about seventy-two hours at the beach to sand down any rough edges on their scheme. They would meet the man in question, get him to confess, and use him as the fulcrum to lift up, see underneath, and finally topple towering Charles.

Amid all this she was actively coming to terms with her return to Pylos, a tiny oceanside village that loomed large on her list of regrets, which was saying something. She'd been anxious about the weekend already, a mood not helped by the showdown in the lab. Still, she was determined to be on her best behavior here and enjoy herself as much as possible. After everything she'd put herself through this year, she deserved a vacation.

Elise, meanwhile, furious at her for forcing some kind of "Kumbaya" moment, was sweating bullets over the idea of Kara turning on her and turning her in. But Charles was with them on the coast for the weekend, so the chances of him finding anything out from Kara were nil. Z hoped against all logic that a fun-filled few days was just what her friend needed to cool down. Ignoring problems had always come naturally to Z, at least; she was somewhat of an evangelist for the tactic.

But the moment they set foot by the sea, her hopes for a carefree weekend vanished.

If you needed to know just one thing about their leader, it was that Charles felt a clipboard was an essential item to pack for the beach. He stood with it at attention on the cobblestone stretch next to the hotel's faded-blue front door, his captain's hat, worn without irony, and a bathing suit short enough to be deemed illegal in several US counties. An irreverent white cat slithered between his legs. The Ugs faced him with their backs to the town's white-stone square, a charming smattering of cafes with sun-faded, yellow-striped umbrellas, archways draped in purple bougainvillea, and souvenir shops that sold postcards of Mykonos and Santorini. The breeze whirled sand around everyone's ankles, and dueling scents collided—fresh sea water from one side and scorched meat from the other, a quintessentially Greek beach perfume. Behind Charles was the short path that sloped down to the gleaming cerulean waves; he stood squarely in the middle of it, legs wide to block everyone's view, lest he suffer any distractions while he doled out instructions. The many rules instructing the group not to fool around were redundant; no matter how romantic the setting was here, feasting their eyes on Charles's thighs was a sufficient prophylactic.

"If you encounter any problem whatsoever, do not disturb me. I am otherwise engaged. Gary here will handle all of your needs, though I would encourage you not to have any."

"Engaged doing what?" Z muttered to Elise.

He took several notes during a talk in which he was the only speaker, then finally announced, "Dismissed." He was promptly trampled by a dozen bare torsos bulldozing toward the water and probably crushing the cat en route. Gary trotted after them with a towel around his neck, shouting something about poisonous jellyfish.

"Elise? Z? A word?" Charles said.

Elise didn't move, forcing him to approach her. Against his wishes she'd already taken a dip, and her long, sopping hair clung to her back. A towel wrapped tightly around her waist, revealing her top half clad in a black Speedo with sturdy straps, as if Elise needed an aerodynamic suit for open water laps. Z wore a red suit beneath poorly chosen green shorts and, thanks to a recent day in the field when she'd forgotten sunscreen, looked like a charbroiled mermaid. She bounced on the balls of her feet, sweating profusely in every conceivable crevice and anxious to disrobe and follow the boisterous band down to the shore.

"I'm delighted by the news," he said with a disarming grin as he surveyed them both coolly. He tapped the clipboard against his hip.

"Regatta this weekend?" Elise tried, crossing her arms.

"Now, don't be modest. It turns out you were right, Elise." His voice was a disturbing mix of joyful and menacing, like he was giddy to deliver horrible news. "It seems you've found something in that trench after all!"

Z's heart dropped through a hole in her stomach. Elise didn't move a muscle.

"Not really," Elise said, ice in her veins. "Don't even know what it is yet."

"Oh, but we will soon. A little bird informed me that the two of you have been quite devoted lately to that trench of yours, Zara. Elise, you were down there investigating, evidently. It's not nothing!" His eyes widened to the point of no return; his bushy white eyebrows, brushed into the electrocution style, leapt from their follicles toward his prey.

Elise and Charles stared at each other so hard, they didn't even clock Z's head sliding back and forth on a swivel while each of them stood perfectly still. She wanted to sprint down that path, dive into the water, and swim home; a propeller to the head would be a welcome break from this chasm of awkwardness. Charles knew that there was something in the trench but not, it seemed, that they'd already removed it.

"Although I must say, Zara," he turned his attention toward her. "I'm disappointed in you." His face wore the same haughty grin. "You told me there was nothing down there."

"No shit," Elise interjected. "We don't come running to you with every pebble. We figure out if it's worth it first. That's my job, to separate the good from the bad." She flattened her lips and drained the open hostility from her eyes in what counted for Elise as a winning smile.

"Your time is very valuable to us," Z echoed the words from the last time she was placed on hold.

Now it was Charles who swiveled his head between the two of them. He seemed to suspect that he was being patronized, but he wanted so, so very badly to be spoken to this way in earnest that he almost willed himself to believe in it.

"Well," Charles smiled even bigger. "Because of how it *shook out* with our late friend Victor, I'll be captaining this ship from now on." They looked at him quizzically. "I'm taking over."

"Taking over," Elise said evenly.

"Don't get hysterical, especially on my one vacation all summer, please. The fact of the matter is it's come to my attention that we've got a thief in our midst. Ian of all people has been stealing pieces from our lab. I know, it's shocking, he's been such a good soldier all these years. In fact, he stole two roof tiles right out from under our noses, and God knows what else. Even the discuses, perhaps!" Charles looked downright delighted, visibly having to stop himself from beaming at this announcement. "So as you can imagine, I'd like to be extra careful all around."

"Ian?" Z balked. "No way."

"Erm . . . way," Charles said, pleased with himself for this hip turn of phrase.

"You said *Ian*," Elise confirmed.

Charles bounced his shoulders. "Who can one really trust these days? Anyway, we'll be working together more closely now. In lockstep. I can't allow anything else to end up in his hands."

"Are you going to fire Ian over this? And Ursula?" Elise asked through gritted teeth.

"I can see that you're mad. I certainly am. But to tell you the truth, we are ill-equipped to take over their duties ourselves. So I may not bring it up until the end of the season. Just keep things as shipshape as possible in the meantime, as I'm suggesting, and then," Charles slid an index finger across his throat.

Z shuddered.

"Good. That's settled then," he said. "Well, you gals enjoy your weekend. A well-earned break from all your very, *very* hard work." He gave them one final assessment, then turned and jogged off.

Z turned to Elise and summarized the situation: "Shit."

"There is absolutely no way *Ian* is the one behind this. Charles just has generational experience blaming the help."

Z looked down the path after him. "That was so creepy," she said. "So, he knows we've been working in there. What happens when he gets down in the trench and finds . . . nothing?"

"We're not going to let that happen," Elise said.

They examined each other, gaging how screwed they were by the worry on each other's faces.

"You think he's got people reporting to him or something? The Greeks, maybe?" Elise asked.

Z nodded. That sounded right.

"We need Kara on our side already," Elise concluded.

Z nodded again. That was definitely right. They both slid their sunglasses back on and walked toward the beach.

ELISE SPENT THE FOLLOWING HOURS TRAILING CHARLES LIKE A PRIVATE investigator, convinced that at any moment he could meet up with a buyer, make a shady phone call or, frankly, steal the hotel towels. She didn't want to let him out of her sight, and if that's how she wanted to spend her days off, so be it.

This left Z and Gary to chaperone a dozen Coppertoned horndogs. She accepted this role with as much seriousness as she took her trench supervision, which was to say she taxed one beer from every six pack that passed her line of sight. The weather was perfect, and she hadn't known she needed a good swim this badly. She wanted to wash the Charles stink off her thoroughly, at least for as long as she could. They were, of course, on the clock. As soon as they returned to Mega, they'd have to sniff out the disc man at the party. Then after that they'd have to find a way to keep Charles from strapping into some kneepads, climbing down the ladder, and seeing for himself that a trophy-shaped hole was in fact missing from her trench—or as he would call it, his trench.

But they were here today, and the blond stretch of sand that sloped down toward the impossibly turquoise bay was more beautiful than she even remembered. It was a narrow slice of heaven, hemmed in on the right side by a small port bustling with the cod trade—giant wooden crates on wheels filled with jiggling, shiny white bellies—and walled off on the far-left side by a sharp cliff, its highest peak extending farther into the sky by an obelisk honoring the Greco-Turkish war. But if you looked straight ahead and ignored the human element, it was breathtaking. The sea rolled out into an exquisite, sapphire expanse, and arched rock formations rose from the water not far offshore, welcoming entryways for ships from every olive-draped nation. Their hotel was a charming white and pink inn that looked tacked onto the side of a gray bluff with weak glue, as if a door kicked open might fling the whole place into the sea. The rooms all had long, shuttered windows that faced the water and didn't entirely close; every morning a slick mist spread on the floor at their edges. Directly beneath the hotel was a short pier with a few bobbing boats in primary colors tied up for rent.

The group assembled at the end of the dock and formed a circle to haphazardly spray each other's shoulder blades with DuPont Chemical's impression of a coconut. Someone forked over an American student ID, which turned out to double as a Greek boater's license. At Z's encouragement, they piled into three rental skiffs.

Gary drove, and Z sat in the front in her bathing suit, warm beer in hand, sun on her face, looking out ahead at the big rock arch they were about to speed beneath. She raised her hands and squealed when they zoomed through and turned around to see Gary doing the same, lifting his hands off the wheel and causing several Ugs onboard to scream. The three boats cruised around the harbor until it was too hot, then anchored in a secluded cove hugged by rocks on three sides, in the cracks of which were tufts of green and purple vines reaching down to graze the waves. The water was a rich royal blue, warm and bracing. They swam for hours, chests pounding, only drying off in long enough breaks to eat half a gyro, leaving the tzatziki smeared across on their chins, swig a Mythos to wash it down, and dive in all over again to wash it off.

Gary sat on the edge of the skiff now, his legs spread-eagle with one foot dangling into the water and one tapping the bottom of the boat. White dots of melted ice cream from the disappearing pop in his hand dotted his thigh. Z felt like she'd traveled back in time into her childhood bedroom, staring up at a poster on the ceiling displaying her wildest fantasy.

"Outstanding idea," he said, licking the last of his treat. "Usually we stay on the beach, and I have to pretend I know how to play volleyball. Why didn't we ever rent the boats before?"

"Because you needed a mind like this," Z tapped the side of her head, the mind that had waved off Charles's extremely logical protests about liability. She fed him some nonsense about being a lifeguard (she had worked the snow-cone machine at a pool snack bar ten years ago), and it seemed he was eager enough to be free of them that he relented. The Ugs' survival rarely cracked his top concerns.

Elise stayed behind too, unwilling to let him out of her sightline and anticipating she'd be unable to restrain herself from shoving an Ug off a boat in international waters.

"Joy!" Gary laughed, bobbing his shoulders and shaking his head like he'd discovered the word. "I haven't felt this relaxed in . . . maybe ever," he concluded and swept his gaze across the horizon. The shrieks and splashes from the other boats sounded far away, though Z wasn't about to point this out, not in this moment. None of them had the first clue how to use the verb *anchor*.

"You guys don't take trips like this? Come on, Gary, that's not how you're supposed to date a rich person."

"Well, we did a classical music tour of Vienna with her stepmother for two weeks."

"I'm so sorry."

She wiped her sticky palms across her bare thighs, then jumped in. He followed right after with a flop. The waves from his jump filled her open mouth with a swell of water that she squirted back into his face. They floated for a long time, smiling like crazy and each straddling the life preservers Z was ostensibly keeping track of, their bodies bobbing and facing each other.

It took every fiber of her strength not to stretch out her legs and wrap them around him like she had the last time they were here together. Her body was rife with these phantom feelings—his slippery back, his hands underwater holding her up, his fingers interlaced with hers in the sand—all of which she could feel right now but *couldn't*.

"You know who I want to be when I grow up?" he asked. "Ursula and Ian."

If he only knew they were about to get the ax, she thought.

"You can't cook," she said. "But I have seen you fix a toilet."

"Seriously, they live the dream. They go from country to country, dig to dig, doing what they're good at. They've traveled the whole world together. They know how to serve these dig teams, and they've got a niche, so they excavation hop. I've always thought that is so cool."

"You are literally trained to work on any excavation you want," Z pointed out.

"Yeah, well . . . ," he started glumly and then sat up straight, interrupting his own thought. "You're right. Maybe Kara and I will travel around to a few more sites next year."

Z slipped off her life jacket and sank down into the water.

The day began to wind down. Ugs were splayed out on the boat decks, defeated by salt, barley, and hops. They hauled up their anchors and began the ride back to shore.

Human-jet-ski Ryan whizzed past them on some kind of redundant Sea-Doo, waving maniacally to let them all know that he was mere minutes away from receiving his third international nautical DUI.

The sun was full on Z's face, her out-of-control hair blown back, and a strong buzz spread to her limbs. This is what she'd been hoping to feel all along when she blasted back a response to Gary's note. It was a revelation to her to be back here, in a fraught place, and feel so excellent about it. It was so colossally mature of her that anything seemed possible. Hey, if she was able to make this kind of perfect, precious moment happen—the kind of moment people made their screensavers at their miserable jobs about—by continuing to tumble and stumble her way forward just like this, then *hell, yeah* indeed, she must be doing everything right.

They repeated the same schedule each day: mornings on the breezy patio with hangovers and the greatest yogurt of their lives, afternoons on the boat, pita-bloated and sublime, then dinner at one of the three cafes on the square—brine time, buttery tentacles, and shells galore. All was washed down by liters of beer and ouzo well into the night. By the third day, Z's face had the sun-kissed glow of a barbecue potato chip.

The first two evenings had required hands-on chaperoning predictably grouped by gender, a role for which Z was more cut out than she'd expected, given her firsthand experience from the client's perspective. Her favorite Ug, Patty, guzzled Mythos at an alarming rate and said yes to every ouzo shot put forth. As she danced around a streetlight with some of the other Ugs, who were taken down one by one by cobblestones, she picked up an interloping cat, used it as a dancing partner for a while, then delivered it to Elise's side and announced somberly, "Elise, I bought you this cat." Z grabbed her by the shoulders and sat her down in front of a pitcher of water with a straw.

By the final night, they'd had it with these knuckleheads and left Ryan exclusively in charge. The Ugs followed him in a conga line to the one haunted, disco-balled bar, leaving Gary and Z alone for the first time here on land. Out of chaperone mode, wined and dined, Gary cut quite loose, as if he'd been working up to it this whole time. As soon as they stood and started walking back toward the hotel, Gary slung his arm around Z's shoulder and pointed forward with the other.

"*Vamos!*" he cried, confusing his Mediterranean nations.

He was unwound enough to touch her, so help her god, something he'd bobbed and weaved his way around all weekend despite close quarters. Now his skin was fully, willfully upon hers, and it made her stomach churn in a tight spiral of alarm and elated anticipation.

"Come on," Gary thought he whispered as they tiptoed their way into the hotel kitchen. When they'd checked in, the proprietress told them all they were free to use the kitchen and should. BYO Everything You Could Possibly Need was their brand of hospitality.

"The mother lode," he said, kneeling in front of a dusty, cobwebbed wine rack. Gary plucked one out, and they stumbled their way out onto the moonlit beach.

The set of circumstances she clocked herself in at the moment had coalesced rather fast. They were at last alone together on the sand, his body was in recent, vivid contact with hers, and he was inebriated. The last time they were here at this hotel, he'd told her that he loved her. Was he about to do something bad and weird, and was she about to go along with it? *I haven't shaved my legs!* was her first wrong thought.

"Let's sit down here," he said.

The beach was most beautiful at night, when the darkness blurred the cliffs to create the impression that the sea encircled them in all directions. The sand was cool against the back of her legs, and side by side they looked out at the horizon, the moon dragging a golden streak across the wine-dark sea. Bands of yellow rippled where the tiny waves arched their backs toward the sky. At the end of the pier, the tired boats rustled and lapped gently against their lines.

Z drew a tic-tac-toe board in the sand with her finger and nudged Gary in the ribs. They played a string of games in silence until the bottle between them was nearly empty.

The next thing she knew she hiccupped. He burped back. She adjusted her seat in the sand, and all of the sudden a flood of dizzy drunkenness and fatigue crashed through her. "I promised myself I wouldn't get hammered on this trip. Again," she drew out the last word.

"Have you met yourself?"

"I haven't even thought about him this whole time," she blubbered.

"Charles?"

"Ew! No," she said. "My ex, the guy who dumped me right before I came here. I completely lost my mind when it happened, and now I don't even think about him. What's wrong with me? I just remembered him, sitting here, because once we went to the beach together and I got sand everywhere and didn't rinse it off before we drove home, and I was insanely itchy. It's the first time he's even occurred to me in weeks. That's horrible!"

"Not really. It sounds good, actually. So you weren't that into him."

"But I was!" Suddenly tears sprung to her eyes. Gary scooted closer. "I was kind of obsessed with him. I told a bunch of people I wanted to marry the guy."

"Did you?"

"Who knows! But then he dumped me next to a wiener cart, and here I am. Now I'm all obsessed with . . ." she wanted to say Charles's scheme and *Heraea* and, weirdly, Kara, but Gary didn't know a thing about any of it, and the three women preferred it that way. "Working here. That's my thing now. There's always a *thing*, and whenever it goes south I do the next *thing*, and I don't even stop to think why the previous *thing* got so fucked up. I think I'm supposed to care more, right? Dwell, or something. I kind of just bounce around. I'm all dribble, no shoot."

She wiped her nose on her wrist. "What should I do?" She asked him, or really anyone within earshot who had a good idea. At this moment she would've joined the cod trade if someone nearby had yelled over offering some kind of direction.

"I tried to be a dance instructor, Gary!" She looked at him with serious eyes for one second, before he burst into laughter. She did too.

"Are you saying there are worse dancers than you, looking to you for help?"

"Why did I do that?"

Their laughter quieted, and Gary sat up straight. "Because you're smart! You're a go-getter; that's what I always liked about you."

Z scoffed.

"Maybe you don't see it that way, but you are. You don't wait around and hope you wake up happy someday. You like how you live, you know how to live, and you're finding out what works. I'm jealous, honestly. You go confidently forth!" He swung his arm out to sea.

"But shouldn't I 'settle down'?" She lifted her fingers in air quotes and rolled her eyes at the phrase, but Gary didn't smile. He didn't move. He looked at her directly and nearly squinted.

"No," he said. "Please don't do that."

Her heart swelled in her chest, and it felt tight, like there was too much there for things as weak as skin and bone to contain.

"Your life is wide open right now. You're not padlocked into a *ten-year plan*," he said the last words in a faux-stern bass. "The funny thing is, I'm about to be finished with this doctorate—finally—and I want to feel like, OK now I can do some stuff I've been holding off on this whole time. Go travel, go try out some real-world jobs, maybe some commercial lidar startup I could get into—but, you know, when you're with someone, it kind of narrows the focus. Which is good! Focus is good. But, wide open sounds great."

Z pressed her lips together.

"Anyway, hey, if whatever happened with that guy is what brought you back here, then I'll take it. It's been . . ." he trailed off. He was often doing this, setting up a thought for himself, then letting whoever he was talking to conclude it for him.

"The best," she finished.

And man, it had been. Even the insane parts with Charles lately (which made her wonder for a fleeting moment if there would even be a *here* to come back to next year) were more exciting than anything else she'd ever been up to. And this, of course: this evening of everything.

"Are you sure you're sure about Kara?" She asked. She hadn't known she was going to ask.

Gary fished a crumpled-up paper towel out of his pocket and handed it over. She blew her nose, but in a sexy way.

He took his time before continuing. "It is weird with you here," he gave each word its own air bath, drawing it out, and she thought he might stop there. "With Kara . . . It's very clear with us and, no offense, there's very little drama. She knows exactly what she wants, and I'm kind of flattered that she even wants me to be like, along for the ride, because she could choose anyone. The only thing is, I do think sometimes, is this a fun ride? Is it one of those scary ones? Can I ever get off and just chill?"

The waves rolled in and lapped at their bare toes. They both stuck out their feet at the same time, pushing further into the sea.

"Being with you up there sometimes when I'm working . . . I do look over to see where you are, and you're already looking over at me, and you smile. There is something. I'll say that. It's a funny feeling. Like I rolled it all back, and it's a fresh slate, and I can do it all over again—makes me feel light, you know? Agile, or something. But no. No, I mean, it is right with Kara. We're really solid, and for me, solid feels really good."

Z nodded, it made sense.

"Did you love him?" Gary asked.

"Who?"

Gary laughed. "That answers that."

And in a flash, that answered it for her too. She hadn't loved her most recent ex, of course. She hadn't even considered looking backwards in his direction. The only force that had ever pulled her back at all was this one, the one with ties so deep into the past she felt helpless against the draw. It was the feeling she got when she'd first seen the metal of the trophy sticking out of the dirt, of a voice calling out to her from underground, *It's me, for you*. That connected her to him, the person who first showed her that a tether through time was possible, the person who understood her well enough to know that having a feeling like that could mean the world, the person she was sitting right next to.

The moon ducked behind the sliding clouds, shadowing the beach and leaving them with only the sound of the waves curling up onto the sand. Z clenched her jaw and wondered if she could really do what she was about to do.

"Gary."

He turned to look at her with an expectant lift around his eyes, waiting to receive a joke, a silly game, or a suggestion for more wine.

"I loved you too," she said.

His eyes drooped, and his head moved slightly back, and for a second she thought anger flickered across his face. She pressed her lips together tight. Then he slid his hand over and took hers in his, cupping a handful of sand between them—it spilled through their fingers so fast. Z squeezed his palm while she could.

"Thank you," he said, then slipped his fingers away. "Better late than never."

And that's exactly the point, isn't it? To correct the record, that's what she was doing. No matter how many years go by—five here, five thousand there—setting the good record straight is the only thing we endless streams of people on planet earth can do for each other.

✈

Later that night, all she could think about was me and how all these pieces had come together from a single movement of her own body. She took a seat, and there I was, rising through the dirt to give her a kick in the pants. She thought about how long and how far they'd had to dig for me (how long the Germans and the Brits dug too, but still managed to miss me) and how if she'd never come here, they never would've been able to put me together.

All that, and you have no idea how fast I had to run to win the trophy in the first place, or to have a statue made of me, how hard I'd had to breathe and push and sweat and how loud I'd screamed at the finish line, and then how long I had to wait, after all that, just to reach these people who knew what they were looking at, and who wanted to see me. Each of you. It was nothing short of a miracle, fragments coming together into a complete mosaic after all this time.

Just think, if we'd been out there all these years in the meantime, if we'd never been pushed back into the stands, think of where you might be.

I swung my shoulder back and hurled my javelin four thousand years ago, and it's just been soaring, soaring, soaring through the air until right now, finally ready to come stab you in the heart. Isn't that remarkable, and isn't that the point of all this, what you really came here to find out, that this life is for you? Maybe, just maybe, come on now, you've got to believe me when I tell you: there are so many more ways you can win.

Chapter

15

On the final morning of the intoxicating Pylos beach weekend, Patty woke up and wished for death.

They had a few hours before the vans were leaving, and while everyone else crawled into town for breakfast, the idea of holding up her end of any conversation right now felt akin to carrying one end of a sleeper couch up a flight of stairs. It was imperative to remain lying down, but the frightening nightgowned old lady had told them to vacate their rooms by ten. Easy for her to say, she hadn't been peer pressured into ouzo oblivion last night.

Despite her current state, she had a very important job to do for Charles.

He'd given her an envelope. It was her first tangible task, and she was supposed to complete it by noon that day. He told her in no uncertain terms that she had to hand off the papers in question to a man in an orange button-down shirt at a restaurant in Pylos called Supergyro's. The man would be waiting for her there, at a table in the back drinking a sour cherry Loux, and under no circumstances was Patty to open or tamper with the envelope in any way. This person required the envelope in-hand at twelve sharp, giving Patty a little more than two hours to find the will to live.

Adding to her queasiness was the guilt she'd been carrying after telling Charles about Ian and the roof tiles. Charles was giddy at the news, but Patty instantly regretted delivering it. The cook and handyman had been nothing but sweet to her when no one else was, and here she'd gone and sold him down the river. It was too much for her to mull over for the millionth time in her present state.

A pile of leftover French fries of mysterious origin greased the top of her hotel room's dresser, and she boldly plucked a few for breakfast on her way out the door, the envelope tucked into her tote bag.

There was no other option but to take all four towels from the room down to the beach and re-create her bed there. She hobbled to a spot on the farthest end of the sand, away from everyone else, and laid one towel down flat, rolled up one behind her head, and covered herself in the remaining two such that only a few inches of her face were visible. As well as she could, she wrapped her torso tight inside the cotton cocoon and pressed her shins into the sand. The only clean clothes she had left were her long jean shorts and the Garth Brooks tank top her mom had taken from her own dresser and told Patty to pack, presciently, for a "good time." This amateur mummification would hopefully force her to sweat out every wretched ounce of alcohol remaining in her bloodstream and bring her back to steady state, she prayed. With a hat brim poking out and sunglasses on, she approximated *Weekend at Bernie*'s chic.

It was all so beautiful here, and she willed herself through the fog to enjoy this beach one last time. Patty hadn't spent this long close to the water, beyond the rare day trip to a sad lake, and she couldn't fathom a more luxurious vista than this. No matter what the other Ugs said about this place being lame (comparing it unfavorably to sainted islands they'd gone to in France: Croix, Tropez, and Bart), she was in complete awe. She'd never smelled air like this, and it made her lightheaded in the best way. The breeze was constant, gloriously cool, and faintly fishy. The water was a shiny-postcard-plastic kind of blue, flowing out into a wide bay gated by large stone formations in the distance, several of which made perfect arches. Boats threaded in and out of these all afternoon, and it was charming enough to look at from afar, but lo and behold—she had been among them! She, Patty, went on a boat. And not a pontoon or hunting skiff like her cousins talked about, but an actual power boat with cushions and coolers, skimming across the Mediterranean Sea. She wouldn't even have known to imagine this kind of beauty; this darling Greek fishing village was the living end. Now, with a towel covering her head, she contented herself with appreciating the colorful soundscape: lapping waves, fisherman haggling over catches, the buzz of boats passing across the water.

In her condition, she couldn't sleep so much as dip down into a kind of haze state. It amazed her that her blood even agreed to flow after she'd treated it so badly. She'd arrived in hopes that the change of scene would liberate the borders of established cliques. It had, to some degree. But now she couldn't exactly remember a single, specific moment of bonding so much as a nautical blur of shouts, splashes, and shots.

Yet early this morning Charles had knocked on her door to hand her the envelope along with lengthy instructions; when a group of Ugs watched him leave Patty's room, the chill descended again. She was too ill to think about it now.

A few voices hummed past her in what sounded like German, after which some Greeks on the pier screamed at each other for a while. Eventually, Patty heard the sounds of English approaching.

"Oh, by the way, meant to tell you, Kal's here. We're gonna get lunch with him before we go. You wanna come?" That was Z.

Somewhere far away it occurred to her that her boss might be seeing her in this state, but there was truly nothing to be done about it. The sand was her home now.

"What? When?" That was Elise's voice; Patty would know it anywhere.

Z laughed. "Bah! I just wanted to see what your face did. And let me tell you, it did not do nothing, I'll tell you that. Not nothing at all, my friend. Come on, lighten up!"

"Lighten up? Lighten? Up? Charles is going to tie us to each other and burn us at the stake if he gets down there inside the trench. And that's if Kara somehow hasn't spent the whole weekend making a federal case against us and telling Chen all about it."

"You're supposed to leave vacation *less* stressed. Have a little faith. I think Kara will come around."

"Did you get laid last night or something? Even for you this is bad. Stop smiling."

The voices turned in her direction.

"Who's that?"

"Who knows. Sheila, maybe?"

There were no Ugs named Sheila, but Patty was flattered they'd confused her for someone else. A boat motored by the beach, and the voices turned away again for a few minutes.

"Man. All this time I was picturing junk, and now I can't stop picturing their boobs flopping all around that track. Ow, God, that sounds painful. Who invented the sports bra? Send this trophy to her."

"Probably hurts as bad as ball flopping."

"Please, that's exactly what they want you to think."

"Where is the trophy by the way?"

"Shut. Up. Are you trying to announce this to the world? Don't worry about it, it's safe—away from your ass."

Then came the sounds of these two women wading into the water. It was a testament to Patty's proximity to death that she couldn't find the strength to lift her head and feast her eyes on Elise in her black bathing suit one last time. At first, the sound of water play soothed her, and she relaxed her shoulders. But soon enough, as it began to crescendo, the sloshing, splattering sounds of wetness horribly began to morph into a repulsive, gurgling percussion. Suddenly, the remaining thin ice that Patty's system had been skating on until this moment cracked.

"Bleeeeuuugh!" Patty shot up at the waist and vomited into the sand. Her sunglasses flew forward and pelted a crab.

"Damn!" Z yelled from the water.

The next thing Patty knew she was flanked by Z and Elise, who was sopping wet and alarmingly attractive at a time like this. Z held a water bottle to her lips.

"We've all been here," Z assured her.

"Thanks," Patty managed. She glanced around the sand and saw that her tote bag had borne the brunt of the barf. "Oh no!" She scrambled to reach the bag and pulled out the envelope from Charles, now coated in a repellent film of last night's Mythos chasers. "No, no, no. Oh, Jeez." She checked her watch. It was quarter to twelve. It was vital that she clean up and get out of here.

Elise eyed the envelope, spotting Charles's unmistakable penmanship: a large, loopy cursive that took up every inch of allotted space. "Did Charles give you that? Give it to me. That's his."

Elise snatched it out of her hand.

"He told me not to show that to anyone," Patty said. "Please, I don't even know what it is. I'm not allowed."

Using the bare minimum of finger contact, Elise peeled open the seal and extracted the papers inside, unfolding each so the three of them could examine the contents together. A tiny thrill of belonging trickled through Patty's chest in spite of her growing fear that Charles would have her expelled once he found out her childish choices ruined his very important documents. Though naturally, she had to admit she was curious about what was inside.

They were printed-out photographs, each sheet a slightly different picture of the same thing; in her haze, it took Patty a moment to understand what she was looking at. It was the bottom of a trench, the telltale bumps of buried pieces, dark and repetitive dirt except one thing, one very different thing: a distinctly gold circle protruding up from the ground.

In fact, it was the very top of a perfect, golden trophy once given to the female victor of a pre-Olympic athletic competition. That old chestnut.

Z and Elise exchanged a glance.

Patty's eyes widened; she'd never imagined seeing anything like that at the bottom of one of the dirt holes they were working in. This was actual treasure. Each page pictured the protruding circle—A gold cup? For drinking or royal testicle protecting? A trophy?—at various angles. Elise carefully leafed through the pages one by one. Finally, the last picture was different. In this photo, there was a man's hand in the frame next to the artifact, making a thumbs up. At the bottom in Charles's handwriting were the words *for scale*.

The wrist was encircled in unmistakable puka shells.

"Criminal mastermind," Elise muttered.

Patty began folding up the towels around her to get ready to leave. She was on the clock.

"I have to go and give these to someone, a guy. I'm supposed to meet him at a restaurant; Charles says he's waiting for me. It's really important that I go give this to him. Please let me just go."

She pulled on the papers in Elise's hand, but Elise did not let go— would not.

"Yeah," Z put her hand on Patty's back for a moment. "That's not happening, kiddo."

Maybe it was the recent expulsion, but Patty suddenly felt lightness inside her body. Her brain, while it remained a spirited sponge, felt clearer. She was terrified to disappoint Charles in this way—certainly she'd have to pay for that. But it seemed that this was her chance to be in the one place she'd always dreamed of being—more than in college, more than in Europe—in cahoots. And so with a deep, foul-smelling exhale, she let go of the pictures and gave herself over to Elise.

Chapter

16

The seasonal nature of the excavations kept Elise circulating, and the unpleasant nature of her personality kept her uninvolved. She didn't get attached; it was clean, and it was what she kept wanting, the life she'd built to be devoid of urgency. There is no urgency to archaeological work. The past doesn't demand to be dug up again and reexamined—except when it does.

Except when a trophy comes flying out of the ground and bites you in the ass.

Time moving forward had been the name of the game, and then it all just record-scratched to a halt and needed to be rewound, started again from the beginning. And she was the one who had to do it. Despite the nature of her job, Elise had never given any thought to her legacy. But here it had arrived for her: she was put on earth to raise women from the dead, up and out and onto an Olympic podium. She was here to correct this record. And she'd be dammed if some pith hat fuck nut was about to come snatch that out of her hands.

The party was that night. Everyone besides the Ugs was getting ready and gussying up as much as possible, given the limited shower situation. The puka-shell swindler Ryan was staying behind with the youth, an inmate running the asylum. The rest of them (Charles, Z, Gary, Kara, and for the first time, Elise) were navigating buttons and zippers, corralling various hairs, altering smells and shapes, all of which felt strange after the freewheeling dirtballery of the preceding months.

Now that Charles was back from Pylos, it was possible Kara could make good on her threat, pull him aside, and tell him everything. *Elise called you a liar. Elise stole from the site. Elise wants you dead.* And he would do exactly what Z said he would do: take one patrician finger and flick her off this mountain like a bug. The only thing she could do was *hope* (a weak worm of a word, in her opinion) that Kara would come around and agree to confront him. It was incomprehensible that she still needed more proof, that she could still give Charles the benefit of the doubt. What more could she possibly need to know?

The photos they found in Patty's hands had proved that Charles not only knew about the trophy but had a plan to sell it to some Supergyro. When they'd first returned to the mountain, Elise had tried to find Kara to show her—puka shells from hell ring a bell? But of course the princess was locked up in her single room, *getting ready for the party*, she claimed, saying she didn't have time to talk. Standing on the other side of her closed door, Elise had never been so furious. She wasn't about to slide the envelope under the door. They had just two hours to rinse off the sand and get their act together before they piled back into the vans for the event; there wasn't enough time to argue. Her hard sell would have to wait.

And maybe, just maybe, Kal could deliver them the man who bought the discuses on a silver platter.

As far as Elise's wardrobe was concerned, there was one dress. Technically, it was a body-length tube of black linen with arm and head holes cut out, which she sometimes wore to sleep when everything else was too dirty and she was too beat to do laundry. The only problem was it didn't have any pockets, and while she didn't mind the idea of holding her pocketknife in her hand all night, Z told her that wouldn't put out a great "vibe." So she clipped on her black fanny pack, rested it on the small of her back, and placed her knife, walkie-talkie, mini flashlight, and some floss inside. On her feet she wore a pair of black plastic sandals, which were held together in a few spots with black tape that, in the dark, wasn't immediately noticeable. The two concessions she made to the impending fanciness were choosing a French braid over a normal one and painting her toenails with polish she borrowed from Patty. When Z saw her in the parking lot, she cinched the fanny pack tighter to accentuate Elise's waist and forced a layer of lipstick on her. Elise did not hate the effect.

At five o'clock sharp she slid into the farthest back seat of the van next to Z, behind the bench containing a sprawled out, beach-drained Gary. Charles drove, and Kara sat up in the passenger seat beside him, where she immediately put on the charm offensive. For Elise's benefit, Kara made a big display of bubbly friendliness toward Chaz, which seemed to confuse him. *See?* She seemed to be saying, *Charles listens to me, to every word I say.* It was chilling chitchat.

They ate dinner beforehand at a restaurant in town. There they met up with Kal, who was a part owner in the place and greeted them as if they were visiting dignitaries, not the day laborers he'd seen last week. She didn't want to deal with him right away; there'd be no way to explain the escalation of circumstances to him, even if she'd wanted to. He looked hurt and slightly annoyed that she was here, markedly not as his date, but he smiled at her once they were seated.

Kal wore a close-fitting khaki suit with bright white sneakers and had trimmed his beard to a respectable five o'clock shadow. His button-down shirt was open at the throat, from which emanated the scent of oranges thrown into a bonfire—and of course there was the ponytail, torturing her. As if she didn't have enough problems at the moment. He'd never looked better.

The restaurant was awash with oceanalia, as if the room itself had been used as a giant net. Traps for various crustaceans hung from the ceiling, fish tanks filled with species native to pet stores packed each corner, and the walls were covered with tacked-on buoys and what looked like critical missing pieces of shipping vessels. The amount of low-hanging nautical line looped in the doorways hinted at suicide, in a jaunty way. The food was standard Greek fare but surprisingly upscale, and the tablecloths were white, with old anchors used as centerpieces that occasionally rusted onto the dishes, mistaken for pepper.

Kal was holding court, announcing his personal mission for the evening to find more financial backers for the Kentro tou Tourismos. Charles cut him off again and again, once even laughing in his face and dismissing the very idea that Mega warranted such a place, as if Charles himself had not come to this land, for this culture. Kal persisted with a good-natured laugh each time Charles shot him down, while the rest of them watched on helplessly. Even Kara, sorceress of small talk, was unable to wedge between the men's parrying.

The next thing Elise knew she was standing. Looking down, she saw everyone's oily lips gaping up at her and Charles's scowl at being interrupted. She held both her glass of beer and a forkful of clam spanakopita.

"*Yamas*," she heard herself say. Charles sat up straighter and began to smile, anticipating his first toasting of many tonight. Elise raised her beer, "To Kal, *efcharistó*. From all of us."

Kara guffawed.

"Kal! Kal! Kal!" Z chanted and Gary joined in.

Everyone clinked glasses, and Kal smiled in a way she'd never seen before: just a small one, sly, lips closed, teeth and lack thereof contained. When Elise sat down, Z kicked her in the shin, impressed.

Snubbed, Charles wrapped up dinner quickly and dragged them out to where he'd be properly appreciated. They drove thirty minutes farther, the tension in the van containing the following sticky wickets: Kal in the front seat, monologuing about his doomed wooing plans for the evening; Kara moving away from Gary when he tried to put an arm around her; Z drooling down Gary's neck like a dog in heat; Elise shifting her eyes in a nightmarish triangle, from Charles, to Kara, to Kal, wondering who would ruin her life in which particular way; and Charles radiating disappointment that this metal box of dolts was his entourage.

Finally, in the spooky twilight, they pulled up to the party venue. Elise wasn't sure what she'd been expecting, but it sure as hell wasn't this medieval castle made from plastic siding material.

The building was lit by a ground-level orange glow from the excessively candlelit entrance, which added to the unknowable size of the place. The massive stone structure appeared to be built out of marble bricks. She immediately marched up to the nearest wall and kicked it.

"Elise!" yelled someone lame.

The rock sounded hollow, as she knew it would. They were on the opposite side of the valley and she looked behind her as they walked inside to see if she could see the excavation from here, which of course she couldn't. This fake castle belonged to one of the faceless goons who worked in a corporate office for the lignite factory, and she wondered if all of them had houses like this, or if the whole executive team and their families just lived here together in this bogus bunker.

The outside wall boasted two exterior stone staircases and a handful of terraces, through which American pop music as interpreted by a local Greek cover band wafted into the night. Two by two, suited-up men and glitter-wrapped women ascended the stairs, shellacked hair and costume jewelry glinting in the stunned moonlight. The scene was as weirdly beautiful as it was bizarrely out of place. They were the bedraggled mole people allowed to come out from their deep, dark holes for one night, and this steep ascent into what was apparently high society was giving them all the bends.

She looked over and saw Kara doing a terrible job pretending not to stare at every unhinged detail. Gary and Z were beyond that, just volleying *Holy Craps*. Charles didn't say a word and stomped ahead, eager to be rid of them. Silently, he handed over the keys to the van to a man standing outside smoking—who could have been a valet, in theory, but probably wasn't. He looked at the keys in his hands, then over at the ridiculous van. His, apparently.

It was just as bonkers inside, and as soon as her eyes adjusted, Elise knew that whoever was happy living here was at the very least cult-curious. Everything was brand new and designed to look like the halcyon days of the Middle Ages, replete with towering stone archways, vaulted ceilings, wrought-iron-legged banquet tables, and flatscreen TVs showing fireworks footage on loop. The cavernous open floor plan was lit with dimmed ceiling lights, plus candles on every conceivable surface. Some were the murky orange fake flames of plastic candles, but some were real. The random intermixing of the two had to be conceived in order to light someone's leg on fire; there was no other explanation. There were about forty or so adults in the room. Every single one was dressed better than the mangy Americans and was thinking exactly that as they filed in.

The fact that these people threw a party for Charles every year without ever having set foot on the site told her everything she needed to know. Any one of these lunatics could be cutting dirty deeds with Chaz. One already had, and Elise was going to hunt him down.

She wasn't normally much of a drinker, but *gia parti mou*, as they say. A waiter handed her something amber in crushed ice, and she slugged it. Z was long gone the moment they were in, helping herself to the loaded bar and striking up a conversation about the Jackie Onassis situation with the first man, in a series, who would be subjected to increasingly specific questions about becoming Greek by marriage. Elise could hear her cackling from across the room, an exclamation point dotted with a snort.

In no time she found herself bypassing Gary's cluster of already-heated conversations about soccer and ultimately standing in a large circle across from Charles and Kara, who were talking about the site's progression. Elise hoped to overhear something—anything—pertaining to the artifacts. Charles didn't acknowledge her when she joined the group. Kara stiffened. God forbid Elise say something that could tarnish Kara's pristine reputation among looters.

"We're making tremendous progress up there; it's been a dynamo season," Charles said. "I'm really pleased about all the exciting new work we're doing. Isn't that right, Kara? I can't begin to tell you how thrilled I am about some potential new discoveries, but I'll try to explain. I'll put my professor cap on, if you will." He really talked like this, and people were really okay with it.

After a few minutes, Elise realized that Kara wasn't following their conversation when it switched from English to Greek. Her laughs were a half beat too late and off-putting. For the girl who knew everything and how, she couldn't speak Greek. Elise lit up inside, delighted.

"It's crazy. It's on me, I know," Kara said too loudly when asked by one of the Greeks. As if there might be someone else she could blame, "Like they say, it's Greek to me! I've tried to learn, I really have."

Crickets, so she kept going, "You know, I'm better with ancient Greek, actually."

In actual Greek, one of the men said, "I hope they put both on the road signs."

After an hour of reintroducing himself to people who'd rejected him for previous projects, Kal joined their circle too. Elise had been clocking him around the room, watching a synchronized refreshing of the drinks dance in which he was the unwitting partner, one after another, as he started his pitch.

Kara kept her body angled away from Elise and blabbered on about the scintillating life that she hoped lay in wait for her at a place like Christie's, a firm that bought and sold antiquities pilfered from countries not at all unlike like the one in which this party was being held.

Suddenly, thank God, there was a pressure on her fanny pack. Kal leaned over and whispered in her ear. "I see him."

They both peeled away from the group without saying a word. Her pulse hurried, and she scanned the room as Kal led her through half a dozen clusters of conversations into which he half-dipped himself—*Yassas! Hello! Yassas! I get you a drink! Hello! Save me seat!*—before they finally slowed and approached a man standing alone at the bar. He looked to be in his fifties, conservatively, and wore a jet-black suit jacket over a purple shirt, which was unbuttoned low enough to reveal a long silver necklace dangling a diamond-crusted dolphin. He was bald, but what dark hair remained rung his skull and was long enough to tuck behind his ears. His eyes drooped slightly from what could have easily been alcohol, resentment, or both; he looked miserable but also slightly amused.

She hoped to at least get confirmation from this man—from an outside entity—that Charles had stolen and sold something. It was a shoring up of ammunition.

"Elise, Cosmo is one of the—" Kal whistled and raised his hand in the air to indicate height, or in this case, corporate stature. "—at the factory. Very important. How are you tonight, sir?"

"Mr. Loukanis," the man acknowledged in a high, flat voice. He neither elaborated nor extended his hand. He looked over Kal's shoulder into the crowd for someone better to talk to.

"Yes!" Kal exclaimed, jazzed just to be remembered. This didn't bode well for the *He will tell me* reassurances he'd proffered earlier. "So I want you to meet Elise. She is one of the Americans, with Charles."

"Charles," the man said, his vocabulary evidently limited to proper nouns. He gave her a lecherous once-over and, unimpressed, continued sipping his drink. Elise, similarly, continued picturing his death. Of course her entire life's purpose would come down to a porpoise swimming through chest hair.

Kal read the room and skipped any remaining pleasantries. He leaned in close to Cosmo and spoke quickly and quietly in English, ostensibly for Elise's benefit. "OK! I saw a discus in your house. I know maybe it was not right for me to be looking around here and there, but I did see. I went to use bathroom, maybe you remember, and I saw it. So I need to know, did you get this from Charles? Is he the one who, you know, you give him money and he gives you that piece? Was it Charles? Yes?"

Cosmo waited until Kal was finished. He said nothing and examined the two of them together, eyes sliding back and forth over the top of his glass. The slightest lip twitch was the only indication that he'd even heard the question.

"We are cool," Kal added, pointing to Elise then back to himself, just to nail the coffin completely shut.

In Greek the man finally responded, "I don't speak any English."

"How about now?" Elise asked in Greek.

"I don't speak any Greek tonight either, not about Dr. Charles," he said in English and shrugged. "Excuse me."

He placed his unfinished glass down on the bar and walked off into the crowd, disappearing behind a wall of slacks and synthetics. Kal started to walk after him, but Elise grabbed onto his sleeve.

Kal let out a big sigh. He picked up Cosmo's glass and finished what was left in it by tilting the glass an inch above his open mouth.

"Let's go out," he suggested. "Follow me."

She drained her own drink and placed it down on the end of the bar. For a split second she looked into the crowd, but the man was long gone. She followed Kal along the outskirts of the party and through yet another domed doorway. After a minute inside a long hallway so dark she had her arms fully extended out in front of her, there was the whoosh of cool breeze and there they were, outside on one of the plastic balconies.

Before her was the mirror image of the view she'd seen a thousand times from home. The midnight Mega valley rolled out before her and in the distance, their silhouetted mountain.

The fresh air hit her like a splash to the face. Her ribs suddenly let go of their iron grip on her chest, and she gulped down the oxygen she'd been abstaining from during that conversation. It had happened, the thing she'd latched onto so tightly for days now, as a way to get some external validation to this whole debacle, which she sometimes felt was nothing more than a nightmare. She'd seen the man, pushed him as much as they probably could (short of throttling him in public), and nothing, absolutely nothing came from it. Nothing she could take to the bank. It all remained maddeningly unreal. But in a way she felt released, the lone wolf left standing; she would be the one to take on Charles.

A few other partygoers stood on the balcony too, draped against the faux stone walls. Kal led her to the far opposite side, where they could be alone, and pulled out his pack of cigarettes. The orange blaze of the candlelit entrance lit them from beneath, and the wind pushed clouds over the bright half-moon one after another, billowing shadows across their faces. Kal stood very close to her, and his skin smelled like grilled grapefruit. Thunder rolled in from somewhere far away, but their air was perfectly warm and dry.

"I'm sorry," Kal said. He hung his head. "That is how all the conversations I had tonight go." He blew a *pfft* sound with his lips and made a thumbs down.

Elise squeezed his forearm. "Hey, at least you got what you wanted," she told him.

His brow creased. "Yes? What did I want?"

Me! He'd asked her to come with him, and now here she was, standing with him at this party. She didn't answer but lifted her shoulders an inch.

He shook his head.

"Elitsa," he said. "I wanted to come pick you up in my car and—"

She rolled her eyes. "You were going to drive all the way up there just to—"

He held up a hand to stop her, which would have enraged her with less booze in her system.

"Yes. Because I wanted to come here together. Not just, oh we are both here and now we are talking, but for you to say to me, *Yes. Yes,* I am here for you. *Yes,* I am wanting for everyone to see me arrive at this event as the date with Kal. To open the door for you in my car when we arrive together and to make you super mad when I say for everyone to hear, *Elise, you look so beautiful tonight.* That's what I wanted."

She tightened her grip on his arm.

"And even though you told me *no,* I still was wanting to help you tonight. I tried," he said. "Because these things—the things you find on the mountain—they belong to us, to you and me. And no, I know," he said before she could interrupt him, "Not like this, not belonging to any one person. But you and me, we are the ones who understand a lot that the pieces you find, they belong *here,* for everyone to see. Me, I can see the future, some place we build for everyone to enjoy. And you, you are the expert, you see the past."

Elise smiled.

"Oh, no. No smiling! I learn this lesson tonight. I go all night and I talk to everybody and I am me, I am joking and laughing and I think, OK, these people, they like me and so they will say yes to helping with the Kentro. Because look, see, we laugh, we joke, it must be yes, we smile, everyone gives a smile. But it is then *no.* All noes. So I will not to be joking with you because I want a good answer here, after many months. For you Elitsa," he took her hand. "No smiles. You are serious person, and so I say, I am very serious for you."

Her mouth hung open. He finished his cigarette and threw it over the edge of the balcony, probably butting the heads of two more people about to make a huge mistake. He gently lifted her hand and slid his palm beneath hers, entwining their fingers together. An electric current shot up the length of her arm and into her chest, coating her insides in neon light. She rubbed her thumb along his and jammed the little webs between their fingers closer together.

"Yes," she said, looking at his determined expression, softened at the edges of his eyes.

And what else in this life could she possibly do? She kissed him.

Chapter

17

Z sipped flat champagne and marinated on the past few days as Charles made his interminable speech at the height of the party in this berserk castle house. On he droned behind a podium, behind a plant, with no end in sight.

Was it pathetic that telling Gary, "I used to love you," turned out to be the most romantic moment of her entire life?

She'd never admitted anything like it before. It was embarrassing that maybe she'd hit her romantic peak years ago and had just been flailing around, in the wrong direction trying to find it again ever since. Saying it out loud made her realize what she'd known deep down all along. She never loved that art guy at all (or any of his colorful predecessors, for that matter). She had just desperately, hopelessly wanted to and had spent a Sisyphean stretch of years trying to make something stick. But where did these feelings leave her? Was she supposed to try and get back together with Gary once he was officially back on the market and ready again? Or was she supposed to let him go and just be comfortable knowing that a love like that was possible for her—someday, with someone else?

She looked at him across the table, sitting next to Kara. They were both diligently watching Charles with a boredom threshold Z assumed grad school raised in them. Yesterday she'd seen Gary dripping wet in swim trunks; now he looked polished and sharp in a well-fitting, navy blue suit, his face freshly shaven. Z tightened her grip around her glass. Kara wore an impeccable short-sleeved pink dress that fit her like a glove and high, narrow heels that would capsize a mere mortal. Z, in a completely wrong, skimpy green number, had cornered Kara in the bathroom just as the speeches were starting and asked her pointedly how her weekend was.

"Fine," she said, not looking her in the eye. "I had a lot of time to think."

"And? Care to share with the class?"

Kara looked up from the sink and met her gaze. "I haven't decided anything, all right? If you must know, Dr. Chen dropped one of my hydria molds, and I spent two days reattaching the handle. And Ursula got food poisoning, ostensibly from herself, so I had to spend the entire weekend cooking for Dr. Chen and Ian." Kara dried her hands and straightened her spine to her full height. "I do not cook," she clarified.

"Oh. All right, bummer," Z said. Kara stood still, so she kept going. "Well, the beach was pretty excellent. Gary and I had a . . . super time." She had intended to say *good conversation*, but decided to keep that moment all to herself.

The corners of Kara's lips lifted and her eyes softened. "Good. He needed that," she said. They both kept going at the same time, interrupting each other. "I'm glad he has you. For when, you know, I—"

"You should know, with Elise, we saw these pictures—"

The door swung open, cutting them both off with the arrival of three women in various states of sequins. Kara shook her head and held up a finger to stop Z from saying anything more. She walked out, and Z followed, back to their table among the crowd.

No fewer than three non-ironically charcoal-suited executives were on deck to introduce Charles, who opened his remarks by pumping two thumbs up into the air toward his long-suffering team. As she had probably been doing when she came out of the womb, Kara smiled and waved, while the rest of them forced smiles and also died a little, knowing that "long-winded" sold their boss short. He went on for what felt like a decade in a maddeningly pretentious mix of English and Greek to guarantee that the fewest people in the room understood him. Z had been promised an open bar but now realized the price she was paying. The idea of sitting at one of the splintery picnic tables with a warm Mythos and a deck of cards was infinitely more appealing to her at the moment than this dress-up lecture.

Meanwhile, one of the young Greek guests Z'd been half-heartedly flirting with at the bar kept looking over at her. Unfortunately, he was seated at a spot that gave them a perfect sightline to each other, forcing her to reciprocate a look of some kind every so often while she debated whether or not to talk to him again if Charles ever stopped. At this point it seemed a real possibility he'd need to be mechanically shut off.

Eight years later, Charles wrapped it up, and her bar buddy wasted no time amid the din of scooting chairs and the checking of glasses to make his way over to her. He either didn't understand or, to his credit, ignored her *feeling flutey* comment about getting more champagne. He was trying to convince her to come along with him to go find the host's secret stash, whatever that was. It sounded like maybe he'd learned the phrase recently and was trying it out.

"All right, I'll go," she said. Then she whistled, "Gary, come on, want to go check out the place?"

Secret stash guy balked, curling up his lip at Gary, who stood across the table cleaning his glasses.

"Absolutely, I do," Gary grinned.

He kissed Kara on the cheek before they took off and it's too bad Stash missed that because it probably would've cheered him up. Grumbling in Greek, he led the way through a dim stone passageway, which looked like an Edgar Allan Poe scene but smelled like fresh tennis balls, and then through a jarringly modern kitchen that displayed an alarming number of knives. They all poked their heads into the rooms as they passed: an empty bedroom, an occupied bedroom, a sad-looking TV room, and a bathroom that Z used quickly, the door through which she heard Gary attempt "So, soccer?" to no avail.

Finally, they corkscrewed their way around and down, all the way to the basement level. There was some chic storage space, shelves upon shelves of terrifying taxidermy and, perhaps representing a preservation step before those items, a row of gigantic refrigerators. At the end of the wide, tastefully lit hallway was one remaining door, with a tiny wrought-iron window in the middle of it. It was the only door they'd tried so far that was locked.

Gary was the tallest, so he peered into the little window, calling, "Hey, wine!" He pulled on the door and shrugged. "It's closed," he said.

Their tour guide would not accept defeat and looked around for a way in. Standing on his toes, he ran his hand above the doorway and all around the wall ledges; soon enough, a small silver key clanged onto the floor. The lock clicked, and they stepped inside.

The ceiling was low, and domed entryways on either side of the main space led into distinct areas with various knick-knacks displayed across every wall and shelf. Z glimpsed a full suit of metal armor, a signed soccer ball on a pedestal, oil paintings, and a bunch of those little mounted engraved glass pieces in weird angular shapes that businesspeople have on their desks. Gary went through one of the archways to the right, and all Z could hear was him going, "Whoa." Stash guy wandered off to examine the labels on a collection of liquor bottles.

Z walked through the arch into the smallest of the rooms. She was hoping to get back to the party soon since they were probably serving dessert. But instead she found herself drawn to the curved corner of the room. There, a white gallery light on the ceiling beamed down onto a Plexiglas box, which rested on a shelf jutting out from the wall.

Inside was an uncanny little statue.

"Pfft! This chick has balls," she said to herself, laughing. "Gary, come here."

"Hey!" someone barked. It was Kara.

She stood in the main doorway and glared at them, hands on her hips. "I just spent twenty minutes looking for you guys. They're doing coffee, and someone wants to take a picture of all of us together. Let's go. Where's—"

Suddenly, her lips stopped. Her head tilted slightly forward, as if someone had magic-wanded her body to freeze. Her eyes were locked onto Z, dead-on, as if she'd just found out something like, *Oh, I don't know*, that her still-fiancé held his ex's hand the other day on the beach. *Oops.*

"Um, Kar?" Gary said, reaching out but not approaching her.

No one moved for a thick few seconds.

Then, reanimated, Kara lunged forward. Eyes crazed, she marched past the table and the suit of armor. She knocked a chair over, blasting through the archway, directly toward Z.

"Kara . . ." Z hoisted up her arms to shield her face.

But Kara strode right up beside her. She stood at Z's shoulder, facing the case that displayed this weird little person, a once crowned athlete with arms raised in a win.

Kara pressed both palms onto the glass. "Victor."

"Oh," Z exhaled and lowered her arms. "You know her?"

✈

Together at last.

Part
Three

Chapter

18

Here's what Kara wanted to do: pull back her elbow high, wind her fist right up around the height of her ear, punch through that glass case like a knockout and blow it up, blasting glass everywhere. Then she'd just grab the statue, her hands and wrists dripping blood by this point, and slam Victor down onto the concrete floor. She wanted to watch him smash-explode into a billion pieces, bulleting white shards and dust all around the room and blasting into the wine racks, shattering those bottles too. She pictured herself standing there in the glass rain, her gushing, raw arm hanging down next to her, her eyes red, mouth foaming, screaming until the stone walls shook.

Instead she placed her hands, one atop the other, on the rose-hued lap of her dress and stared straight ahead, unblinking.

"Take this," Kal said. Somehow she was in the backseat of Kal's car, with Elise in the passenger seat, whizzing back up the mountain after the party. Without taking his eyes off the road, he twisted his arm behind him to where Kara now sat. She accepted the flask and took a long, scorching slug without even asking what it was. Questionable drink was the least of her concerns. She still could not grasp it: Victor was alive.

Kal veered dangerously close to the switchback edges in this ersatz hearse he called a car; Kara didn't so much as twitch when she saw him remove his only hand on the wheel to light a cigarette. In fact, she heard a voice that sounded distinctly like her own asking if she could have one of those. It was all over for her now anyway.

"*Now* do you want to ruin him?" Elise yelled above the sputtering motor. The car was a perfect venue for their exchanges insofar as they didn't have to look at each other.

She grunted, a begrudging affirmative. She continued staring off in a catatonic daze, until whatever was in that flask fully hit her bloodstream and she could consider breathing again.

"Finally," Elise said, all vim and vigor. "We'll do it during Field Day. He'll be up on the track with everyone, and I'll get Z and Patty to keep him there. If we're lucky, someone gets injured, and it takes forever. That'll give you and me time to talk to Chen and Newkirk solo. Those two weirdos probably love you, so hopefully they don't lose their shit once they see what we've got. Once they're clued in, he's toast."

The details of this master plan washed over her; she was finding it very hard to focus on any words in particular, however critical they all seemed. Though she'd always felt she would be the kind of person who'd be good in a crisis, she was realizing now that theory had never been tested. Elise took the news of Victor's ongoing existence like a boxer took a punch; it reeled her back just enough so that she had even more momentum to pounce forward and punch even harder. But Kara was still absorbing the blow. That little stone face, the jumble of junk, those two raised hands drifted inside her skull like an apparition. All she could do was play the tape back over and over and over again until she could see it clearly: He was whole. He never broke. No one broke him. Charles had very intentionally broken the two of them; he'd wedged a statue between Elise and herself, so they couldn't see each other.

Elise filled in the gulf left by Kara's inoperable state with additional details, perhaps to prod her back to life. "We've got the trophy and Deb's journal, the one I showed you. Plus Kal's going to try to get the discs, at least one of them."

"I will succeed," Kal said, an unnecessary guarantee that implied the opposite.

"When he comes down, the four of us will meet him. Charles always goes full throttle at Field Day, so he'll be exhausted and caught off guard and boom!" Elise clapped.

Kara flinched. She needed that.

"What is 'boom'?" Kal asked.

"They'll have him fired," Kara monotoned, at least now able to speak. "Strip his degrees. Revoke all his research and essentially eviscerate anyone who was involved with it, like me. Like Gary."

The instant she saw Victor behind the glass, her whole life flashed before her eyes. Poof. Done-zo, just like that in a pretentious, moldy basement. Charles being a looter, bowdlerizing this history, insinuated as much about her by association; he was her mentor, and now everything she'd been working toward was utterly compromised, scandalized, and vaporized. It would obliterate all her credibility forever. How was she supposed to end up at a place like Christie's now? What had seemed inevitable was now impossible. It was also unfortunate that Elise had been right.

"Shh. You can figure this out all by yourself," whispered whatever had been in that flask that was now coursing through her limbs.

It was easy to imagine what Evelyn would say under the circumstances: *Smile, raise your chin up, wrap up your research already, slim down for the new pencil skirts I've just bought you, and move back to civilization. You'll be off this godforsaken mountain in a few weeks to spend the rest of your lucrative life advising women like me on how to add dimension to their collections of historically significant vases.*

"You're so wrong." Elise said. "This is going to make your goddamned career."

Elise has been right about Charles. Maybe this was the key Kara needed to open the doors that had stubbornly remained closed with her existing resume. It was certainly a major blurb addition, if handled properly. She'd have to massage the narrative of course.

Yes, that was it. She was a whistleblower. She was doing the right thing. She *was* the only one of these people who really, truly cared about the artifacts. She was their savior, their protector, their champion. Any of the auction houses would be lucky to have her.

"Exactly," said the flask. "Yes, you're in command. You'll be fine. You are currently, already, fine, forever."

"We have to get Victor back," she thought she thought, but had in fact said.

"It's Victoria," Elise corrected.

"You're a star," the flask whispered.

"I want to murder him," Kara said.

At last, Elise turned around to face her and smiled. "Now we're talking."

HERE WAS THIS BIG GIANT THING, A RIP IN THE SPACE-TIME-GENDER continuum, and nothing else compared. Kara had never understood the word *transcendent* before, not until right now, not until a tiny plaster man changed into a tiny plaster woman right before her eyes, slapping Kara silly with her tiny plaster hands. Kara's life on this earth was on a plane of higher purpose now, and from this vantage point it became absurd to her that she was still tethered to a human man, let alone one she didn't deeply love. The idea of sharing with him this moment, the most momentous of those in her life probably, historically speaking, felt laughable. Indeed, she laughed like a blubbering loon in the back of Kal's car until he came to a stop before the gravel parking lot. She floated out, leaving Elise inside to continue, curiously, holding hands with the ponytailed man.

They had a plan now. The evidence was gathered. The authorities were here, Chen and Dr. Trudy Newkirk, the other visiting scholar, fast asleep in the farthest corners of the boys' and girls' rooms, respectively. The bad guy was headed to bed, scotch-buzzed and unaware that in the very near days the chauvinist chateau he'd spent his life constructing would come crashing down to the ground.

Later that night, still in her party dress and heels, Kara stood at the steps to the lab, yet again watching her fiancé trot toward her like a Labrador. But this time, rather than feeling filled with dread and determination, she felt light with the promise of flying higher still any moment now. Her blood was spiked, thanks to Kal, and she knew the time was right to have this conversation. It was now or never.

"Want to go for a walk with me?" She asked.

It was pitch black in the patches between streetlights, and the cicadas were on full blast. The two walked downhill in the middle of the road she'd just driven up, and Gary reached for her hand. She let him take it, soaking up the warmth while she still could, oh-so-selfishly taking comfort from the very person she was about to demolish.

The half-moon rose above the tree line ahead of them. It felt like she'd toggled between dimensions, broiling in the open skillet of the patio that very morning, then seeing a ghost at the party, and now walking this plank into the darkness. She'd spent the hours while everyone else was at the beach trying to convince herself that Elise was wrong—and failed. Now, having seen Victor, it was undeniable. The cicadas squealed in anticipation.

As they walked, Gary recounted for her exactly how he'd ended up in that wine cellar with Z, as if that were the interesting part, as if that were the part that required an explanation. The fact that this discovery didn't rock his world was exactly what upset her. Gary was maddeningly even-keeled and contented, a silver-lining loyalist who didn't try to change things when they didn't work out. He just savored the good and endured the bad. To her, he did not want enough from life. In a way that felt impossible to explain to anyone; the ease of his happiness always made her feel furious. Couldn't he want more, for her sake? Didn't he realize how much more she needed him to want? She'd tried over the years to sink down into the warm bath of this undemanding outlook, but simply couldn't. There were oceans to cross! Rungs to climb! Connections to be made! There was so much to pull off each and every day, and things never, not once, just magically shook out. You had to take the tree by the trunk and do the shaking yourself if you wanted a single coconut to fall into your lap. This felt especially true at the moment.

"Other than that, Mrs. Lincoln, how was the show?" He laughed for himself. "Man oh man. Maybe this is good though. I mean, not good—don't get me wrong—but now for sure I'm going to have to distance myself from the Charles track. I can start looking at other jobs, spread these old wings. Charles, sheesh. The crazy part is I was actually having a pretty damn good time this summer. Which means I guess I haven't been paying enough attention."

She couldn't possibly reply to that, and after a moment he jumped in again. "You know what? Before tonight I was thinking we could maybe do the wedding here. Greek destination, break some plates, take some of the work off Evelyn, but now—"

"Yikes," she interjected, despite never having used the word before.

He pursed his lips. "Yikes? Are you all right?"

She took a big step backwards and watched the shadows on his face ripple through a muscle sequence of droops and squints.

"I don't mean yikes." She put air quotes around it like that was the debate they were about to have, *jeez* vs. *yowza* vs. *zoinks* and which one means your life is over in this specific way.

She lifted her chin and tightened her ponytail, the source of her power. This part she had thought about a lot; she was determined to say the difficult sentence only one time and not have to clarify syntax at a moment like this. The *why* and *how* could be up for discussion, and would be no doubt, but not the *what*. The tone would be clearly set at the start; that was critical to her.

The right emphases eliminated what less direct sentences would invite as next questions, like, *Should we just postpone? Do you not believe in the institution?* or *Do you want to marry someone else?* Clear as sharp glass.

"Gary. I don't ever want to get married to you. I'm sorry."

He bent toward her as if he'd heard wrong. "What?"

"I'm sorry," that part she was willing to repeat, because she was.

The cicadas shrieked from the trees like a live audience riled up by the drama unfolding on the street below.

"What are you talking about? Did you talk to Z?" He shifted his stance with every question, moving his weight from foot to foot.

"Z? No, no, that's not . . ." she trailed off and waved her hands once in front of her face.

"Where is this coming from? Wait, how long have you been thinking about this?"

Before Gary, there had only been one other boy, her high school sweetheart who outgrew his role a year after they entered college. He approached the subject of their breakup much like she was doing now, logically and methodically. She had agreed with him; they'd each received what they needed from the relationship—the certainty of prom dates, virginity losses, and the crutch of long-distance phone calls during freshman year—and now it was time to move on. They'd shaken hands at the end of it. To this day they still occasionally sent each other messages about any news at their prep school. But Kara had a slumping certainty now that if, in the future, she ever sent Gary a message about something to do with Mega, he might not respond at all; he might see her name and simply delete it. Her hands started to quiver a little, and she clasped them together, willing the almighty pill-flask combo to keep up its end of the bargain. This was no time for her support system to wear off.

"I do love you. I think. But—"

"You think?!"

She hadn't expected for him to be this angry at her. He had to understand. "But it isn't what I want, forever. I don't feel what I'm supposed to—Like you feel, it's not the same," her voice lurched from one logical lily pad to the next, then fell right into the murky waters.

"Oh my God. What were you waiting for?"

She stiffened; her bullet points were bleeding together, and she felt off balance.

"I'm so sorry. I shouldn't have said yes. I should have told you this sooner, but I didn't know. I thought, maybe, that something like getting engaged would change me, or the way I felt at least, make it more real or deeper, or something, I don't know! But it never happened for me. I'm not articulating it well."

He nodded and crossed his arms.

"I knew it," he started pacing back and forth across the street. "I knew it as soon as you stood in the door of your room here and wouldn't even let me stay inside, not once. Who does that the summer after they get engaged? And then I think I pulled back some and looked around, or something. I've been spending all this time with Z, and you saw that and you didn't even say anything—you didn't mind—but then I didn't say anything either. I figured we'd talk about that at some point. I thought maybe that's why you wanted to talk to me tonight, actually. I didn't think it was just . . . over." His voice trembled then broke.

He wiped a tear from his cheek. Kara's heart seized, and her throat filled. She lifted her chin all the way up, as if the water was rising inside her and she needed to save herself from drowning. But she was wrong; she was going to cry too. It couldn't be helped.

"I'm so sorry," she choked out.

"I'm sorry too," he sniffled. "I wanted this to work, so much. But you wouldn't do this if you weren't sure. You're always sure. And there is something missing with what we both want, I know that, but we have time and I just thought . . . it was solid." He shook his head.

"Gary."

She slid off the ring and extended her hand. He opened his palm, and she dropped it in like an arrow to the chest.

The earlier boozy lightness just made her feel extra vulnerable now, unprepared when she should've been cloaked and fortified. She pulled at her dress sleeve and wiped her nose on the edge; she didn't care. The liquor was plummeting in her system, crashing and dragging her down with it. She'd never felt so low.

Even the cicadas seemed devastated, as there was a long and total silence during which they both wiped their faces on their clothes.

"Can I at least hug you?" He asked.

She nodded and pressed her cheek into his chest, feeling hollow and nauseous and trying to hold her breath because if she took in one lungful of his smell for the last time it might put her over the edge. She closed her eyes and pushed herself to think about the hours before this one.

Victor was alive, Elise was right, and she was free—all of which made her feel emptier at the moment than she'd ever felt before. The world was not as she knew it to be, and she wanted to rush back in time and reel it all back in somehow to start over from scratch and set it right.

The thunder they'd heard from far away at the party boomed closer now, and the wind picked up, swishing the leaves all around them. She and Gary released each other and, without a word, turned to walk up the dark, tree-lined street back to the sleeping village, each alone, each palpably wanting to reach for the other, and each willing themselves not to. The first fat drops of rain smacked the leaves above their heads, and for one simple second the branches caught the water for them and kept them dry. But naturally that didn't last.

Chapter

19

The whole time they'd been there it hadn't even rained once, not so much as a wet leaf from an overnight drizzle. But now they were two days into nonstop downpours that didn't seem to be stopping any time soon, and everyone's nerves were soggy and frayed. They were trapped there, all twenty or so of them in that tiny village designed for six—max—being steamed like vegetables. No one was allowed to go to the site or could have even made it up there anyway; the streets and pathways were flooded. Trench work was suspended indefinitely, and Charles marched around the village in flustered figure eights, furious at the sight of so many of his charges unable to do his bidding. The mood throughout was exceptionally tense.

This wet weather triggered a series of miserable events.

Patty woke up the first morning to one of the girls crying, *My straightener!* and Elise swatting it out of her hand into the puddle from whence it came before she electrocuted herself. There was a thin layer of water on the floor of their room, like someone had come in and hosed it down overnight. Elise immediately ordered them each to go down behind the lab and retrieve two of the flat construction rocks. There was a whole jumbled pile of beams, nails, and white stones down there, most of which was used by Ian—or would be when the village was chosen for a home-makeover contest. They used the rocks now to prop their suitcases a few inches off the ground. So much for whichever items were already soaked.

At breakfast, Patty nursed a sense of foreboding as she slurped her

not-warm-enough oatmeal and watched Charles talking in the corner
to Gary and a new woman she'd never seen before. She looked to be
about Charles's age, but she wore her gray hair in two unsettling pony-
tails and had those bright red glasses frames that people wore when
they wanted to frighten you with their quirkiness. The scene was dis-
concerting, to say the least, and didn't bode well for Patty's wish for
them all to be given the day off.

Charles had laid into Patty when they got back from the beach; he
said he'd have to review her *status as a student* since she hadn't been
able to handle an assignment as simple as dropping off an envelope
(specifically an envelope that hadn't been vomited upon). She con-
fessed that she'd had to throw the envelope away, which was true, yet
she neglected to mention she'd shown its contents to Elise and Z. He
was livid, and she was positive he was going to have her expelled. For
all she knew these were her final days before getting booted back home
for life, and she was spending them in a monsoon of guilt, shame, and
actual rain. On the plus side, for the little it was worth, she felt like a
supremely stealth double agent.

The next thing she knew they were all crammed into the lab, their
heads atop the single holes that had been cut in the clear storage bags
that were handed out as ponchos. No one had thought to cut arm holes.
The rain pounded on the metal roof so hard Patty was sure it was about
to pour in. Charles and the new lady stood up at the front, facing the
group.

He gave a loud *ahem* to begin. It was like every now and then he remembered that he had some sort of vague instructional obligation to
them here, and then he really overdid it.

"This is Dr. Trudy Newkirk, our visiting botanist."

"What a morning!" She exclaimed, a scream over the rain.

"She's the reason you've been saving up all this dirt all summer long,
which we so appreciate. After her analysis, she'll be able to tell what

kind of flora grew in this environment and re-create, digitally of course, a 3D landscape of the beautiful green trees and bright colorful flowers that make this mountain here so verdant and vibrant." It seemed that he'd prepared these remarks before the weather turned but for some reason was unable to adjust them now. Without turning their heads, everyone shifted their eyes out to the window. Thunder rumbled.

"It'll be a hoot!" Dr. Newkirk said, introducing herself perfectly.

Now the group shifted their eyes inside and toward one another again. Lightning flashed, and Nuts started barking outside. They'd forgotten about him. Someone opened the door, and he trotted in and shook off. He didn't have a collar, so all they heard was the sound of his ears slapping against his head and an Ug saying, *My pants!*

"So, shall we begin?" Dr. Newkirk asked.

Before they could find out what starting meant they were divided into smaller groups, so that once they heard what the task was, they could less effectively riot.

The everyday routine at the site was this: one group shoveled dirt out of a trench into a giant pile, while another pair stood near the pile and sifted that dirt. Very rarely, they found something. Very often, they found something that they thought could be something but never was. So by this point, if a gold nugget ended up shining through the dirt, they would throw it over their shoulder out of sheer muscle memory. This dirt—the post-search, rock-free, artifact-free dirt—was then shoveled into a one-hundred-gallon drum. Seven of these drums were lined up behind the lab at this moment, all of which were presently filled with carefully sifted mud. Their mission, which they had no choice but to accept, was to dip the top halves of their bodies into the drums, remove every last puddle of mud into hundreds of three-inch plastic vials, and label each one with a permanent marker, without contaminating the drums or vials with any outside dirt.

Oh sure.

At first Dr. Newkirk insisted that they keep the barrels upright, though no one was sure why beyond this woman's misreading of the Geneva Convention. But then a few of the Ugs dipped their top halves in so far that their feet lifted off the ground. In one case, a girl fell in completely and had to be yanked out by the ankles by Gary. She flipped out of the drum looking like a drowned bear, the whites of her eyes wide with shock, and she got to take the rest of the day off. Everyone hated her.

Then they put stools next to the drums so people could reach in farther.

When Patty first heard, weeks ago, that a kooky plant lady was coming, she'd been looking forward to it. That was a person she could relate to from her previous line of work. They did not prepare her for the "Seed Queen," the moniker Dr. Newkirk had bedazzled on her backpack in pink little jewels with a crown on top.

It was clear this woman was disappointed in the weather, but instead of just saying so she kept circling around past one sad-sack group after another, cheerleading. Patty wished she would just sit down and say to them, *This sucks*, and let them all exhale. Those two words would at least make this week make sense.

Upside down inside a barrel full of mud, she began to wonder if this was the best summer of her life. Something had to click forward. Something, so she'd be able to say, *Oh, that summer? Man oh man. That was the summer I . . .*

The third morning when she woke up in her cot, she felt she might actually cry when she opened her eyes and heard the rain still coming down. In the cafeteria she was yet again slurping her oatmeal, which Ursula had at least allowed her to improve in the microwave (by this point Patty had crossed the thin-but-helpful line of looking not just pathetic but pitiably pathetic), when Elise came over and sat down across from her.

"Hi. I need you up at the site today," she said. At that moment the clouds parted, and sunlight streamed down from the sky in the tube of airspace right above Patty's head.

"Really? Are you allowed to go up there?"

"Don't get so excited. And yes. It'll go faster if I have someone to hold the stakes for me." She glanced around at the damp and downtrodden ragamuffins. "This sucks."

And there were those magic words, a glimmer of sense, starting to click.

"Yes. Please, take me with you."

"Don't let Charles see you leave. Meet me at the van in ten." Elise was always saying cool stuff like that.

When they reached the excavation, they left the van and trudged through the maniacal rain up the hill past most of the trenches, both slipping in the mud every few steps, coating their gloves in sludge. Normally this would have been *torture*, but after Barrelgate the term was all relative. Each trench was covered up with a heavy-duty brown tarp with small holes in the edges, through which Elise had nailed in stakes over the past two days. The shiny brown patches gave the hillside vista the look of an image that was still loading, blurred smooth in squares and textured in detail on the rest. No one else had set foot here since the rain started—it was too dangerous, which was exactly why Elise was here.

They headed over to Z's trench, and Elise climbed down inside, instructing Patty to stay put and hold the tarp. Once she was down at the bottom, completely invisible, her voice called up, "If this wall goes down while I'm in here, take the van and go get Gary. The keys are on the seat. Don't waste my time screaming, just go."

Patty stared ahead and pictured her own body flinging around inside the van as it flipped end over end down the mountain. There was no way she could ever drive that giant thing by herself—let alone in a flood, let alone once Elise was crushed in a mudslide, let alone with Charles's mix CD soundtracking the end.

After ten long minutes, Elise's red visor brim poked up from the depths. The rest of her rose up the ladder, to which she clung one-handed. In the other hand she clutched three vials of mud.

"Newkirk's little power trip reminded me that we hadn't taken any samples yet," she said. "Got to match the soil samples on the piece to the trench it came from, and now we've got every last thing we need." She grinned, and Patty did too. Cluelessness enhanced her feeling that she was part of something exhilarating and vaguely punitive toward a man who'd been less than kind to her.

They walked over and sat down beneath the stone shelves that jutted out from the locker room wall, giving them a small roof from the pounding rain. Elise unzipped and removed her rain jacket, revealing her standard tank top with the built-in bra that tormented Patty. Goosebumps rose across her arms where the tiny hairs stood on end like a field of lightning rods ready and willing to be struck.

"Nasty," Elise said. "It's a fucking sauna down there. And it stinks. I don't know what the hell that is, but it reeks," Elise fanned herself.

"Well, dead people," Patty suggested. Not wrong.

Elise laughed. Patty had never seen her do that before, and it made her laugh too. She relaxed her shoulders.

"Charles reamed me out," Patty admitted. "He said he might pull my scholarship or something. I think I should've delivered that envelope for him."

"Fuck Charles. You did the right thing. And trust me, he's not kicking anyone out any time soon. It's our turn to do the kicking out. You're going to get your degree, which, believe me, is more important than you even know right now. Don't blow it."

Patty nodded. The rain blew harder, and they squished their bodies tighter to stay beneath the rock. "Why didn't you get yours? You're the smartest one here." She turned to face her.

Elise scoffed. "Because I had the brilliant idea to go for a boyfriend instead. Biggest mistake of my life."

Patty kissed her. It happened so fast she couldn't explain it. She just leaned over and did it, no hands, just pushing her face onto Elise's and hoping that's where her mouth was. Elise's lips were warm; while they didn't exactly open to receive hers, Patty noted in the blink of an eye that they didn't shut closed either. The brim of her visor created a tiny, perfect room for the two of them that would stay built forever. In a hundredth of a second Elise had her hands on Patty's shoulders, pushing her away.

"Jesus Christ, what the hell was that?" Her voice soared over the rain hammering the tarps.

Patty's eyes stayed closed through the end of the question. When she opened them she saw that Elise wasn't as mad as she could have been—probably should have been—not as mad as Patty had seen her get before.

"I—I don't know? Sorry. I'm really sorry," Patty tried. Despite being yelled at, her stomach was awash in a thrilling acid mix of excitement and shame, laced with tenderness. She had no idea why or how she did what she'd just done.

"God damn it, people!" Elise railed like there were unrelenting crowds at the gate: men, women, and children clamoring to smooch her. She stood, zipped her rain jacket back up, and dropped the vials into its big side pockets.

"Come on," she waved. "And keep it in your pants." Before Elise turned away, Patty caught the beginning of an eye roll.

Oh, that summer? That's the summer she had her first kiss.

Inside the tense van, Elise's walkie-talkie crackled to life. Kal's voice came in through the plastic yellow square.

"Elitsa, are you here?" he said. "We have some problems."

Chapter
20

The rain was a mixed bag.

On the one hand it kept Charles off her back for another few days, preventing him from coming anywhere near the trench. Elise had spent the monsoon up at the site trying desperately to tarp everything down before the entire arena slid down the mountain like chocolate melting down a chin. Given the mountain grade, the site location was precarious on a good day, and now that the walls and edges of each deep hole were soggy and loose, it was all the more dangerous. Charles hadn't thought about this—or worse, he had and was pretty comfortable with knowingly, accidentally killing them all.

On the other hand, the rain meant that every last sap was stuffed into the village for days on end, giving her zero chance to talk to Kara or Z alone. Group crankiness ran at an all-time high, and Ursula chose this moment to put them all on a liquid diet of orzo soup and Ovaltine, which she thought would act as comfort food but instead inspired mutiny. By the time the sun came out the starved, mud-ravaged Ugs were howling at the doors to the van, wielding shovels and pitchforks like the rioting villagers they were.

To make matters worse, Kal's dolphin-dangler friend Cosmo had tipped Charles off. Charles had called Kal to ask him about it and luckily Kal played dumb, a strong suit.

But now the site was dry again, or as dry as it would be for a while, and Chaz was chomping at the bit to get down inside the trench and ruin everything.

"I put your dirt samples in storage bin B," Kara told her. The two of them stood on the roof of the cafeteria. The roof might have seemed to be the most public place to have a secret chat, but in fact it was encircled by some kind of exotic purple flower that was catnip to bees and thus surrounded by a deafening buzz. Most sane people were too terrified to climb the metal ladder up here in the first place, but if they did they were rewarded with a soundproof conversation, gorgeous flowers, and a panoramic view of the entire village, mountain range, and valley below.

"Sure," Elise said. It seemed to her that trust was when you decided to care slightly less about something in order to let someone else care about that thing a bit more for you. In this spirit, she'd handed over the dirt samples she'd retrieved with Patty for Kara to place inside the lab's labyrinthine storage system. It had been a leap, but one she'd willingly made once Victoria, that wily bitch, revealed herself and revealed the two of them to be allies. The trophy was now safely ensconced in the lab as well.

"Evelyn can keep him on the phone for hours," Kara continued, explaining her plan to keep Charles hamstrung down in the lab for the day. Tomorrow was Field Day, the day they'd execute their plan. "And then for the afternoon I've planned to tell him that the rain may have damaged those VHS tapes of all his TV appearances, so we'll need to watch them all to see if any can be recovered."

"Damn," Elise said. "You're a genius." Elise jumped forward to avoid a particularly angry-looking bee. She was convinced it was the same one out to get her, rather than one of the ten thousand identical alternatives in her midst.

Kara preened. "I know."

"How are you, uh, doing?" Elise squirmed. She couldn't bring herself to make eye contact at this moment, but she couldn't not ask. Gary had been conspicuously comatose since the night of the party.

"Oh," Kara said. Her lips and eyebrows fell in parallel. "That. Not great, actually. I guess I feel kind of lucky, in a weird way, that this is all going on at the same time. Otherwise, if I had to think about it anymore than I already am, I might die. Elise, I just feel sick. I've never felt physically ill over something like this. Not even when I brought up ancient Roman latrines at the Sotheby's interview! Do you think I did the right thing? Have you talked to him? What did he say?"

This was already so many more words than she'd wanted to get back. But Kara's eyes were so sad, so hopeful that Elise might throw her a bone, so not evil now, it was like looking at a new person completely.

"Gary's fine," she said, despite a tremendous amount of evidence to the contrary. The rain had cleared the air, and she looked out over the valley, able to see for millions of miles in every direction, the sloping little house-filled hills, the city center bubbling with busy little buildings, even the tiny red and blue specks of cars containing people humming to and fro about their bizarre little lives. "Trust me, whenever in doubt, get all the way out."

Kara wiped her eyes and nodded, then she looked up. "You and Kal . . . ?"

DIGGING AT THE ALTAR NOW FELT LIKE AN ESSENTIAL RITUAL, LIKE A player slapping the same side of the locker room wall each and every time before running out of the tunnel and onto the field. She needed this time up here to settle herself before she did what she was about to do tomorrow. It was crazy to think she'd even come this far; yanking something out of the ground and hiding it was absolutely insane, and she'd just gone ahead and done it, on instinct.

These might be her last moments here. She took a deep breath; she would savor them in peace.

"Yoo-hoo!" Trudy shouted. She was making her way up the hill toward her.

Trudy wanted to collect another dirt sample, as if an ancient sneeze sent a snot-encased seedling up to the top here and it blossomed into a slightly lighter shade of pink than the flowers down below. *We must find out!* There had to be some things science could survive without knowing, but Elise hadn't heard of them.

When Trudy reached the altar she, like everyone else, sat down on the grass for a while to recuperate.

"Lord, no wonder you're so in shape," she said. Her gray pigtails sagged and clung to the sweaty sides of her neck.

Elise continued working to give Trudy both time to catch her breath and a sense of her enthusiasm for their exchange. She wasn't going to say a word about tomorrow, even though in no time she'd be throwing herself at the mercy of this maniac.

"Is that safe, do you think? I mean health wise, the air?" Trudy huffed out, pointing to the smokestacks.

"No."

"Well! Good thing we're not trying to grow anything up here in the current century, am I right?"

She remained seated and wiggled out of the straps of her backpack, slumping it onto her lap. On the large outer pocket, the words "Seed Queen" were spelled out in hideous rhinestones. She pulled on one of its dozen zippers, but it only budged an inch, then continued to snag, and she met its resistance with harder yanks as if to convince it otherwise.

"I'm not sure I've properly accounted for the air quality in the samples," she said, her elbow jerking back again and again like a tragic dance sequence. "This is a good reminder to ask Lou about that. Between you and me, by the way, he's quite a dish. This damned zipper!"

Elise knew that right now, all over the world, people were talking to themselves; in her experience, the majority of people never required the green light of reply.

"Though I have to say, the other samples are turning out just beautifully, mmm," she added.

The backpack still wouldn't open, and Trudy now had both hands pulling in opposite directions of the zipper itself.

"They're right there. I can feel them, just a little more muscle, all that Tae Bo I've done and yet—"

Suddenly her elbow swung back, and with it the large, bedazzled *D*, *Q*, *E*, and *N* that adorned the obstinate pocket released their rhinestones, all of which flew into the sky and then rained right down into the trench. They both stared, watching a hundred-piece rainbow of plastic jewels tumble and nestle into the far nooks and crannies of Elise's work.

Trudy froze, her elbow still angled into the air.

"What!?"

"Oh. Uh, oh, Elise, I'm very sorry. Oh," she mumbled.

Elise picked a rhinestone out of her braid.

"Here, I'll take that. And, well, I got them out!" She held up a plastic bag containing a few vials.

She continued. "Well so, I guess, would you mind? I'm sorry, I can do the scooping myself if you want, of course, but I imagine . . . Then I'll be out of your hair, all of it."

Elise was doing some imagining herself right now, a pinwheeling See- -u-e- down the hill.

She snatched the vials from Trudy's hand and made shallow scoops from the side of the trench, making sure to include as many beads in the process as she possibly could. The rest would be plucked out by a future techno-archaeologist version of herself who would do a dissertation on what kind of royalty, exactly, had deposited these here.

Finally Trudy stuffed the samples into her slightly less regal backpack and scooched back down the hill with a curt wave, drift finally caught.

Elise grimaced and harkened back to the last moment she'd been freak-free, in the fleeting minutes she'd had alone with Kal that night after the party.

He'd brought the car to a screeching halt on the road just before they reached the gravel parking lot and got out. With one hand indicating the direction of the village, he urged Kara away. For a moment Elise's stomach seized; she wondered if she'd been completely stupid and was about to receive a dry hump attempt under a walnut tree.

"You don't want her in the car anymore," Kal told her, getting back behind the wheel. When it wasn't an absolute nightmare to have someone tell you what you wanted, it was kind of nice.

"No, I don't," she agreed. "This was plenty. Even though I probably have to stop hating her now."

He turned toward her. "A big night for you, yes? For us?"

"Victory," she grinned.

When he laughed, he did it with his whole upper half. His chest pumped out, and he barked toward the roof.

He turned and kissed her on the cheek, which somehow felt intimate, mundane, and straightforward in a way she had never experienced before.

"Thanks for the ride." She squeezed his fingers. Before she could pull away for the evening, Kal lifted up her hand and kissed the back of it. His scruff bristled her skin, and his wild black and gray halo of hair dipped in front of her face, and it smelled like a lime aflame, and she wanted to sink down into a bath of it.

The last thing he said to her before he drove off was one of those supremely obvious statements he often lobbed that she'd previously viewed as proof of his naked idiocy but now realized were these narrow, deep pools of truth.

"It is me," he shrugged. "For you, it is me."

Of course it was.

Ever since, she felt filled to the gills with light, like she might blind someone when she opened her mouth. It didn't make sense to her that she could feel this way, but here it was, happening. She was powerless to tamp it down, even though she dearly wanted to before anyone saw her and asked what was up; then she'd have to explain that her skin, all along, had the ability to glow in the dark. She had no idea how and wanted to hate it.

A wolf whistle suddenly sliced through the air. One of the overalled Greeks had two filthy fingers in his mouth and waved for Elise to come down.

En route she passed Gary, who looked like he was about to hurl himself off the mountain, as well as Z, baldly staring at him. Both were nearly in tears. The Ugs were lounging about in their lack of sentient oversight, but Gary's incapacitation, at least, meant Ryan had to pick up the laser slack. He was walking down the processional along a red beam line with some measuring tape. Elise stuck out her boot and tripped him without breaking stride.

As expected, the Greeks, with the help of some Ugs, had moved the wrong boulder in the wrong direction again and wanted to show her. They stood there staring at it, wondering how this had happened. The rock was the size of a mini fridge and, thanks to their handiwork, now sat precariously at the edge of the burial grounds, exactly where Elise had warned them it shouldn't go. After the trenches took a beating in the rain, it was extremely dangerous there. They discussed this for a bit then finally agreed on the only day they ever agreed to do anything: tomorrow.

When the vans returned to pick them up at the end of the day, Elise felt herself unclench. They'd made it without Charles getting up there, thanks to Kara. Instead of him coming to fetch them, Ursula of all people flopped out from the driver's seat.

"Elise!" She shouted, waving as if everyone couldn't see and hear her. She waddled over and continued to wave the whole time, like maybe if she stopped, Elise would leave. She might.

"You've got to be kidding me," Elise muttered.

"Five minutes!" Z shouted, as if the Ugs needed one before they were in the van seats and complaining about being starved.

"Ursula," Elise acknowledged, once the woman was standing in front of her. Her white cooking apron was splotched with a shockingly inedible shade of blue.

The woman panted and looked around to make sure that no one was listening in.

"I've lost Ian," she said and pressed her fingers into her cheeks, smushing them up into her eyes.

"He's dead?"

"No! Oh, God. That's what I'm worried about. He just walked off all by himself with nothing but a hammock and twenty sandwiches."

Elise dreamed of doing that at least twice a week.

"Oh. He'll be back," she assured Ursula. "Doesn't he usually go for a nap or something? I mean, we've all seen him nap." Specifically, they'd seen him snooze in the buff down in the orchard.

"No," Ursula said, "Yesterday. He walked off yesterday."

Oh shit.

"That's why we had the beef at lunch!" Ursula's eyes widened with the word and grew glassy. "He took the sandwiches! Can you help me look? I've got to get back down now."

"Did you tell Charles?"

Ursula's face darkened. "No, no, no. I can't, I can't do that. He's already threatened us right and left about being thieves; he thinks Ian—nevermind. I won't tell him. And not *her* either, that new lady with the pigtails. She saw him in the orchard days ago, and she's been going on and on about how she's appalled. Wacky prude," she scowled.

"Right," Elise looked at the vans, now waiting impatiently. "OK, yeah, fine, I can go look."

Ursula shoved a few granola bars into her hands then put a warm, wet palm on the side of Elise's neck, "Nuts is looking for him too," she assured her, then turned to go.

Z gave her a quizzical thumbs up from the driver's seat, and Elise returned a demoralized one, a lexicon that would have to do for the moment.

The granola bars were a warm, chunky mush inside the green plastic, but she ripped one open and slurped it down anyway. If she found the naked handyman, at least he'd have a sandwich for her.

She didn't trust Charles not to come up here after they were all gone anyway. Ian was bound to be somewhere nearby, and this way she could guard the site with all her heart for a little bit longer.

Chapter
21

After dinner, the four of them—Kara, Elise, Patty, and Z—assembled down in the orchard deep among the walnut and fig trees to proverbially pile their hands on top of each other and shout *Break!* They were destined to be here: sufficiently wound up, athletic, and aggrieved. This and a well-timed sitting-upon was all it took to finally get to the best part of the Olympics: the four woman, four lap, four sweaty palms around the baton relay.

A lot could go sideways, and none of them were prepared to execute their respective responsibilities. On this they all agreed. Equal time was spent in this discussion on both archaeological data sets and the terminal velocity of water balloons. The whole thing made Kara nervous in a way she never knew she could feel before—that her future was heavily uncertain. But beside that feeling was another new sensation: the pleasant ballast of being part of a group.

"So we're good," Elise said at the end. Maybe it was the wind, but none of them could tell whether that was a question or not. Either way they all bobbed their heads, importantly, in unison.

Sleep was out of the question, so Kara spent the night scrubbing every surface of the lab building. Only two to three times did she think to herself, *I probably shouldn't get bleach on my ring*, only to remember.

Elise burst through the door just after dawn. "Good God!" She lifted the collar of her shirt over her nose. "You trying to poison us?" She went around the room pushing the shutters open to air out the chemical scent and save Kara's life.

Kara stood and removed her rubber gloves. "I couldn't sleep."

"I slept like a rock—not. Z snored like a freight train, only because she has no skin in the game. Unlike us."

Kara smiled. "So, what's the status?"

"Vans are leaving now. Z's got them so hyped they're gnawing each other's shorts off. Our two are coming down now. Patty broke the coffee machine though, so the mood's not great."

"Now?" She thought she had a few more minutes to prepare—or at the very least, to panic.

From the doorway Trudy trilled, "I am an addict!"

"Good morning," Chen yawned as he swung the door open and the two of them stepped inside. "Trudy, I think I can use the chemical boiler here for some water and stir it into the de-encapsulated Folger's. Though, I suppose there could be some blood residue."

"I don't mind that," she said.

The two researchers sat down at their respective centrifuges and began their usual silent routines. Various chemical compounds— plant, mineral, human, potable, and otherwise—bubbled pleasantly in the library-like atmosphere as they geared up for the workday. The delicate sounds gave Kara a wonderful sense of calm, and for a moment she imagined they didn't have to do any of this. It would be like any other day, a relaxed, rigorous investigation into largely inconsequential tiny things.

"Smell you later!" Z screamed from the van window for their benefit as she revved the van engines. Kara looked longingly out the window and remembered how a week ago she would've said that Field Day was her worst nightmare. Charles was right where he should be, driving the second van. As soon as the wheels skidded off the gravel, Elise began to cough. She stood in full trench warrior regalia at the center of the room, arms crossed and impatient.

"Blerrgufhugh," she subtly prompted.

The time was nigh; coffee or not, there was no use in delay. Kara's ponytail was as tight as it was ever going to get. "Dr. Chen? Dr. Newkirk?"

They both turned around in their chairs and pushed their giant plastic safety goggles up onto their foreheads.

"Tea makes me queasy, if that's what you're about to say," Chen said.

"I wouldn't mind just sucking on some espresso beans at this point," Trudy added.

"We'd like to talk to you about something," Kara forged ahead. It was the second time this week she was delivering a blow in a set of prepared remarks, scaffolding around a burning building. "It's about Charles. Elise and I have come to understand that he has been systematically lying about the facts of the Mega excavation for years by selling off a series of artifacts clearly indicating that women, not men, were the primary athletes here. We believe he poses a continued threat to the site's sanctity and thus to our own careers. Due to his pattern of looting, we have removed an artifact from the site without his knowledge, which we believe will be critical in confirming the new gender framework of the excavation once and for all."

All three of them stared at her in stunned submission. A loaded several seconds of silence hovered in the pristine room. Kara wasn't sure what to say next. She'd reached the end of her talking points.

"Delivery!" Kal swung open the door holding what looked like two pizza boxes. "My discuses," he sang.

"Meniscuses?" Chen squinted at the boxes.

"Now hang on," Trudy whipped off her goggles and pinched the bridge of her nose. "You took what? You're saying Charles is stealing from here? And I'm sorry, but who are you?"

She turned on Kal, who stuck his cigarette in his mouth and extended a hand.

"Kal Loukanis, mayor of Megalopolis. I am with Elise, we are together," he smiled. He turned to Elise and went on. "I work miracles to get these. Cosmo and I, we see eye to eye now, but a problem is I explained to him we are borrowing, so we may need to think again or, maybe Kara, you could talk to him?"

"OK." Kara held up her hands. "Let's all sit down. Kal, please take those and put them on the table there. Elise, please get the trophy and put it under the light at my desk. And please, Lou, Trudy, let me explain." She could, and would, please everyone.

One by one Kara went over the facts of the case in great detail, accepting all questions. As the researchers donned their glasses and leaned down to examine the pilfered artifacts, their inscriptions, and the journal, they listened carefully to Kara's measured words about Charles's request to meet collectors, the discs, pictures with puka shells, rumors, Cosmo, and finally, about Victoria.

Trudy crossed her arms. "Let me get this straight. He blamed the both of you—tried to stop you from coming together on this." She huffed. After more than an hour of discussion, the Seed Queen was coming around first. "Charles. I have to say, I was never a fan of the whole macho muchacho sports thing. I was a bulldog tennis player, you know. And he never wanted to hear that, of course! Good gravy, I tip my hat to you ladies."

She looked down again at the trophy and shook her head. "I'll be damned," Trudy said. Her eyes glassed over, and she wiped her cheek. Kara's heart surged; she felt, finally, like she was on firmer ground with someone else—someone pedigreed—on her side.

"You shouldn't have removed this," Chen admonished.

"Well, what the hell was I supposed to do?" Elise asked. She'd kept a lid on it this whole time, ceding the floor for Kara to deal, appropriately, with her own ilk.

"It could have been compromised, though," Chen went on. "And it needs the right documentation, you know. You need the corresponding soil samples."

"I've got all that," Elise growled. Kal placed a hand on her shoulder and squeezed.

"Actually," Chen said, "this does jive with those bone samples you gave me, Kara. I did run a few tests."

She held her breath.

"Looks like they're female," he said. "It's neat all right. I used this new centrifuge setting that's got these compounds you'd need to examine—"

"Shut up, Lou." Trudy snapped. She punched the palm of her other hand with a loud smack and looked toward the windows, to the open road. "Give me the car keys. I'm going to butcher him."

Chapter

22

Because American Independence Day fell inconveniently early in their working calendar, Charles personally moved the holiday forward a month to August fourth and called it a field day. Everyone was riled up to have some good old-fashioned fun and hardly noticed at all that Patty's frenetic energy had an edge of panicked terror to it. All she had to do was keep it together for a few more hours while Kara and Elise convinced the others to join in on the scheme. How hard could it be, really, to play a few rounds of dodgeball with someone who wanted her dead?

They'd hauled up a folding table, from which Ursula served her three signature American dishes as interpreted by someone who said on the van ride up, *Well, I've only been there in my mind, America, and let me tell you, it was wild.* There were sausage slices dropped on top of liberally ketchuped white bread that were meant to approximate hotdogs, and an extremely literal interpretation of frozen yogurt that had been stacked in the freezer in red cups for weeks, now impenetrable by the human mouth. Patty frantically snacked on everything in a misguided attempt to calm herself down, ignoring the repercussions of such pre-exercise intake.

"Welcome to the Hellish Games!" Z blew a penis whistle from Charles's suitcase that hung around her neck, with a go at geographic accuracy turned Freudian slip. She was their air traffic controller of fun for the day, a role she'd been threatening them with for weeks.

"Zara! Get down from there. And my God, put that away!" Charles put his hand over his heart, and just in time.

The pledge of allegiance began as Z and Gary doled out bandanas indicating whose team everyone was on. After this, Charles stood before them and gave what, even for him, was a lengthy speech on the importance of this event. He explained to a dozen sweaty teens in nylon the historical significance of what they were embarking upon here today: reenacting the ancient rites of the Greek forefathers, the militaristic parallels that connected and cleaved the very nations they lived in, the downright religious imperative of sport to tether man, specifically, to a higher purpose through the physical, spiritual current that ran uninterrupted through the centuries, culminating unto today's male athletes.

Z made faces and did air humps at Patty throughout this speech, and it buoyed her mood. Patty perked up; after all, organized fun was where she thrived. Someone could tell you what to do with your hands, and sometimes they even helped tell you what to wear; she appreciated being instructed on how to have a good time in groups. This would be no different. She could handle this. Elise was depending on her. With every move she made she thought of her new friends, huddled in the lab over important documents, saying something like, *Don't worry, Patty's on the case.*

She also thought of Charles's words to them from their first training day: *I implore you to picture the exceptional athletes.* Patty did. This time she could picture herself among them.

They hurled water balloons, carried raw eggs on spoons, spun around blindfolded, and generally made the aforementioned forefathers proud. As the activities ticked down, Patty had a growing sense of dread about how well it was all going and therefore whether she was doing her job. She and Z hadn't needed to distract Charles at all; he was engrossed in the day's demands. He'd ignored them both, entirely aligning himself with only the tallest Ugs or the ones who displayed so much as a swirl of chest hair, treating every activity seriously enough

to warrant cursing and stomping when he didn't come in first. But after he worked himself up into a fury over losing the cornhole round-
robin, Z made her move and assigned him Patty as a partner in the
three-legged race.

They were angled as far away from each other as tied ankles allowed,
forming a human *M*. His leg hair felt inappropriately soft against the
side of her shin, and her stomach was an accordion of cramps dangerously close to audible. Z was shouting instructions about which there
was apparently some confusion, as if less than one hundred percent of
these people had been a child in America before. The unnecessarily
long directions, plus a lovers' quarrel that broke out between two Ugs
who were very mistakenly paired up—proving that Z had paid no attention to any of the summer's lower class social dynamics—gave Patty
and Charles an excruciating five-minute void to fill while they waited.
This was Patty's moment to kick it into gear, but before she could think
of something that would take him four minutes and fifty-five seconds
to expound upon, he turned to face her, twisting her ankle.

"Ow!"

"I know you know where it is," he said slowly in a raised whisper.
"Do you remember a single one of our conversations, Patty? Have you
retained anything?"

Her cheeks burned, and she clamped her mouth shut. She would say
anything, admit anything, to throw him off the scent of their plan. He
continued.

"You came up here with Elise. Ryan saw you leave together. And
now it's gone, and let me guess, Elise swore you to secrecy. Well, whatever the two of you have going on, I can assure you it is illegal."

Was it? She desperately tried to get Z's attention, but it was pointless; Z had her head down and was crawling on all fours, from ankle to
ankle to ankle, tying and untying Ug legs to one another based on their
stated sexual allegiances of the moment.

"For something like this—you have no idea. I could have you both punished very harshly by the international authorities. Did you know that? I do not like the cut of this jib one bit. Had you even considered—"

"Go! Go! Go!" Z squawked at them at last.

Immediately Charles launched his bony body forward, thrusting out all four limbs at once and in so doing slamming unprepared Patty facedown to the ground.

"Up! Up! Get with it, woman! Come on now! Up you go! Up!" He gripped her by the arm and yanked her vertical. They were up and sprinting, and she was panting, dazed, red, and Charles was crushing the side of her rib cage with his fingers, and she didn't know what to do with her inside arm, and so she gripped the back of his shirt enough to choke him, and she was breathing so hard through a film of dust on her face and coughing the dust back out, and she thought her knee might be skinned, and around the track they went, around at a speed that shocked her, and she remembered that Charles had been a track star in his day—or something that explained this preposterous speed—and she'd never walked in this circle before, which was funny because that was sort of the whole point of them all being here, so this was cool, and she was glad she'd done this at least once, and then they picked up the pace even faster, who knew how, so impossibly quickening her heart might explode, but around and around, and how many laps were they supposed to do? and people were screaming, screaming to either side of them, and then finally Charles hurled out his limbs and flung them both over the finish line.

"Yes!" Charles screeched right in her ear and blasted up both fists in victory. They came in second to last.

The last pair, an Ug plus Ryan, hobbled in behind them, all four of their knees skinned. "Damn, Unc," Ryan said, patting Charles on the back.

Charles smoothed down his disturbed hair and held it back as the others all made their way to the water station, to which Patty now required a visit in order to remain alive.

"So, do I make myself clear?" Charles asked her, hair back intact.

Patty could not have been less clear. She looked around to make sure no one was within earshot. Everyone else was circling the lunch setup where Ursula leaned over the table, red-faced and terrifying above the perspiring meat discs, fisting a plastic knife in each hand like the lunch lady from hell.

Patty wasn't entirely sure what Charles was accusing her of, but she did her best to allay him. "I'm not going to kiss her again, I swear."

He opened his mouth to reply, then cocked his head sideways, a response she'd received often. Not a word came out. Instead he stood up straight, faced the crowd, and made one of those loud, meaningful coughs indicating someone's about to say something no one wants to hear.

"Kids! Now, picnic responsibly, and then I've decided we're going to remain here for the afternoon," he called. All of them groaned back. "I know you expected the remaining day off, yes, but there's work to be done, and we only have two weeks left. It will only be a few hours. Patty here has reminded me how much there is still left to learn this summer."

He kneeled down and untied their ankles. Upon returning upright he said, "Thank you, Patty." His droopy lidded grin sent a chill down her spine. Then he bypassed the lunch table completely, marching to the back of the van to fetch the buckets and, of course, the iniquitous clipboard.

There had been one plan and one plan only—map Charles onto a simple schedule today—and Patty had botched it. In every moment she dropped the ball, it seemed; only the consequences this time were much larger. Z looked over at her and sucked in her lips, eyes agog. There were no walkie-talkies in sight, none other than the one strapped to Charles's belt, presently bobbing its way toward the trenches.

Chapter

23

Well, this threw a trowel in their plans.

Dehydrated and stuffed with sausage, the team resumed their work in the trenches with betrayal in their hearts. Groans and grunts filled the air. They accepted their fates with disdain, stripping off colorful bandanas and headbands into a rainbow stench pile of forgotten fun, and sank to their knees, shovels in hand, to reminisce about the glory days of five minutes ago. The music was off, and gentle sounds hovered above the hill of poking trowels, brushing stones, wet knees in rubber pads, and mellifluous Greek swear words from the men who'd recently sat watching college women run around the track and were now tasked with moving the boulder back yet again.

There was no way for Z to reach Kara or Elise to let them know they wouldn't be coming down. The showdown was off, and she couldn't tell whether it was because Charles was on to them or if he was just inspired to be an asshole by the day's joie de vivre. Either way, all the energy she'd ratcheted up between Field Day mayhem and the confrontation anticipation now was channeled to her only goal: keep him away from her trench. She paced in anxious circles around its perimeter.

Luckily Charles was taking his sweet time. Having spent the last few weeks in the lab with the visiting scholars, he was now walking around each section of the site and taking stock, jotting down ominous notes at every turn. Z clocked him as he circulated.

In all her exuberance, she'd forgotten to apply sunscreen that morning and now, suddenly hyper aware of her body, she could feel the skin on her lower back burning. When she reached around, it was tender to the touch. The strip between the top of her shorts and where her T-shirt rode up was leathered into a narrow brown hide. Last week, one of the Ugs got so badly sunburned that he had to sleep with his whole red body soaked in lotion topped with Vaseline; the next morning he woke up coated in bugs, some of which were large and still writhing in the slime. Z hastily pushed her sports bra straps aside, shoulders pressed forward and elbows akimbo, and reapplied SPF. Summoned by the smell of tropicalia, Ryan appeared beside her.

"Lemme get some of that," he said and started rubbing the stuff all over his exposed midriff, the white goo pooling in his bellybutton.

"You down to roll with me to Costa Rica this year?" he asked.

"Kindly go screw yourself," she said, looking around for Gary.

Gary had gone through the motions earlier in the day—even a gracious display of sportsmanship once whacked in the sack by a cornhole bag—but had now exhausted his reserves. At the moment he simply sat on the grass all alone at the top of the altar, staring out into the distance. There was a wheelbarrow up there next to him, full of the stakes they'd been told to mark trench corners with. He'd single-handedly pushed it up there and then just plopped down next to it, done.

The guy couldn't catch a break in this place; he had one dating pool, and people kept peeing in it. In a miraculous turn of class, Z had decided to give him a few days of mourning before she "accidentally" grazed his butt or made a similar opening salvo to restarting anything romantic between them.

One thing at a time. Kara and Elise had to be wondering now where they were, and it was fully Z's responsibility to keep an eye on Chaz. For some reason the sight of him flipping up his prescription sunglasses was frightening to her; the seemingly dweeby man wasn't exactly that at all.

With a giant camera dangling from his neck, Charles periodically crouched down or did that thing where he put one foot on top of a rock and leaned in, which he must've thought made him look serious and limber at the same time. Occasionally he'd ask an Ug to hold up a number with their fingers before the camera, as if he'd been hit in the head.

"Gary!" Charles called up to the altar, as if just noticing that his survey man was camped out up there. "Come down here, will you? Yes?" He suggested as the answer.

Instead of answering, Gary picked up one of the metal stakes from the wheelbarrow and raised his arm high. Then he stabbed it into the ground beside him with a disturbing force and level of accuracy. Z hadn't necessarily thought about it, but that relationship probably wasn't going great for Gary either.

Charles blinked then emitted one of his canonical harrumphs. He moved on and finally, terribly, started marching straight toward Z's trench. It was as if all this time he'd waited until she relaxed, like all his meandering around was just for show when he knew exactly what he wanted all along, but sought to give everyone up there the false impression that this was merely a day like any other. He tightened the strings on his pith helmet as if heading into battle.

She stopped pacing and made a split-second decision. There was only one way to get in and out of the trench.

He was down at the far end of the processional, and it was uphill from there, giving her two minutes max to destroy the ladder. Bending down, she grabbed the top of it. She walked backwards fast, bent at the hips and pulling it out sideways, ruining the trench edge in the process (but what the hell else was she supposed to do?). Then she hoisted it up diagonally and stomped her foot onto the wooden side. It splintered in half immediately—bastion of sturdiness—and then she took a half in each hand and sprinted toward the far side of the site, where there was a steep drop off.

"Z! Stop!" Charles shouted behind her. Not that she did before, but she certainly didn't care now.

She threw the ladder pieces off the edge, watching them tumble and land not all that far away. They were completely retrievable, and yet she'd accomplished what she set out to do; he couldn't get down in there now.

The Ugs clapped and cheered, readily enthusiastic about conflict of any kind. They understood nothing.

"Why did you do that?" Charles asked when she returned, unaware that this was the single silliest question in human history.

Z panted. She hadn't run this much in years.

All of a sudden Nuts, asleep nearby, lifted his head off the ground like he'd been called. He stood up and started sprinting down the processional, barking at top volume in every direction at absolutely nothing. He zoomed back and forth in long laps, howling and yowling endlessly. Charles couldn't get a word in.

"Nuts!" Charles shrieked.

Down on the track, a white car sped up behind the vans and skidded to a halt. Z's stomach did a backflip. Here they were! Here it is!

"Now what?" Charles yelled over the dog.

All four of them—Elise, Kara, Chen, and Trudy—spilled from the car and advanced uphill directly toward them.

Charles cupped his hands and yelled down in their direction. "Trudy, I told you there would be no hotdogs left over!"

"Charles!" Trudy shouted, walking with both hands on her hips for maximum sternness, elbows aswivel.

"Trudy! We are out of hotdogs!"

"Charles!" She yelled again, undeterred. It's possible they could've gone on like this for hours.

The four of them drew closer, advancing in an apoplectic line. Upon seeing their four furious faces more closely, Charles began to step backwards.

"What is this? What's going on?" He asked.

"You tell me!" Trudy screeched, pigtails levitating. "You have been stealing from this site! How dare you involve myself and Dr. Chen? We trusted you all these years and defended you against these things people would say, and now you don't even have the decency—"

"You're done, scumbag!" Elise cackled.

"We should chat," Chen suggested. "It's come to our attention that there are some pieces missing. I'm mostly wondering about my bones. It's no good to blame the postal service, you know."

The idea to conduct this conversation in the lab made perfect sense now. The Ugs had all poked up their heads from their holes like meerkats and turned to watch the proceedings with commentary galore.

"—the decency to admit it! And the women! My God, the women!" Trudy cried.

"You did this to me." Kara was the first to come with tears. Her eyes glassed, and she spoke at a menacing lower volume that silenced the rest of them. Even Nuts piped down.

"Now, just hold on one minute!"

"No. I held on for years. Years, Dr. Barton. And you lied to me, you lied to them, and you lied about all of this," without moving her head, she waved an arm wildly about the site. "None of this is real!"

Her crazy eyes were widening by the inch with every word, her hinges coming undone. Z loved to see it.

"You are all making an enormous mistake! This is not right! This is supremely unprofessional!" Charles looked around, as if one of the gobsmacked Ugs would suddenly rush to his defense.

"Hello, mates!" Suddenly Ian appeared on the ridge just above them by the burial grounds. So that's where he was. "Don't you worry. I'm putting it all right back where it belongs, how it used to be, just like I said I would!" He gave a thumbs up and a huge smile. He lifted his other hand high, holding up two red roof tiles.

"Ian!" Charles screamed. "Ian! Dear God, man!" He began scrambling up the hill. "Get him! This is the thief! I told you! Ian, get over here! Ian! Ryan, go get him!"

No one moved a muscle.

"Thief! Stop this instant!" Charles sprinted forth. When he finally reached the man he grabbed for his hands, but Ian wouldn't let go. "I've got him!"

The two of them wrestled, all four arms extended, and Charles's white hair came loose in great white stalks above his head.

Nuts took this opportunity to trot toward Dr. Chen, jaws open in a disguised grin, and make a slobbery lunge for his ankle. It was that time of the year.

Suddenly the vans wobbled side to side. A hair-raising roar rumbled up from the ground. The tools rattled against the rocks. Z's thighs started to vibrate.

"Get out!" Elise screamed and heaved her open palms up in the air like she was riling up a crowd. "Everybody, get the hell out!"

She ripped the walkie-talkie off her belt.

The metal stakes at the altar clanked inside the wheelbarrow like a maraca, and at those starting guns the entire earth beneath her boots began to shake violently. Everyone started wailing. The mountain jiggled all at once, and it sounded like thunder, a deep rumbling boiling up from under them that loosened every single strigil and pebble and stake and body, drizzling them all down the hillside at once.

Z tumbled to the ground.

The sharp tool edges clattered; limbs scrambled up and out of the trenches and onto the grass, then stumble-collapsed back down just as fast. Someone screamed for help. To Z's left, Patty was knocked to the ground, kicked like a doll into a pile of bodies containing Ryan and several of the Greek workers. Her elbow jammed into one of their lit cigarettes, and she screamed.

"No, no, no, no!" Gary was on his belly with his arms extended after the wheelbarrow. It rocketed down the hill. Side to side it wobbled, tightly self-correcting, then picking up speed and aim together, zooming down the hill between the trenches, heading straight for a cinder block. It guzzled the distance in no time, and the rubber wheel flash-melted into the rock with a gunshot pop. The back wooden handles vaulted up into the air. Upside down, body open to the field, it cleared the cluster of dancing stones that marked the parking lot. The wheel's rubber skin flapped in the wind. Then the wheelbarrow javelined the back of the van, shredding the metal and shattering the glass with a breathtaking explosion that was neither the coup de grâce nor the pièce de résistance.

The Ugs were down on their stomachs, gripping onto chunks of grass like handles on a sled. Someone new cried out, and one of the workers did too as the boulder next to them tottered over onto his hand and then began rolling down the hilltop. The fingers made a revolting crunch.

The tips of the factory smokestacks shimmied in the sky, and the leaves on the trees shook like they'd gotten it wrong, like they'd been told it was wind. The stone wall of the locker room wobbled and dropped slabs of itself onto the ground, like the thumps of giant footsteps approaching.

The rolling boulder reached the burial ground trenches with a booming *whoosh-whump*. A massive dirt cloud bellowed above the trenches there as the center tracts of land collapsed, swallowing up the hillside edge.

It was the sound of a door closing behind the earthquake. It was over. The rumbling stopped, and another door opened to a new place. In the relative silence everyone was yelling and wailing and crying all at once.

"I'm OK!"

"Oh my God!"

"My arm!"

Elise was up on her knees. She stared at the burial ground and shouted into her walkie-talkie, "Feet! *Different* feet!"

Gary was speed-crawling down the hillside headfirst. Then he popped up diagonally and sprinted toward Z, who was vertical again, though she couldn't remember standing up, trembling hard and covered in dirt. They wrapped their arms around each other and sobbed. And what else in this life could she possibly do? She kissed him.

"Are you OK?" She asked him.

Someone else answered, "No, man!"

The trenches were all filled in, hers included, and it looked like shovels and hammers and red roof shards had rained down from the sky instead of coming up from beneath them.

Following the sound of Elise's voice, Z looked over to the burial ground ridge. She saw two legs ending in two completely different shoes sticking up from out of the ground at incomprehensible angles.

Her stomach rolled, and her knees buckled. The edges of her vision bled to black, and she slipped through Gary's arms, swiveling back down to the ground.

Chapter
24

They were managing to dance with one another from twenty feet apart. Whenever Gary moved around the perimeter of the liberally tasseled library, Kara did the same in the opposite direction. They hadn't spoken in the three months since they'd returned from Greece and were keeping their distance today. In between them were several dozen white-haired biddies, Charles's wife Terry's set, all circling a mahogany table offering up the pantheon of WASP cuisine: square slices of cheese across the full spectrum of white to yellow and crab dip with buttery crackers. Almost unrecognizable in a suit and tie, Ryan stood helping himself to the latter, straight from the silver serving dish.

Though it was only early October, the fireplace had been insisted upon. Everyone in the room kept blotting their foreheads with the napkins that were monogrammed with a gold *C.B.*, bindis of which adorned them all.

Charles's retirement party was funereal. The turnout had been low enough to prompt a gentle suggestion from the Club staff about moving them all into a smaller room. The honoree sat hunched in a far corner in a leather wingback chair, staring vacantly at the built-in shelves full of decorative books and mallards. A green hat dotted with golf balls proclaiming *Par Tee Time!* clung limply to the side of his head, covering his remaining bandages. A group of guests standing nearby chatted with their sides turned to him. He'd suffered a head injury plus a dozen broken bones from the earthquake, whittling him down to a husk of his former athletic self. There was apparently some memory loss, though glimpses of his previous charm shone through with abrupt non sequiturs of *You're not a member here* to passing guests.

At various points, teenagers would walk straight up to Kara and hug her out of the blue. Apparently they were Ugs, but it was impossible to recognize them in these clothes, under these circumstances, in this economy. Over by the bar a gaggle of them huddled around Patty, who was dressed in a shockingly decent jacket and cashing in her new social currency of having been Charles's gofer during the scandal.

There were rivers of gin to be forded if one wished to reach Terry herself, who sat by the fire surrounded by Main Line originals who came with the tartan furniture. This event was clearly being held for her benefit; few attendees had ever worked with Charles. The attitude among Charles's colleagues was that his death would've been the preferable amount of distance between him and the department. For those who had absolutely no idea what was going on (a group Terry thrived in), this get together was a lovely way to vaguely transition Charles out of his career without putting too fine a point on it. The investigation into his crimes was quietly ongoing.

Kara wished to avoid a prolonged exchange with her former professor but could not bring herself to ignore him altogether. She hadn't seen him since the day of his near-death tectonic experience and hoped, irrationally, that perhaps he would have cultivated some contrition in the meantime. Certainly he'd been brought low: the university had demanded his immediate retirement, stripped his name from all department material, notified his publisher (who recalled his books from stores), and launched an investigation into his research led by Trudy and two women from the University of Athens. Furthermore, much to the delight of local gossip, his home was searched twice by officials from the State Department's cultural antiquities task force.

Kara politely weaved through the crowd and approached his perch in the corner.

"Charles," she said, sitting down in the chair beside him, which had long remained empty.

"I've been trying to get your attention this entire afternoon," he began.

"I hope you're feeling better," she said evenly.

"Certainly I'm not. That's exactly what I need your help with. Someone sensible has got to listen to me."

She folded her manicured hands in her lap and said nothing.

"You are my protégé, Kara. You understand better than anyone how devoted I am to the field. Tell me, all these years, has anyone worked more tirelessly than you and I on the Megalopolis excavation?"

"Elise," Kara answered.

Charles scoffed. "Monster. She is the one they need to be going after, which I have informed them of repeatedly. These authorities," he snarled, "have tarnished my decades of commitment with this excessive investigation while a pirate goes free. Nay—continues to work! She stole a piece from us, Kara. Now, when you speak to these investigators, please tell them the protocol and how Elise willfully removed something from the dig—something over which she has no authority, whatsoever."

"Dr. Barton, I believe they're keenly aware of who has authority over what." Kara had spoken to the task force extensively—all of them had. Everyone had been forthcoming, and none were under investigation except for Charles, who had called upon his every connection to assist him out of this jam and been universally turned away.

"It has been a nightmare." He raised a hand and snapped his fingers at a passing waiter for another drink. "If you can believe it, they removed my articles from every academic journal I've ever published in. They're eliminating my book from the university bookstore. My very name—poof! As if my entire life's work has just disappeared, into the wind. Is this acceptable to you? Someone you've worked for?"

"It's almost as if they're erasing you," Kara said.

"Precisely!"

"You worked very hard to accomplish something, and now someone has come along and removed your achievements from the record."

"Yes!" He brought his hands together in front of his chest and clasped them. "I knew you would understand."

Kara nodded, then stood. "Goodbye, Charles."

AS SOON AS KARA HAD LANDED BACK IN THE STATES, SHE RECEIVED AN additional interview request. Trudy had heard about where Kara wished to work and reached out on her behalf through a string of connections. Through this game of telephone that led her to the Sotheby's office, the narrative became about Kara's diligent unraveling of the mystery of the missing pieces and how she put them all back together, correctly, crucially. Charles had made a palimpsest of the mountain, and Kara was its restorer. She did not amend this description of events. She accepted Sotheby's offer, and though it was a less prestigious role, she asked if they would place her in the restitution and repatriation department. They agreed.

At Evelyn's insistence, Kara had taken yet another small pill prior to this party. Though she was loath to eat in front of strangers, she took a delicate bite of crackers and crab dip from her tiny plate to keep pace with the white wine she was sipping. There were parallel murmurings of a toast that Charles wished to make at some point and of the many wishes for that not to occur.

Kara smiled tightly to whomever was speaking to her at the moment, one of Terry's pottery dealers.

"If you'll excuse me," she said and turned away with a chilly smile. She went out into the hallway and found an upholstered bench, worn in the middle from years of its service providing respite from the party room. She leaned back against the wall, resting her head against an oil painting of a horse.

"How are you holding up?" Evelyn stood in front of her. She'd come for moral support, which Kara had needed more than ever in the past weeks. She was even learning, finally, to request it.

Kara sat up straight, nodded.

"Good." They exchanged the requisite pleasantries about how little they'd enjoyed the food. Then they wrapped up with some light commiseration around the appalling injustice that was legacies having to submit the very same application to clubs as brand-new members these days. This chat steadied her.

"By the way," Evelyn said. "There's a dentist involved, I'm afraid."

"A menace?"

"Dentist," Evelyn enunciated. They were trying to keep their voices down. "Although you might be right. It's a bit vocational in my opinion. Gil is his name."

"Mmm," Kara hummed. Evelyn had been helping her corral capital for Mega. Elise and Kal were finally opening the Kentro, starting with the handful of pilfered artifacts they'd recovered, and had nearly enough at this point to welcome any visitors. They merely lacked a building. Much to Kal's delight, Kara was single-handedly orchestrating the necessary patrons without a coal factory goon in sight.

There was no one, as far as Kara knew, that Evelyn couldn't convince to become more involved in ancient history.

Evelyn continued now in a raised whisper. "Though I don't know that he's a dentist himself, per se. I think it's more that he's involved in dentistry, the business of dentistry devices, or something along those lines. Anyway he's Greek, or so he claims, even though it's Gil Schermenhorn. Don't ask me to get into that, but supposedly, regardless, he's wild about this kind of thing, the sport of it all, so he's quite keen. Though he didn't look like much of an athlete to me, I have to say. Again, I won't get into it. It is all pertaining to sports, isn't it?"

"Yeah," Kara confirmed for the thousandth time. "Yes," she corrected herself.

"Good girl. Now I haven't said a thing about . . . the Charles of it all, naturally. I merely brought to this man's attention a rare opportunity to lend his prowess—be that medically, regionally, or athletically, whatever the case may be—to our nascent gem. As I was gauging the depth of his willingness to pursue those interests with a dedicated set of resources, voilà. I believe we've got our final patron. As they say, *He's in*. You can tell your friend Elise."

"Kara?" Terry walked toward her. "May I have a word?"

It had been years since Kara had seen her, but Terry looked the same. Her clothes were those very loose-fitting, jewel-tones that were never clearly either pants or skirts, making it impossible to find a limb in women of a certain age. The blurb for Terry contained multiple lines on wine collecting and hobby ceramics. Misreading the mood, she bobbed her limbs energetically, elbows and knees triangulating around her like a Keith Haring sprung to life. Her copper hair was tied back high and tight into a ballerina's bun, and her chunky, colorful jewelry flopped atop her chest and jangled around her wrists. Her eye makeup choices spoke volumes.

Terry guided Kara down the hallway, wrapping a stretchy shawl tighter around her bony shoulders as Kara held the door open to the parking lot, where she'd indicated they were headed.

They walked around the corner and stood out of the eye of the valet, shivering and performatively lambasting themselves for not appreciating the fire before.

Kara crossed her arms in front of her chest. "How are you doing?" she asked, in the right way, unsure why Terry had dragged her out here.

She wished for the tenth time that day that either Elise or Z were here with her, doing what they did best: shortening conversations.

Terry fiddled with her bracelets and looked nervously behind her to the valet stand.

"I just need to know if Ryan's going to be okay. Can you promise me that? He's my nephew, you know."

Kara scrunched her brow. "Oh. Well, I'm sure he could always join another dig. I mean, he does have . . . experience. Or, there are so many other outdoor opportunities for someone like him, I assume."

Terry looked around her again and, seeing only shrubs, began. She spoke every set of two words as if each were its own sentence.

"I know—that he—assisted Charles."

Kara's mouth froze in an open, upside-down crescent. This was the first time today that anything remotely pertaining to the theft had come up. "Right," was the only sound she could make come out of it.

Terry kept going, "It's my fault. I'm the instigator here. Blame me!" She put her hand over her heart. "Because I just wanted more from him. We were trying to travel all over the place, and his TV appearances dried up, and Ursula! Ursula kept telling me to pursue what excites me. You know she can read palms? And that's what she told me once, and so I said why not. Sue me! One minute your husband's on television, the next you can't even follow your terracotta passion. I made him put all this money into the pottery studio. And, well, he went ahead and invested the rest of it in that damned squash league because they promised him he could be an announcer. And there it all went. What were we supposed to do? Squash is the new lacrosse, they said—they promised!"

She'd raised her voice above the acceptable decibel of cocktail chatter. The valet poked his head around the side of the building. Kara waved and close-mouth smiled, the universal gesture of *Go away*.

"I just don't want Ryan to have any trouble," Terry said, putting her hand on Kara's bare arm.

With great poise comes great responsibility, an Evelynism for the ages.

Kara stood up straight and tightened her ponytail. Then she un-crossed her arms to clasp her hands at her waist, no matter how cold it was.

"I'll keep that between us," she lied. She would make sure Ryan never set foot on another dig as long as he lived.

"Oh, good. Thank you, sweetie." Terry's shoulders relaxed.

"Of course. And I'm obviously not privy to your material circum-stances," she returned a strategic freezing hand to Terry's bare arm. "But that will be easier for me to do if you were to sell your pottery studio, and perhaps these lovely bracelets you're wearing and anything else you may no longer need, and make a sizable donation to my friend Elise at the Heraea Center."

Terry looked stricken. Kara beamed.

"Would they display my ceramics?"

No, they would not.

Chapter

25

As soon as Z saw the humongous freezer full of ice cream pops, she had her vision: all the food here would be served on sticks. This included kebablava, a kebab of Ursula's signature baklava, a javelin of phyllo. This inspiration du cuisine was a historical nod to the ancient sports fans whose footsteps their guests would be following in—those early adopters of such a resourceful method that combined the cooking and serving apparatuses in one. For drinks, which was the bulk of what they sold since kids were always running around here, she felt that straws were in line with the theme as the sticks of liquid.

She stood behind the grill on the patio outside the Heraea Center, beneath the white sheet that Kal had rigged up for them to provide some shade after Ursula had nearly fainted last week. Nuts licked the ground around her feet for meat drippings as she fired up the charcoal and started assembling the day's kebabs.

Without a clear role for Z, Elise had her helping out Ursula and Ian for the time being. She would be here for a few months getting them set up, and then Elise had made arrangements for Z to take over her trench jobs in Corinth and Crete for the next two seasons. In those places, Elise had never been willing to take on the responsibility of managing the latest crop of Ugs or interns, but Z was happy to do that, whistle at the ready. She realized she loved that aspect of this work the most—the teachable moments, the coaching and camaraderie—and the dig bosses were delighted to have the help. The nicest thing Elise had ever said to her was *You could probably handle that.*

In the meantime, Z was rather enjoying cooking. Grilling, specifically, allowed her to ensnare visitors in her chicken-scented web for
conversation. Ursula read her palms and talked crystals most days, and
Z would take all the free divination she could get. When would Gary
come back? That's what she wanted to know the most.

On the van ride to the Athens airport, they'd held hands and had a
circular conversation about timing and distance, returning rings and
returning home. Gary had one more year before he was finished with
his degree, and then they would see. Time would tell; he would visit;
they needed time; they wanted each other; give it a minute; give it a
month. *See you soon*, he signed his emails.

She felt like she had to stay here; for the first time in her life she
didn't feel remotely over it. Some days she believed she'd personally
caused the earthquake. She'd sat on history and corrected it—that
woke the dirt up all right.

The grounds here were T-shaped with a long, narrow basketball
court at the top. An oval track beneath it encircled the entirety of the
small building. There was no fencing around the court, so balls were
always bombing the landscaping and pummeling the walls with a constant symphony of boings and smacks and cat screeches. On the opposite side, below the track, there was just dry grass stretching as far as
the eye could see into the open valley, dotted with four soccer goals.

The courts and goals and round track were all Z's idea. Let them do
what we've been supposed to do all along—the whole reason we're
here: play. It was a Kon-Tikian twist on their mission, to stretch beyond
an exhibit and lead those little girl visitors by example with sweat,
blood, and cheers.

After all, we lit the torch, baby.

Z drove visitors up in the ice-cream-branded vans, past the village,
all the way up to the original track excavation, where they could see
the ground from which the pieces came. She loved to watch the kids up

on the track there, running around like wild, not listening at all to her as she explained what everything was. They collected little scraggly bouquets of flowers to bestow on each other as they took turns standing on top of the podium that Kal built.

Visiting the excavation was the highlight of their offer to guests. The tiny inside of the Dr. Gil Schermenhorn, D.D.S. Heraea Center for Women's Athletic Archaeological Exploration was nothing to write home about. It was mostly taken up with the aforementioned ice cream freezers and a large Poseidon fountain, both of which Kal had previously committed to.

The important part was a large glass enclosure with the gold Ἡραία trophy in the middle, surrounded by the discuses carved with H. Of course, there was also Victoria with her gold crown, raised arms, and husky little body that curved almost exactly like Z's did. There was even a display of bone dust from the burial grounds, most of which was retrieved when they'd frantically dug out Charles and Ian.

They'd been flooded with other small pieces when the investigation into Charles concluded. The US and Greek authorities had jointly brought trafficking charges against him and each of the men he'd sold pieces to—the men who thought they could own a piece of the original Olympics for themselves. Jail time and six-figure fines were on deck for Charles's crimes. The pieces were all delivered to Kal and Elise here, and Kara was visiting shortly to monitor their progress and inflict an organized storage system.

Ursula waddled over and used her fingers to rotate the meat skewers. She told Z the story again of where she was when the quake hit, up on the roof of the cafeteria. The roof turned out to be as solid as a fortress, and from there she watched as the back wall of the lab just dripped down the side of the mountain, stone by white stone, like a melting ice cream cone, frankly. After Ian had been nearly buried alive beside Charles, the two of them, spared, decided to stay put here.

Some days on their rides up the mountain—more and more lately—Ursula and Ian would join Z, and they'd pull into the village and spend a few hours cleaning up. Elise told them this was pointless, and Kal told them it was dangerous, but neither warning had stopped anyone before. Each of them would grab a stone and heave it into a large pile, hang a shutter back onto a window, or sweep up glass and splinters and whatever else had been left behind.

"Heck of a time for whoever's next," Ursula said, surveying the scene.

The grill hissed, and Z stood up to tong the sticks onto a plastic platter. The kebabs were a bit charred on one side, but it was nothing a glob of tzatziki couldn't mitigate, a pool of which she'd dolloped at the end of the tray for rolling the meat hunks around in. Today there was another school group coming to visit them. Then Kal's niece's soccer team would be here, and she'd promised to play goalie. Z flicked a piece of chicken fat onto the ground for Nuts then carried the food inside.

✈

And I'll be honest with you, it wasn't the worst next chapter for me, as far as those go, staring out through the vanilla and chocolate smudge fingerprints on the glass out at a view of the track. Not my track, but close enough, and where every year someone new might come to run around and around in those tight little loops that seem to go on forever. Every so often they would come in the evenings, when the sun spun nectarine and silver across the outrageous sky, and no one else was watching them but me. They'd finish a fast lap or two, or four, or ten, and even though they'd just blown their lungs out, legs throbbing, heart bursting, they'd always manage to stick out their burning chest and hold up their arms high and scream, "Hell, yeah."

ACKNOWLEDGMENTS

I started writing this book in 2015. Both it and I have lived about a thousand lives since then. If anyone reading this is working on something you're not sure will ever see the light of day, hear me now and believe me later: keep going.

To this end, thank you, Claire Friedman. You are the catalyst for all of this, and I am insanely lucky and grateful to have you in my corner. You are the best in the biz, hilarious, sharp eyed, the right kind of weird, and greatest of all, zero-nonsense. Thank you for pushing this book to be better early on and for not giving up on it. I can never thank you enough for that. Remember when you thought it might be about sharks? You rule. And thank you to the whole team at Inkwell for your support.

Thank you, Daniella Wexler. You made the big dream come true, and some days I still can't believe I get to work with you. From our first breakfast, I knew I was in the smartest, funniest, best hands. Your clear vision, passion, and dedication to what the story is all about made working on this together an absolute joy. Thank you for championing this at every step and for totally getting it; it's been such a privilege to be on this ride with you. Here's to the marathon runners.

Thank you to the wonderful, smart Ghjulia Romiti for your tireless work and skilled notes. When the chips were down, a <3 in the margins kept me going. We couldn't have done this without you.

I'm so grateful and proud to have a home at HarperCollins and HarperVia. Thank you to the incredibly talented and hardworking team there: Judith Curr, Juan Mila, Tara Parsons, Paul Olsewski, Brieana Garcia, Almeda Beynon, Yvonne Chan, Janet Evans-Scanlon, Suzanne Quist, Kate Lloyd, Terri Leonard, Mary Grangeia, Elizabeth Sullivan, Anna Brower, and Stephen Brayda.

Thank you to Berni Barta, Will Watkins, and Norris Brooks at CAA for believing in this story.

Thank you to Paragraph in New York, Brooklyn Writers Space, The Office in Brentwood, and Writers Junction in Santa Monica. I wrote parts of the book in each of these places, and I couldn't have finished a page early on without that very special mix of quiet and community. Special thanks to Joy Parisi and Lila Cecil from Paragraph, and to the whole Paragraph family for giving me a home in the city and making me feel like a real-deal writer.

Thank you to the Penn Museum, Dr. David Romano, Dr. Mary Voyatzis, and the Mount Lykaion Excavation and Survey Project.

Thank you to Melody Wukitch at Park Books for all your support and insight.

Thank you to Cheryl Dolins from our time at CBS in New York; I learned so much from you. Thank you to my excellent teachers Tom Worthington at Severn, and Dr. Louise Krasniewicz, Dr. John Jackson, and Kathy DeMarco at Penn. Kathy, yours was the only writing class I ever took, and your encouragement over the years meant the world to me. You told me once to quit my job and go do something interesting so I'd have something to write about. You were right. Parents, you can blame her.

Thanks to fellow authors Matthew Thomas, who told me to keep trying, and Teddy Wayne, who told me to cut bait and start over; you were both right. A deep thanks to Zach Sergi for endless texts and talks about the wild west of the publishing process.

There is no doubt in my mind that I have the greatest friends on the planet, all of whom have cheered on the sidelines as I ran through these years. Thank you Ashley Templeton, Bridget Gummere, Anastasia Radford, Anastasia Olowin, Ashley Graf, Ali Mendes, Rachel Abrams, Kerry McHugh, Shannon Pasch, Ariel Colangelo, Carly Daucher, Sasha Silver, Zandria Haines, Max Nacheman, Anna Nelson, Selena Strandberg, Shane Romero, Jenny Pelaez, Lauren O'Connor, and Justin Tackett.

Thank you to my hero Serena Williams.

Any parents out there still reading this? Nothing is possible without childcare, so thank you to Natasha and everyone who's ever helped with Banana. Special thanks to my mom for countless hours of grandmother time and support while I was editing, and to the makers of Bobbie formula.

Thank you to my parents for raising me in a family of voracious readers, to my dad for a love of history, and to my mom especially for teaching me to love poetry and mostly read *The New Yorker* for the cartoons. I love you both with all my heart, and thank you for everything.

Thank you YoYo, Noodle, and Jack, in that order. I love you. Thank you Alex, Ray, and Joanna for your love, support, bagels, and pasta; I am so lucky to call you my family.

To Anna, thank you for all those hours in the middle of the night when I was awake to come up with ideas and jot down notes. You are my whole world and everything is for you.

And finally, the biggest thank you for last, to my one and only, Paul. I tricked you into marrying me when I still had a real job and when the pandemic rolled through and I said, *Actually, I think I'm going to edit this manuscript I wrote*, you set up my office, brought me coffee, and closed the door so I could work. You get me. Thank you from the bottom of my heart for your love, every single day, for being the best father to Anna and the most supportive, encouraging husband I could ever dream of. I doubted myself a million times, but you never did. You made this possible, and I love you forever.

A NOTE ON THE COVER

In book packaging, there is so much opportunity to explore different avenues of design. Incorporating illustration, for example, often gives a book's cover originality and highlights the energy and spirit of the story.

From many editorial conversations digging through potential imagery for this novel, showcasing the main characters felt like the most effective approach, and I began by illustrating them on screen. To elevate my flat digital graphics, I slowly cut out each shape from a low-quality print and then re-layered them all in Photoshop, keeping paper texture and rudimentary edge quality intact. I felt like I was engaged in a process of discovery much like the characters in *Excavations*.

—STEPHEN BRAYDA

Here ends Kate Myers's
Excavations.

The first edition of this book was printed
and bound at Lakeside Book Company in
Harrisonburg, Virginia, June 2023.

A NOTE ON THE TYPE

The text of this novel was set in Freight Text Pro, originally designed in 2005 by Joshua Darden—the first African American type designer, according to *Fonts in Use*. The Freight font superfamily is known for its innovative approach to optical size and stylistic versatility, and Freight Text Pro provides its sturdy center. Aptly named, Freight is a workhorse font that can handle standard text sizes for small and large amounts of copy. Unique but easy on the eyes, Freight is a go-to typeface for everything from magazines to cookbooks to data-driven documents.

HarperVia

An imprint dedicated to publishing international voices, offering readers a chance to encounter other lives and other points of view via the language of the imagination.